About the

R. J. HEALD grew up in Amersham, on the outskirts of London. She attended Merton College, Oxford University, where she studied Economics and Management, before pursuing a portfolio career spanning nuclear decommissioning, strategy consulting and television. In September 2010, she founded Five Stop Story, a small digital publisher, specialising in short stories by new writers. In September 2011, she won the Next Big Author competition. Her debut novel, 27, was shortlisted for the Amazon Breakthrough Novel Award in 2012.

www.rjheald.com
www.fivestopstory.com
Twitter: @RJ_Heald

DPP

First published in Great Britain in 2012 by Dancing Parrot Press (UK)

This paperback edition published in 2012 by Dancing Parrot Press (UK)

Set in Palatino

A CIP catalogue record for this book is available from the British Library.

ISBN: 978-0-9573447-0-9

R. J. HEALD

27

DPP

DANCING PARROT PRESS

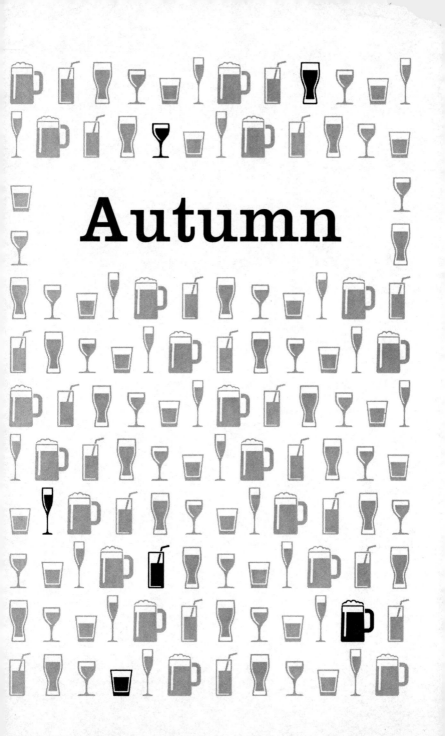

Autumn

1

Dave's twenty-seventh birthday started well, but then went downhill quickly.

It was a particularly bright September morning. As Dave dragged himself to work he imagined sitting outside the pub at lunch and having a birthday pint with the sun on his face. Birthdays at work were always good. You got away with doing less work than normal, people came over to congratulate you simply for getting older, and after work vast quantities of alcohol were consumed. This year, for the first time ever, Dave had even stopped off in Tesco Metro and bought a chocolate cake to share with the office.

Once he'd settled down at his desk, Dave decided he would release the cake when the clock reached ten thirty. He had just returned his attention to his computer screen when his manager, Peter, came wearily over to his desk to observe Dave's unique approach to multitasking: simultaneously browsing Facebook and emailing a friend. Dave considered quickly clicking on an excel spreadsheet and hoping it would expand to cover his screen, but he decided that that would probably look more suspicious. Such rash behaviour could lead Peter to think that he had been looking at something much worse. Anyway, the concept of management in the office was quite a relaxed one; Peter was both a manager and a friend.

Dave looked up at Peter, expecting a "happy birthday" but receiving none. Dave cracked a lame joke about age, but Peter didn't respond.

"Dave, it's your turn."

"My turn?"

"Yeah, you know, the HR talks. We're talking to everyone individually."

"Right." Dave scanned his memory for what Peter might be talking about, and vaguely recalled a staff meeting where things had been rather downbeat and they'd mentioned redundancies. Everyone in the department was at risk, but it was going to take them a month to decide who would go. Had a month passed? Maybe it had.

He followed Peter into a side room.

"Take a seat, Dave."

Dave laughed nervously at his formal tone. Hopefully Peter would relax in the pub later, when they were out celebrating his birthday. Dave frowned for a second. Would people still come out to celebrate? Or would the redundancies overshadow things?

"You're still coming out for a drink later?" he asked. Peter looked up from the bundle of papers in front of him on the table. Dave saw a vein in his forehead pulsing in a way he had never noticed before.

"A drink?"

"Yeah, it's my birthday."

Last year Dave's birthday had gone down in company history. They had ended up clubbing until four a.m. and eight people, including Peter, called in sick the next day. It was a company record.

Peter shuffled the papers in front of him. "Let's just get this over with first," he said.

Get what over with? Wasn't this just a formality?

Dave's stomach started to knot uncomfortably. He watched

the green-grey vein protrude from Peter's head, pump and then retract, and then pump and then retract.

"So, you know why we've called you in?"

"Yes." Dave wanted it to be lunchtime already, to be sitting outside the pub.

"Good, well, I'll be quick." Peter was speaking at twice his normal speed. "Unfortunately we've run the numbers and all employees at your grade are being made redundant."

Dave stared.

"There'll be a good package, a fair package. It will give you enough of a cushion to find another job."

Dave nodded. Shit. How long had Peter known about this? They had had a pint together yesterday after work. How come he hadn't warned him? If Peter had told him this was going to happen, he could have spoken to the directors himself and persuaded them not to fire him.

"Do you have any questions?" Peter looked like he wanted to bolt from the room.

"Err . . . no." Dave had only been promoted six months ago. How could they promote him and then make his grade redundant? Had he only been promoted so he could be fired? No, that didn't make sense.

"Right, then." Peter interrupted his thoughts and set off again, speaking quickly. He smiled nervously as he rushed through what appeared to be a script written on his paper. "Well, you've got a lot to think about, so we suggest you clear up your stuff and take the rest of the day off. You can come back and collect any personal effects next week. We've got some boxes you can put things into."

"So . . . I won't be coming back at all?" But what about his birthday drinks? He couldn't leave now. He needed to be around for the evening.

"Think of it like a holiday. You're on one month's notice so you get one month to do whatever you like. Paid. And then the redundancy money on top of that. It's really a very good deal. I almost wish it was my grade." Peter smiled and Dave felt slightly sick.

"You do?"

Peter looked embarrassed. He was always shooting his mouth off, saying the wrong thing. This was clearly why they'd given him a script.

"Well, I suppose not, not really; the job market's pretty tough at the moment." He seemed to realise he was putting his foot in it, and added quickly: "You'll be fine though, someone with your skills."

What skills? A bit of PowerPoint and pissing around? Doing the minimum possible in the day? Shit. A new job wouldn't let him get away with that.

"Yeah. Thanks, mate."

Peter left the room and Dave sat on his own for a while staring at the wall. What was he going to do?

After ten minutes he got up and returned to his desk. The office was eerily silent. He sat at his computer. Facebook was still on the screen and his page was littered with birthday messages. He scanned them, and then shut down the computer. He glanced up at his friends sitting across from him, but they looked back at their computer screens. He supposed they must know by now.

"I'm off," he said to no one in particular.

He picked up his rucksack from under his desk and headed out the door, down the stairs and into the sunshine.

Across the road he saw the empty wooden picnic tables of the pub. If he wanted to, he could go and have a drink there now. At eleven a.m.. He was free. The thought didn't please him as much as he expected it to, but he wandered over anyway. He pushed the door, but instead of giving way and welcoming him in, a chain rattled. It was closed. It didn't open until twelve. There was nothing to do but go home.

2

For Renée, Facebook was a self-imposed purgatory, a means of taunting herself with the success of others. Perched on the sofa in her flat in a suburb of Wimbledon, she idly scanned through the collective lives of friends, acquaintances and people she'd been to school with.

Clicking through baby photos, holiday photos and the news about job promotions and engagements, she took another sip of wine. Her forehead wrinkled as she stared at the screen.

She had planned everything so carefully: work hard at school and university, find a decent man, get a good job, get married, buy a place to live. And at just twenty-seven, she had accomplished almost all of it. She had a First from Bristol, and a well-paid job in the legal department at the local council. She owned half a flat in Wimbledon. Not only had she settled down, she had settled down with Andy, who had been widely acknowledged as the most attractive man in the university tennis team.

However, there was no denying the evidence spelled out to her in parallel lines of text on her Facebook news feed. Not only were other people having more fun, they were also more successful. She could cope with them having more fun. That was OK. She had accepted at university that she would work hard in the library while others went out and got drunk. She would get good grades while others scraped through and had to retake exams. But there was supposed to be a pay-off. She was supposed to get the best job and earn the most money once she left. Wasn't that what the teachers said at school? Work hard and you'll be rewarded?

She clicked dejectedly through her friends' Facebook profiles. Work-shy Dave had recently been promoted. Steve, the university drop-out, now ran his own business turning over millions. James, who had always been more interested in drinking than academia, had had a meteoric rise to senior management in a financial services company and was father to a new baby. Katie was still travelling round the world without a care.

Renée took a sip of the generous glass of white wine on the table beside her. Just today, she had been overlooked for promotion.

She vaguely heard the scratch and then click of the key in the front door, and a gentle thud as it closed, but her distracted brain hardly acknowledged it.

I'm lucky, she told herself forcefully, as she took another sip of wine and looked around the tastefully decorated room. *I jointly own a nice flat in a premium location and I'm married to a handsome, caring man. I can wait to get promoted.*

A woman who'd only recently joined the council had been promoted ahead of Renée. Her boss had sat her down and promised that she was next in line, but Renée found it hard to believe. She'd heard it all before. Renée had sat watching the clock in the office for the rest of the afternoon, and then, at exactly five thirty, she had got up and left. She never usually left the office before seven, and her colleagues had looked up in surprise. Today someone else would have to turn out the lights.

Andy's shadow appeared across the doorway, and Renée

jumped. She pulled her eyes away from the screen and looked up at him, neatly dressed in his grey suit and pale blue shirt. She put her laptop down beside her on the sofa, tucked her long dark hair behind her ears and got up obediently to give him a peck on the cheek.

"Hello."

"Hi, darling."

Renée's shoulders tensed. *Darling* made her think of country houses, hunting guns and the smell of a Sunday roast, not the supposedly modern life they were living in London. After eight years, the original appeal of Andy's eccentricity and old-fashioned values had started to wear thin.

She gritted her teeth and sat back down.

"How was your day?" she asked.

"Fine, thanks."

Her eyes turned back to Facebook as she half-heartedly waited for him to ask her the same question.

Another of their friends was engaged. *Samantha Evans.* She struggled to place her in her mind. The picture didn't look that familiar. She flicked backwards in time through Samantha's photos and saw her morph from a slim blonde into the mousy-haired, overweight girl who had been a vague acquaintance of Renée's at university.

"How was your day?" Andy's voice faded as he started to walk away.

"Fine," Renée mumbled under her breath as she tried to find a picture of Sam's fiancé on the site. She found one. He was tall, with dark curly hair like Andy's. He beamed into the camera as his arm rested round Sam's shoulders. That wasn't going to make her feel better. She probably needed more wine.

Somewhere in the flat a toilet flushed. She glanced up and saw that Andy had left the room.

She sighed. Without Andy, she didn't know what she'd do. He was always there at home waiting for her every evening when she finished work late. He cooked for her when she was too tired, and listened to all her worries.

She scanned through the smiling, happy photos of her friends, and felt increasingly irritated. She felt conned by all the people who'd advised her: the teachers who'd promised she'd do well if she worked hard; her mother, who'd told her she was doing the right thing in marrying Andy; the careers adviser who said there was always demand for lawyers. Even Andy himself, for suggesting that a law job in the public sector was the right way to maintain a work-life balance.

She heard footsteps, and then felt a pressure on the sofa beside her. Andy picked up the remote and turned on the television. Renée's attention flitted quickly to the flashing colours and voices coming from the television, but she couldn't absorb them and she turned back to her computer screen.

She browsed through her friend James's photos of his baby: baby with rattle, baby in bath, cute baby with food all over her face. Not only did James have a happy family, he was also the Head of UK Strategy at a huge American conglomerate. A few weeks ago Andy had come home holding a copy of *Management Tomorrow* magazine. In the centre pages there was a feature on the top thirty businesspeople under thirty. James had come in at number seventeen, and his perfect white teeth and casual smile had mocked Renée from the glossy pages. While Renée had studied relentlessly at university, James had spent most nights out drinking with the rugby team. It just wasn't fair.

She stared at the photos blindly, flicking through and trying to fight back the tears.

"Renée." Andy's voice interrupted her thoughts.

"Yeah."

"How long have you been home?"

"I dunno, a couple of hours."

She looked up into the kitchen and saw what Andy saw. The house was exactly the same as when he'd left that morning to go to work. The dishes were still piled in the sink from last night. She supposed she should have washed them up.

She watched as he opened the fridge door cautiously. Renée could picture the inside perfectly: bare white shelves, empty except for a bottle of wine and some cheese. Wine and cheese seemed perfect as dinner for her tonight. She was watching her weight, and skipping dinner in favour of wine calories and small quantities of cheese sounded far more appealing than a light dinner. She knew Andy would disagree, and when she had passed the Tesco Metro on the corner of their road, she had known that she should go in. But she had seen the long queue spiralling round the shop, and something akin to exhaustion had washed over her and she had gone straight home. The previous night, Andy had been tossing and turning in bed and his movements had disrupted Renée's sleep. Once she was awake, she couldn't calm the uncertainties about her promotion that raced through her mind, and she spent the rest of the night staring at the ceiling.

She heard the jangle of Andy's keys as he left the house without a word. She listened to the door close again, knowing he would resist the urge to slam it, even though he was angry. Repeated slamming had led to a cobweb of cracks creeping up the paintwork above the frame. Andy had spent last Saturday afternoon painting over them, and a faint smell of fumes still lingered in the house.

She turned back to her computer screen.

Katie is having an amazing time in India.

Renée felt a compulsion to click on Katie's profile and trawl through her photos: Katie's blonde hair and pale face centre-stage in a sea of grinning Indian children jostling to get closer to her; Katie smiling serenely in front of the Taj Mahal, a flowered sarong wrapped around her legs; Katie posing with the other English teachers at a local bar. Renée clicked and clicked and clicked, her mind casually absorbing the sights of someone else's life.

Katie had been at university with her and Andy. But while she had been studying and seeing Andy most nights, Katie had just seemed to potter through the course. After university, Katie had spent six months living at home with her parents in Beaconsfield, before going travelling around the world to teach English. She still hadn't come back.

Renée hadn't seen anyone from university in ages. Thumbing through their photos online, she couldn't remember the last time they'd been together in person. Had it been last year? Or was it the year before?

She needed to get out more. She should organise a reunion. She went into the kitchen and topped up her empty wine glass, before starting to compose a message. She'd invite James, Dave, Steve . . . and Katie, of course, even though she doubted she'd come all the way back from India. They had been such a close-knit group. How had she let them drift away from her?

Andy returned from shopping and she heard him in the kitchen, noisily unpacking.

"Andy!" she called.

He ignored her.

She paused for a second to type a message to Katie, and then walked into the kitchen. She observed him unwrapping a meal for one and spiking the clear plastic seal with a fork.

"What do you think of a reunion?"

"A reunion?"

"Yeah a reunion, you know, all our uni friends . We haven't seen them for ages."

"Why?"

"To catch up," she said, unimpressed by his lack of enthusiasm.

"Don't you know what they're doing from Facebook?" Andy put the plastic tray in the microwave.

"Yeah, but, you know, I want to see them myself."

"OK then. Well you don't need my permission, do you?"

Renée went back to her computer as Andy set the timer on

his food and then followed her into the living room. They sat beside each other on the sofa.

Renée sent the message about the reunion, and looked up at Andy. She observed his blue polo shirt and jeans.

"You're not in your suit?"

"No, I changed."

"Right."

He had deep bags under his eyes and his expression was strained. He looked exhausted. She suddenly felt a wave of love for him. They had both worked so hard so that they could afford to buy this flat. They were in it together. The tiredness, the work, everything; it was all so they could build their life together. She suddenly needed reassurance. She leaned in towards him, but he leaned away. She glanced up at him, and obediently he put his arm around her, without taking his eyes off the TV.

"You haven't asked me what happened at work today," she said, accusingly.

"What happened?"

She thought of the talk with her boss about the promotion. How they'd chosen to promote someone else instead of her. She thought about telling Andy that everyone seemed more successful than her, that she felt lonely and insecure. That she was starting to think her life had taken the wrong path.

"Nothing much," she said, hoping he'd enquire further.

"Great. Nothing. Everything's always fine isn't it?" He let his tongue roll over the words as if they were an insult.

"What's wrong?" Renée said impatiently. Surely he should be asking her that.

"Well, I don't think things are fine at all." His eyes were on the television, and Renée wondered if he was actually talking to her.

Had he read between the lines? Did he realize she was unhappy?

"What?"

"This! This is our life. This is our future. And it's not fine."

"What's not fine?"

She felt the need for the security of his body, the security of her marriage, her place in the world as Andy's wife.

"I don't know," he said.

"I love you," Renée said.

A pause.

"When I married you I thought I was so lucky. I didn't deserve you."

She looked back at her computer screen. Couldn't he just say it back? She didn't want to have this conversation. Not today.

He pulled away from her, and leaned back into the sofa.

"I am lucky," he murmured under his breath. He sounded like he was trying to convince himself. He turned to her, and gave her a sudden hug. She felt his fingers gripping her arms, as if he was drowning.

"I love you," Renée said again, trapped in the intensity of his embrace.

"I'm lucky to have you," Andy repeated into her hair, more to himself than to her.

3

Katie squinted up towards the bright lights of the departures board, scanning the list of flights. Boarding. *Right. She could do this.* She checked the gate on her ticket, then eased her way up from the hard seat, each movement seeming to jar her stomach, sending it into another spasm.

She made her way slowly through the airport, her hand clutching her belly. She hadn't realised it was possible to feel quite so much pain. She noticed a shop and realised that she'd need water to take her pills. She picked up a bottle from the fridge and went to the counter. When the price rang up on the till her heart sank. 100 rupees. At the most she had 70. She scrambled around in her handbag, pulling out coins. Eventually she found enough. The till assistant smiled serenely at her, and the man behind her coughed. She took the water and continued her painstaking journey towards the gate.

When she arrived, the board was lit an angry red: Final Call. She hurried to the desk and showed her boarding pass and passport, walked a few steps, and found herself in a queue to get on the plane.

People grumbled and chatted around her as they edged into a smaller and smaller space. After a few minutes Katie sat down on the floor. If she had known she was just going to join a queue she would have stayed sitting down in the waiting area until the last possible minute. Her stomach was killing her.

She had loved India until precisely three weeks ago. Everything about it had delighted her: the incessant bargaining and negotiation, the hot, sweet, milky tea they served at the roadside stalls, the bright colours of the saris. And the noise: the constant noise and chatter and honking of horns had felt like a soundtrack to her life.

The pupils at the school where she'd taught had been well-behaved and diligent. All of them were so keen to learn, keen to get things exactly right. They always did their homework, and if they got things wrong they would practice and practice until they got them right. Katie had never taught in the UK, but she expected that it would be quite different. She'd read enough stories in the papers of happy slapping and gun crime to know that she never wanted to teach in Britain.

What she had loved most about India was the food. The curries were delicious, and in the three months she had been there she had attempted to try every type of curry, bread and dahl.

Until she got ill.

The first day it had just been a headache, and she had gone to the school as normal. But by the end of the day she had been worn out and the noise of the children was getting too much for her. When she came out onto the crowded street and hailed an auto-rickshaw, she didn't have the energy to argue with the driver over price, and let him rip her off in order to get home to her bed just a few minutes earlier than normal.

That night the diarrhoea started, and the next day she called in sick.

Her accommodation, which had seemed so nice when she'd first arrived, now seemed less attractive. The toilet was a good three doors away, and as she had to make seven or eight visits a night this became a problem. When she'd first arrived she had just been pleased it was a Western toilet; it had seemed a luxury after her travels. She had stayed in places where the toilet was simply a hole in the ground, enclosed by nothing more than a waist-high fence. But she'd never had diarrhoea this bad.

She just wished the toilet was clean, and she began, in her more lucid moments, to fantasise about her toilet at home: white, shining, with an intact seat and a sink right next to it with a soap dispenser. She wondered if she was going mad.

Later that night the fever started. She became so cold that she put on two pairs of trousers (one pulled up as far as it could go over the other, the zip left undone,) and five tops. She wished she'd brought a jumper. As she lay shaking and shivering, she started to sweat. She felt goose pimples all over her body. Between shivering and trips to the toilet she hardly got any sleep.

The next day she had little appetite and could hardly look at a curry. Instead she opted for a sandwich from a local bakery. An hour later she was throwing it up. And she continued to throw up. The vomit soon lost its texture and became a waterfall of yellow-green liquid, which a fellow teacher helpfully informed her was her stomach lining.

That was two weeks ago. Her friends had helped her get to a doctor and she'd been prescribed pills, but her symptoms had persisted. It wasn't long before she had swallowed her pride and phoned her mother to tell her she was coming home. In six years of travelling she had hardly thought of her parents, and they had been lucky if they had got a postcard from her. But suddenly she couldn't imagine anything better than going home and staying in a nice clean house.

The queue started to move, and Katie stood up and eased her way forward until she was at the front. As she showed her boarding pass to the flight assistant, she felt a twinge in her stomach and she bent over in pain.

"Are you alright, ma'am?"

"Yes, I'm fine." She just about managed to force her mouth into a smile.

She went past the assistant, through the double doors, onto the tarmac and towards the plane. Then she felt a wave of nausea. She had no choice. She bent over on the runway and threw up. And then threw up again.

The assistant reappeared beside her. "Are you sure you're alright?"

Katie nodded and then threw up again.

The assistant stared at her, her eyes narrowing as she looked at her watch. "I don't think you should fly."

Katie's heart sank. She had to get home and see her family. She had to lie in a nice comfortable bed and be close to a toilet. She wanted to live with people who cared whether or not she was well and would look after her. She needed to get home.

"I'm fine," she said again.

But the assistant was already radioing for medical help. She went back into the airport for a moment, and Katie started making her way determinedly towards the plane, following the other passengers.

She reached the steps and another assistant came over to her.

"We need to shut the doors. Are you OK to fly?"

"Yes, yes, I am." She didn't attempt a smile this time. Instead she began to slowly climb the steps, focusing all her energy on getting to the top and onto the plane. She reached the last step and crossed into the comfort of the air-conditioning, took several deep breaths and then made her way to her seat. The airport staff didn't catch up with her, and the cabin crew busied themselves with shutting the door. As the plane pulled away, Katie smiled with pure relief, and immediately felt a rumbling in her stomach. It was going to be a long flight.

4

Steve paced his office, too tense to sit down at his desk and concentrate on his work. It was ten past three, and Harry's appointment had been at three. What would he do if he didn't turn up? It wasn't the sort of thing you could say over the phone, and Steve really didn't want to leave it until Monday.

Although, a part of him did want to put it off. Maybe it was best if Harry didn't turn up. Maybe they could just forget the whole thing. But of course they couldn't. Steve had to act decisively. After all, he was the boss.

There was a timid knock at his door and his PA stuck her head into his office.

"Harry's here."

"Right." Steve paused for a moment and straightened his tie. He could feel the stares of his staff through the windows of his office. He picked up his folder and strode purposefully out to the reception area.

Harry stood up as he walked towards him. He was wearing a suit. Steve didn't think he'd ever seen Harry in a suit before. Although he was a salesman, he always claimed that the casual look connected with his clients. It worked for him. He had had the highest sales in the team.

Steve reached out to shake his hand. Harry's eyes scanned

his face, as if looking for clues of what was to come, and Steve had to look away. Harry had been caught with a hard drive full of porn on his work laptop, and he was back to hear the inevitable findings of the disciplinary panel.

Moments like this were the hazards of being self-employed. You had to fire people. You could try and avoid it all you liked, but sometimes you had to. "Follow me," Steve said, and Harry meekly followed.

Steve shut the door of the meeting room behind them and took a deep breath.

They sat down and went through the formalities quickly. Harry looked at Steve hopefully, and Steve had to tell him he no longer had a job.

Harry's face went red and blotchy. Steve expected anger, perhaps even a punch (he had asked Miriam from HR, petite but firm, to be on standby to deal with this precise situation). But Harry's face crumpled and curled in on itself, tears formed in his eyes and he started to bawl. Steve could only watch, helpless, and wait for it to stop. He wanted to leave, but he couldn't open the door and share Harry's shame with the rest of the office. His cries were already permeating through the thin walls of the meeting room and Steve didn't want to make things worse.

This was the last thing he had expected from Harry – from one of the others, maybe, but not Harry. Harry was always the centre of attention in the office, the one who made all the jokes. Steve had never wanted to hear one of Harry's politically incorrect jokes as much as he did now. If Harry would just make a joke and then leave, Steve wouldn't have to feel the guilt that was curling in his stomach. He looked at Harry hopefully. Harry's head was still on the table, in his hands.

Steve leaned over and patted Harry awkwardly between the shoulders, a half-hearted display of sympathy. Harry didn't shake him off as Steve had expected, and Steve continued for a little while longer, before stopping and standing upright again. Harry's sobs subsided enough for Steve to quietly excuse himself from the room.

*

Half an hour later, Steve watched through the frosted glass of his office as Harry left the meeting room, body slouching, head down. He made his way across the office and began to clear his desk under Miriam's watchful eye. Harry filled the box methodically, his face swollen. Steve watched as Harry's life went into that box: first his dirty "best dad" coffee mug, which no-one had dared to move from his desk since he'd gone on disciplinary, then the "top salesman" gong that he'd been awarded at the Christmas party, then a picture of his wife and two boys, followed by a pile of CDs and memory sticks. Steve wondered if he should stop him taking the memory sticks. What information was on them? Was there anything confidential? He sighed. He didn't want to confront Harry again. He watched Harry finish packing the box, heave it into his arms, and make his way across the office to the exit. He didn't stop to say goodbye to anyone. Miriam held the door open for him, and then he was gone.

Steve had never thought about these moments when he had spent months working into the night to set up the business, an organisation that taught other businesses to harness the power of social networks. He ran a hand through his sandy hair and went back to his desk. He should get on with his work. He had a pile of CVs to review, all recent graduates looking for a job at his company. He picked up the first one half-heartedly and scanned the black and white pages. The candidate had been at Bristol University at the same time as him. He smiled to himself. The guy had done an MA and then a PhD. Now he wanted to work for Steve. Moments like this made dropping out of his Law degree worth it.

Even so, he felt restless. He had everything he'd worked

for, his own business and his own house, but somehow it didn't feel like enough. He wanted to move on and try something different, but it was his company. He couldn't just give it up. And in the recession, times were hard enough as it was. Marketing budgets had been slashed and clients were unwilling to take a risk on a big, innovative campaign. It was frustrating. Sometimes he thought that he might as well be an employee rather than the CEO; at the end of the day he still had to bow to other people's demands.

He sighed. Perhaps he needed to try something new. Refresh himself. But he wasn't sure if he was good enough. Since he dropped out of university, he'd only worked for himself. He didn't know how to work for someone else. Perhaps he should have stayed on and completed his Law degree. Who, these days, employed people his age who didn't have a degree?

He thought of James, his closest friend at university. He had stayed the course and got a good job in an American company. He'd worked his way up and had featured in last month's *Management Tomorrow* magazine. What Steve did was small-fry in comparison. Then again, James was always destined for success. He was the only person Steve had known who had been able to drink until three a.m. and then get up at seven to play football for the university third team. And still get by academically. By comparison Steve was always going to struggle.

He sat at his desk and flicked idly through Facebook, looking for new ideas for his business, new ways to use the site to market his clients' products. Firing Harry had made him feel slightly off-kilter, and he couldn't concentrate. Maybe today he would leave early and get home before seven, order himself a takeaway and relax in front of the TV.

He saw he had a friend request and clicked on it half-heartedly. It was from a girl called Caroline, who he didn't recognise. It was accompanied by a message.

U R fit.

That was all. Did he know her? He didn't recognise the name. He studied her picture intently. It seemed to have been taken at a party and it was a bit blurry. Had he met her somewhere? He hardly went out socially, but she didn't look like a client. Perhaps he had met her at a business event. But then, if he had, her message didn't seem appropriate.

He closed the screen and pulled up a project proposal he was working on for one of his oldest clients, about new ways to use Twitter to attract new customers. He wrote a paragraph, but couldn't concentrate. He went back to Facebook and looked at the girl's picture again. She was heavily made up and clutching a drink. She had big, wide eyes that were staring into the camera, and she was wearing a top that only just covered her chest. She was laughing. Who was she?

"Fuck it," he thought, and clicked accept on the friend request. He accompanied it with a message.

How do I know you?

There, that would do. He would forget it now and concentrate on the proposal for his client. He would get it finished and leave early.

In the corner of his screen he noticed he had an event invitation. He clicked through and read the details of Renée's reunion quickly. She wanted to meet up again and relive the old times. In two weeks' time. Steve didn't need to look at his calendar to see what it said. It was always empty, every evening reserved for urgent work that might come up. The mouse hovered over the "not going" button . . . But it would be good to see everyone and catch up. He'd only seen James once since his baby had been born. They both had such hectic work lives. He would go to the reunion. Why not? One evening out wouldn't kill his business.

5

Sam laid everything out on the table: the delicate ivory wedding invitations, two black fountain pens, the printed guest list, the envelopes and the purple ribbon to tie round each invitation.

She had been learning the art of calligraphy for just over a week, so that she could write the invitations herself. She'd taken a book out of the library and had practiced tracing the names of the guests over and over again in the notebook she kept on her bedside table.

She could hardly believe she was getting married. It had been a childhood dream to walk down the aisle of a church lined with blue hydrangeas, in a huge white meringue dress, admiring friends and family watching her every move. She had been planning her wedding since she was ten years old and she knew exactly what she wanted.

Patrick had proposed three months ago, and since then she'd bought every wedding magazine in WHSmith, studied the internet religiously for advice, and spoken to her mother daily on the phone about each tiny detail of her big day.

She had finalised the venue two weeks ago: a picture-perfect church near where she had spent her childhood, the centrepiece of a quaint English village of stone houses and cottages. The reception was in a hotel down the road. As soon as she had booked the church and reception, Sam had felt so elated that she had gone out and bought the materials for the invitations. The wedding wasn't until the summer, and she had toyed with the idea of sending out "save the date"s rather than invitations, but as the timings of the day were already planned down to the last detail, it seemed silly not to go straight to the invitations.

Sam sat down at the table and took the first invitation from the pile and started to write out the name of the first couple on the guest list. By the tenth invitation, her concentration was waning. She forced herself to focus, and began to etch the name of an elderly relative, Niamh, on the paper. She concentrated intently on writing each letter just right, crafting each curl and flourish with care. She leant back and surveyed her work.

She'd missed out the "a".

She felt her jaw tense in annoyance. She put the invitation to one side and decided to take a break.

She made herself a cup of tea and sat back at the table. She pulled a wedding magazine off the shelf and began to flick idly through it. There was a four-page spread of formalwear for the groom in the middle, and Sam began to fantasise about Patrick waiting for her at the end of the aisle. With his curly dark hair and strong jaw-line, Patrick could have carried off any suit perfectly, but it had been decided that he would wear a kilt, as a nod to his Scottish roots. Sam smiled at the thought.

She put the magazine to one side and went back to the invitations. Apart from Niamh, she had ticked off all the members of her small family: her mother, a couple of aunts, an uncle, two cousins, and Niamh. And of course her father. Although she didn't expect him to turn up. She frowned for a second as she tried to shake the image of her walking down the aisle alone alongside the crowd of uncles and aunts and long-lost cousins on Patrick's side of the church, and the contrasting empty pews on her side.

She doubted her father would have any interest in her wedding. Her mother forced him to leave when Sam was young and she hadn't heard from his since. Her mother had made it very clear she didn't want him to have anything to do with her or Sam. That hadn't stopped Sam from sending a letter to his last known address, asking him to walk her down the aisle. As Sam had expected, he hadn't replied. Despite this, she had carefully written out his invitation, just like the others.

The next names on the list were her friends from university. She wrote the first two invitations quickly. They were for her two closest friends in the world. Next came more names from uni. She hesitated. She worried that they wouldn't turn up, or else they'd turn up, but only for the free food and drink. Each invitation represented an expense, and although Patrick had told her that he would pay for everything she wanted, she was worried about waste.

She wrote Katie's invitation first. They had studied English Literature together, and although they hadn't been that close, they had remained in touch. After Katie, there were the people she'd occasionally talked to at the pub, people she had tagged along with rather than her close friends. She looked at the list: Renée and Andy, James, Dave, Steve. If it wasn't for their Facebook updates, she'd have no idea what they were doing now. They had faded away into their own lives. Would any of them come to her wedding?

She wanted them there so they could see how much she had changed. Gone was the fat, shy, insecure girl she had been at university. Now she was a slim size twelve, and she was marrying a handsome older man. She imagined the door opening to the church, and the group from university gasping at the sight of her expensively styled blonde hair and huge flowing dress. She knew she was being melodramatic, but the thought of it always made her smile.

She started carefully writing the name Renée out on the ivory invitation. Was the accent over the first e, or the second? She reached across to pull her address book from the shelf to check.

In doing so, her arm caught the half-full lukewarm cup of tea that sat beside her, and she knocked it over the pile of unwritten invitations. She jumped up to get a cloth, but by the time she got back to the table the tea had seeped through each and every one of the fresh invitations.

Sam felt her eyes brim with tears, and told herself to be strong. She wasn't that person anymore. She could laugh off these kinds of things.

She went to get some kitchen-roll and dabbed at the remaining invitations. They were beyond rescue. The calligraphy would have to wait until she'd bought some new ones.

*

The door banged behind Patrick as he came in from work.

"How was your day?" Sam asked.

"Fine," he murmured, reaching down to kiss her head and breathing in the scent of her shampoo. He grinned at her. "I'm horny. Shall we go straight upstairs, my future wife?"

Her heart lifted; then she smiled apologetically. "The dinner's already in the oven."

He stroked her back. "I guess I can wait until after dinner, then. It smells great; you're shaping up into a great little wife."

Sam smiled, buoyed by the compliment, and that word: *Wife.* She repeated it over and over in her head. It summed up everything she wanted, everything she could be. It made her giddy that in less than a year she would be marrying this man.

"How was your day?" he asked, picking up his post from the kitchen counter and flicking through the envelopes.

"Good and bad . . . I made a start on the invitations, but . . ."

He turned sharply, hearing the hesitation in her voice. His intense blue eyes were on her. "But what?"

Sam's heart beat faster and she clasped her hands together nervously. "But I . . . I spilled tea on them."

The slap came quickly, and she felt the blood rush to the spot where his hand had met her face.

"Stupid girl."

"I'm sorry," she said, but he was already calm again.

"It doesn't matter, I suppose. We can buy new ones." She knew him well enough now to know that he wasn't being sarcastic. His anger was like a bolt of lightning, and it was often over before it had properly begun. He didn't see anything wrong with it.

It was a part of him, and it was something she just had to accept. When you truly love someone, you love them in spite of their weaknesses. She'd read that in a magazine once, and she knew it was true. And she certainly loved him. Their love could survive anything.

6

A wave of relief flowed through Katie as the taxi pulled up in front of her mum's semi-detached suburban house. She paid the driver with the last of the money she had managed to take out of the cash machine in the airport. She was so far into her overdraft that she had felt an intense emotional relief when the machine had returned both her card and the cash.

She got out of the car and watched as the driver lifted her mud-spattered rucksack out of the boot. That rucksack had been her life for the last six years. And now it was accompanying her home.

She didn't have the energy to lift it and put it on her back, so she carried it in her hands as her shoes crunched slowly over the gravel.

Her mother opened the door before Katie knocked, and held out her hands. She took her rucksack and then gave her a big hug.

"Are you OK?"

"Yeah," Katie said, trying to sound stoical in the face of her illness. She needed to sit down soon or she might be sick any moment.

"You look awful," her mother said, reaching out and touching Katie's lank, greasy hair. Katie moved away quickly.

Washing her hair had been the last thing on her mind over the last few days. She tried to smile at her mother as she bent over to untie her trainers. She placed them carefully on the shoe rack next to her mother's high heels.

"I'm just going to the toilet." She rushed off to the bathroom.

Ten minutes later she went into the kitchen to find her mother, who had poured her a glass of water.

"Here you go," she said.

"Thanks," Katie said, although she wasn't sure she'd be able to keep it down. She picked up the glass and held it in her hands without taking a sip. "I'm just going to go and lie down."

"Is there anything else I can get you?"

"No, I'm fine."

"Do you want any dinner?"

"No, thanks; I'll just go upstairs."

Katie was about to climb the stairs when she noticed parallel rungs going all the way from the bottom of the stairs to the top. At the top was a stair lift.

"What's this?" she asked her mother.

"It's your grandfather's stair lift."

"Right," Katie said, confused. Why did her grandfather need a stair lift in her mother's house? Or was there something she wasn't remembering?

She started a gradual climb up the stairs.

"Katie, you remember my email, don't you?"

Her mother had sent her at least three emails a day in the six years she'd been away. Katie had no idea which one she was referring to, but she didn't really want to have this conversation now. She was just too tired. "Yeah," she said. "I'm just going up to my room."

Her mother reached out to touch her arm and spoke softly. "You can't go to your room. It's where your grandfather sleeps now. You'll have to sleep in your brother's room."

"Grandad's staying here?"

"Yes. I told you in the email."

"Why?"

"You remember he had that operation, a couple of months ago?"

"Yeah." Katie vaguely remembered something about a "minor op". It hadn't sounded serious.

"Well, afterwards he wasn't quite the same. He wasn't really well enough to go back and live on his own, so I said he could stay with me a while."

"OK." Katie was too tired to think about this now. She began to slowly climb the stairs under the watchful eyes of her mother. The house around her was spotlessly clean, and for once she appreciated it. She knew that by the time she went to bed her socks wouldn't have picked up dirt from the floor and she wouldn't need to wash her hands from touching the banister rail. She was glad to be home.

When she opened the door to her brother's room with the trepidation she had had as a child, she found it neat and tidy, with clean sheets on the bed. She had imagined it being just as it had always been, with her brother's boxers spread round the floor, books and fag packets everywhere.

There were still remnants of her brother in the room. The wallpaper was the red Man United paper he had chosen when he was twelve, and there were posters of long-forgotten pop stars on the wall. Katie lay down on bed and stared at them. They stared back.

She had thought she'd get to sleep instantly, but she lay awake on top of the sheets. She should really change her clothes. In the last few days she had got into a cycle of sleeping for a bit, going to the toilet, throwing up, sweating with fever in her bed, then sleeping a bit more and repeating the cycle. She hadn't changed her clothes or showered for days. She reached down and scratched her leg. She felt so greasy that she thought she might be leaving an oily stain on the bed.

She heard the sound of her mother's footsteps on the stairs and then the door to her room creaked open and her mother came into the room and stood over the bed. She placed Katie's rucksack on the floor.

"Are you OK, Katie?"

"Yeah. Thanks for carrying that up." There were no clean clothes in the rucksack, but at least she would be able to change into something less dirty.

"Is there anything I can get you?"

"No, I'm fine." And with that she closed her eyes and fell into a restless sleep, before she'd even had the chance to open the rucksack.

7

Dave wove his way through the crowds of tourists and shoppers in Tottenham Court Road. He turned the corner into the street marked on Renée's map, and caught sight of the pub sign protruding from a brick wall. As usual, Renée's directions to the reunion had been nothing if not precise: as well as the Google map, there had been written instructions and a list of notable landmarks.

They had discussed the venue over Facebook; Renée had suggested a bar, but Dave and Katie had pushed for a pub. None of the others seemed to care. Renée had gone with the majority and chosen the Rose and Crown.

Dave pushed open the wooden door and felt the gust of warmth hit him. The Rose and Crown had a long bar down the left-hand side, backed by a mirrored wall. A board on a pillar advertised two for one cocktails, and sharply dressed barmen shook, threw and caught cocktail shakers with elaborate movements. In the cavernous main room the music was pumping. There were low sofas filled with people, and small tables dotted around what looked like it might be a dance floor. Despite its traditional name, the Rose and Crown was a carbon copy of every other modern bar in London.

Dave thought wistfully of the nooks and crannies of his local as he fought his way through the hordes by the bar, scanning the tables for the others. Eventually he spotted Renée and Andy sitting at a table in the corner. Despite himself, he felt a familiar flicker of attraction when he saw Renée's long dark hair and oval face. There had always been something about her.

Renée and Andy were surrounded by empty seats. Was Dave the first? It seemed unlikely. He was forty-five minutes late. He approached cautiously. At university Renée and Andy were the kind of couple that took you by surprise with their sudden and seemingly random affection for each other. Without warning, and mid-conversation, Renée would lean over to kiss Andy, while Andy's hand crept up her thigh alarmingly, in full view of their friends. Being the third person at the pub with them was never an attractive option.

When Dave looked closer, he saw that Renée's usually pale face was flushed and she was talking heatedly at Andy, while Andy sat back with his arms folded. Perhaps things had changed since they got married.

He pushed past the final crowd of people and reached their table. It had a big "Reserved for Renée" sign in the centre. He coughed, and they looked up. Renée stood up immediately, and Andy was a couple of seconds behind.

"Hi, Dave. How are you?" Renée asked, her voice strained with false enthusiasm, her mind clearly still on her argument with Andy. She manoeuvred her way round the table and reached over to give Dave a kiss on the cheek, while Andy stood awkwardly.

"Good thanks, good." Dave nodded.

"I'm so glad you could make it; it's been absolutely ages."

"Yeah, it's been a while."

Andy was leaning forward in an attempt to hear the conversation over the noise. Dave reached out and shook his hand. "Alright, mate. How are you doing?"

"Good, mate, good."

"Do you want a drink?" Dave indicated Andy's half-full pint glass.

"No, I'm fine," Andy said.

"Renée?"

"No, I've got a bit left." She pointed at the half-empty bottle of wine beside her on the table. Dave smiled and raised his eyebrows.

"I'm going to share it with Katie, when she arrives," she said, indignantly.

Dave grinned, unsure whether the alcohol had been the cause or effect of the argument she'd been having.

"I *am,*" Renée insisted. "Anyway, James and Steve are at the bar. If you catch them, you might be able to scab a drink from them," she said, in attempt to get him back.

Dave grimaced and chose not to rise to it. Everyone thought Dave was tight. After a first year at university constantly buying rounds and lending friends money, his credit cards started to be declined, and out of sheer necessity his second and third years had been rather more frugal. But the reputation stuck.

He considered challenging Renée's view of him by staying where he was, but instead he swallowed his pride and headed to the bar. When he'd checked his bank account this morning he'd discovered it was nearly empty. The redundancy pay was already almost gone. Anyway, it wasn't like Steve and James couldn't afford to buy him a pint. They were both doing well for themselves.

Dave eased his way through crowds, trying not to knock into anyone. He scanned the groups pushing themselves forward to be served. Why did the men's backs look identical? Women, with their distinct clothes and hair, were easy to recognise, but the men were just a sea of pale shirts and short haircuts. It didn't help that Dave hadn't seen either James or Steve for at least six months.

Eventually he spotted Steve's sandy blond hair at the other

end of the bar, close to the front of the queue. He barged his way through, and reached them just as they were ordering.

He slapped Steve on the shoulder just as Steve pulled his credit card from his wallet. Steve turned, irritated by the distraction, and then grinned when he saw it was Dave.

"Ah, Dave! What do you want to drink?"

"Are you sure? Pint of Stella, mate."

"And a pint of Stella please," Steve said to the bargirl.

Dave turned to James.

"So, how are you, mate? Haven't seen you for ages."

Of all the crowd from uni, James had been the least good at keeping in touch. As soon as he'd left, he'd landed himself a job in strategy at the UK branch of a big American company and had worked day and night to sweat his way up the corporate ladder. Dave could count on one hand the number of times he'd seen James since university. He was almost always distracted by some last-minute crisis at work.

"I'm good," said James, lifting his whisky and coke from the bar and taking a controlled sip. "How are you doing?"

"Yeah, good," Dave said emphatically. There was no need to mention his redundancy. James and Steve would never understand. Their matching designer shirts were enough to let everyone know their place in the world.

*

Two hours later, Dave had drifted off into his own world as the conversation ebbed and flowed around him. He considered a group of girls perched on bar stools by a tall table a few feet away. He couldn't quite tell whether they were looking at him or not. They giggled to themselves and he looked away. He knew he wasn't the best looking bloke in the room, but he'd mastered the art of careful eye contact and comic self-deprecation, and he usually found it easy to charm women. But today he just wasn't in the mood for it.

He turned his attention back to his table. His pint had been hovering around the quarter full mark for some time now, but no one had offered him another drink. Steve, James and Renée were engrossed in a detailed comparison of how they'd each been screwed over at work. Renée's tone was indignant as she described how she'd missed out on a promotion. James's company had failed to secure a new client, despite James letting him win on the golf course, and Steve was annoyed that his clients hadn't recommissioned him for a new project. That was the problem with them: they were just too competitive. No one asked Dave about his job, and he idly wondered what they'd say if he told them he was unemployed. He would surely win the competition for being the most hard-done-by.

Andy was checking his phone and frowning. He seemed as uninterested as Dave. Dave tried to start a conversation with him. "So, mate, what have you been up to?" he shouted across the table, trying to make himself heard over the noise of the bar.

"What?" Andy asked, leaning forward.

"What have you been up to?" Dave gesticulated, emphasising each word.

"What?" Andy shook his head apologetically.

"What have you been doing, mate?"

"Yeah," Andy shouted, nodding emphatically, clearly unable to hear.

"Never mind," said Dave, leaning back into his seat, his head making contact with the shirt of the guy standing just behind his chair.

Dave turned, to feel the full force of the guy's glare. They should never have gone to a busy pub in central London. It was impossible to have a conversation or get to the bar. He frowned to himself. When had he started to have a problem with noisy pubs? He used to like noisy pubs. Was he getting old?

At the table, the conversation had moved on to marriage. Dave fiddled with the beer mats in front of him, wearing away their damp edges and separating the cardboard between his fingers. He wished Katie would show up. No one had expected her to come, but Renée had said she was back from India. Katie would liven things up; perhaps talk about things other than work and marriage. Anything was preferable to this.

Dave looked at his empty pint glass sorrowfully.

"So how's she getting on?" Renée was asking, leaning towards James.

How was who getting on?

"She said her first word the other day – dada."

Renée practically squealed with delight.

What? Dave's mind was struggling to process this. James had a baby? James, the guy who had run naked round the biology block after consuming five bottles of wine? That guy was a father?

The others were leaning towards James as he narrated story after story about his daughter. Dave hadn't quite caught the name of the baby, so it was difficult for him to join in, but it didn't matter, as James didn't need any encouragement.

Dave looked at them. How and when had they all got so old? And how come the same thing hadn't happened to him? Had they just aged faster and seen the delights of marriage and children before him? Was it like growing your first pubic hair? Maybe some men just matured quicker than others.

He shivered. If this was the future, then the future scared him. He couldn't imagine living their lives, or even having these conversations. James was reaching into his wallet and bringing out the inevitable baby photos now. It was getting a bit too much.

Katie suddenly appeared at the edge of the table, dressed in a long, flowing, hippy-style skirt and loose cotton top that she must have picked up on her travels. She was carrying a woven bag. It was a bit tattered, the edges were fraying and some of the colours had run into each other in the rain outside. Dave grinned to himself. At least she hadn't changed.

Katie greeted them enthusiastically, kissing each of them in turn on the cheek. "I'm going to the bar," she said. "Does anyone want anything?"

Dave got up quickly, eager to escape the conversation, and Renée laughed.

"After a free drink, Dave?"

Dave glared at her. The bottle of wine she had supposedly been going to share with Katie seemed to have disappeared. He turned to Katie. "I'll come with you," he said.

Katie gave a quick look round the others. "Anyone else want a drink?"

James nodded. "Double whisky and coke, please."

Andy added: "Pint for me."

Dave turned and headed for the bar before anyone could add any more drinks to the order. Katie quickly followed.

"So, how's it going?" she asked.

Dave pulled a face. "Well, I'm not having the most thrilling evening of my life. They're all talking about marriage and children and their jobs." He was aware that he sounded like a spoilt child.

Katie laughed. "I meant how's it going with *you*? You know, in your own life?"

"Ohhh..." Dave stretched out the sound to avoid answering the question, but she waited patiently. He might as well be honest with her. "Well, I was doing alright, you know, getting by, reasonable job. But I lost it. So now I'm unemployed. I'm not married and I don't have children. A failure, in fact." He grinned at her and she laughed.

"Well, we're in the same boat: no wife and three kids for me yet either. We could sit on some kind of separate children's table for the people who haven't quite got their lives perfectly planned yet."

Dave caught the eye of the barman and ordered the drinks. As they were being poured he looked fearfully into his wallet.

"£14.20," the barman said.

Dave produced the last tenner from his wallet reluctantly and looked at Katie.

"I'm a bit short of cash."

"Me too," she said. "But I think I've got a tiny bit of room on my credit card, so I could pay by card."

Dave felt guilty.

"It's OK, I've got a tenner. I just need £4.20."

"Don't worry. It was my round anyway."

The barman coughed impatiently.

"Why don't we split it?" Dave said.

"OK. I'll put it on my card and you can give me a seven quid when you have change."

They carried the drinks back to the table and sat down.

The others were immersed in conversation, and although Dave leant in to listen he couldn't pick up the gist of what they were saying. He turned to Katie. "So, how was travelling?"

"Great. Well, mostly great I mean; I got a bit ill in India."

"Oh." Dave said, trying to picture what a bit ill might mean. A cold? Traveller's diarrhoea? Hospitalisation?

"Are you better now?"

"Yeah. I spent about a week just lying in bed when I got back, but now I'm definitely feeling stronger." Katie smiled, and then added quickly, "But don't let that put you off going to India. Other than that, I had a great time."

"I'd love to travel," Dave said wistfully.

"Why don't you?"

"I don't know."

"What's stopping you?"

"Well, I suppose my job was."

"But now you're unemployed?"

Dave glanced round to check that no one had heard.

"Yeah," he said.

"So you could travel?"

"I suppose so."

He frowned at her. She was implying that he hadn't travelled because of some kind of lack of initiative, rather than any real reason. Even if it was true, he didn't need her to tell him. A minute ago they had been in the same boat, but now she was kind of suggesting she had one over on him. The evening was going from bad to worse. Did he have anything in common with his friends anymore?

"Do you want to see my photos? Maybe they'd give you some inspiration for where you might want to go."

Dave cringed. He had no desire to see a string of photos of landmarks he didn't recognise dispersed between photos of someone else having fun. But he couldn't say no.

"Sure," he said.

"Well, I don't have them here, but I can definitely show you them another time." Katie seemed to brighten at his interest.

"Yeah, another time."

"Have you been to Israel?" she asked.

He had been on holiday abroad twice in his life: once to Gran Canaria with his parents and once on a lads' holiday to Corfu. "No," he said. He supposed that while Renée's thing was "success at work", Katie's thing was travel. It was kind of her specialist area, something you weren't allowed to be better than her at. He supposed everyone had their niche, their specialist subject. But what was his?

*

Renée studied the photos of James's daughter on his mobile. She'd already seen a lot of the photos on Facebook, but she somehow felt obliged to look through each one again, just to be polite.

"She's adorable," she said.

James was looking over her shoulder. "I know. Look how determined she looks there; she's trying to pull herself up to crawl."

"Yeah."

The photos saddened Renée. Three years ago when she'd been pregnant herself, she'd imagined herself in this position, proudly showing baby photos to friends, discussing all the things her child was doing. Part of the reason she had taken the job at the council in the first place was that it was secure and it was supposed to have sensible hours and good maternity pay. The life of a lawyer wasn't usually like that.

"That's her favourite toy. Steve bought it for her."

Steve glanced over and smiled when he saw the photo of the baby with the toy.

The baby was about six months old now, but Renée hadn't bought James anything when it was born. She hadn't even seen James since it was born. Was she the only one who'd lost touch with her friends?

"So, are you and Andy planning any little ones?" Steve asked conversationally.

Renée glanced across the table at Andy. Before the miscarriage, they had both been excited about being parents. They studied books of baby names religiously, and looked at cots and prams in John Lewis. But since the miscarriage they hadn't discussed a baby at all. Renée had started taking the pill again. She'd told herself they'd try again when she was ready. Yet three years on, she still didn't feel she was.

Steve asked the question again, presuming she hadn't heard.

"Maybe," she said, as Andy replied, "Not just now."

Andy held Renée's gaze for a split second, and then they both looked away.

"So, James, where are you living now?" Andy said, changing the subject.

"Richmond."

"Ah. We're in Wimbledon, so quite close; whereabouts in Richmond?"

"Parkside."

Renée sat up a bit straighter. Parkside was one of the most expensive roads in Richmond. Andy and Renée would never be able to afford to live there.

"Wow. That's nice."

"You should come over and meet our daughter. We'd like that."

"Sounds good," Renée said.

There was a lull in the conversation. Renée glanced over at Katie and Dave, who were immersed in each other. Some things never changed. Dave still had that cheeky look about him; not handsome exactly, but boyish. He had been quiet earlier, but now he was grinning broadly.

Renée found a pencil in her handbag and used it to clink her glass. It wasn't very effective against the noise of the bar. James, Steve and Andy had become engrossed in a conversation about football, and Dave and Katie didn't even look up.

Renée stood up and raised her glass. They all turned to her.

"I wanted to propose a toast." She paused as they raised their glasses. She noticed that Andy and James's glasses were empty, but they raised them obediently.

"To us," she said. "And to friendship."

They repeated the toast, and returned to their conversations.

Renée sat back down. She was lucky to have friends like these, but she should really spend more time with them. Especially now Katie was back from India; they should catch up more often.

Renée became distracted by the conversation that had started up to her left. She overheard the name Sam, and strained her ears to hear what Steve and James were saying.

"Yeah, it came in the post last week," Steve said.

"Are you talking about Sam's wedding?" Renée asked.

"Yeah," James said.

Renée and Andy had also received their invitation. Renée

had been baffled at first, struggling to recall who Sam was. Eventually she had remembered. *Samantha Evans.* Renée had seen she was engaged on Facebook. Sam had hung around with them sometimes, sitting with them at the bar, going out clubbing with them. She was often in the backs of their uni photos, but Renée's memories of her were fuzzy,

"You guys got an invite too?"

"Yeah, it came the other day," James said. "It should be a good wedding."

"Do you remember her?"

"Yeah," said Steve.

"I do too" Renée said, "but not very clearly. I was surprised to get an invite." She frowned. Perhaps she should have invited Sam to the reunion tonight. It hadn't even crossed her mind. "Has anyone heard from her in the last year?"

"I have," Katie said. "We've sent a few emails – you know, she's lost a lot of weight and met a man she's fallen in love with. It's like a fairytale ending for her." Katie smiled.

Renée herself had only received the occasional email from Katie when she'd been travelling. Did that mean that they'd grown apart? Had she been too preoccupied with her marriage to Andy and her job to notice? "So, is everyone going then?" she asked.

There were mumbles and nods round the table. She smiled. The wedding would guarantee that they'd all see each other again in the summer. They could talk and laugh and catch up again while they drank wine in the sun.

Thinking of wine and sunshine made her feel sleepy, and she stifled a yawn. She suddenly felt tired of trying to make herself heard above the noise. But the evening had been a success. She'd caught up with everyone's news. The only person she hadn't really talked to was Andy, but then she talked to him every day.

*

It was the nearing the end of the night. The bar was empty-ing around Dave and his friends. On the tables around them, people downed the final dregs of their pints and rose to leave.

James had left an hour ago, to get back to his family. Dave had seen him drink at least six double whiskies, and yet by the end of the evening he hadn't even been slurring his words. He had walked out of the bar perfectly straight, waving a cheery goodbye. Dave was impressed. Even now James could still do it. Just like at university, where he had managed to get a first in Business Studies, play for the university football team and still drink everyone else under the table.

Renée was putting her coat on while Andy waited for her, stony-faced. Dave wondered if they had had another argument.

"We're off now," Renée said.

Katie got up to give her a hug. Dave raised his hand, goodbye, from where he was sitting. He was getting that feeling that he sometimes got towards the end of the night, when he just wanted to keep drinking. He felt full of energy. He didn't like the thought of just going home to his shared flat and going straight to bed. It was a Friday night. It was eleven o'clock. The night was still young.

Maybe the others would fancy going out. He turned to them as Andy and Renée retreated out of the bar waving their goodbyes.

"Does anyone else fancy going on somewhere?"

Only Steve and Katie remained. Steve was already putting on his coat.

"Not this time mate – I've had a busy week; I'm tired."

Since when was a busy week an excuse for not going out on a Friday? "Alright mate. Next time then." Katie was his only hope. He looked over at her. In the bright light of the pub, the highlights in her hair looked almost fluorescent. "You coming, Katie?"

"Er . . . I'd like to." Katie fiddled with her hair, a habit that she'd had at university ". . . but I don't have much money. Can we go somewhere cheap?"

Dave could only think of a dodgy club in Battersea that was usually empty. As long as it wasn't busy you could usually persuade the bouncers to let you in for free. And it was never busy. The club was mainly used as a front for a middle-class drug dealer. Clients tended to go in and out pretty quickly.

"Yeah, sure. I know somewhere, and it's free to get in. So are you coming?"

"Yeah, why not?" Katie's face split into a smile.

*

Forty-five minutes later, Dave already wanted to leave the club. The music seemed to just repeat itself over and over again and he suspected you had to be on a lot of drugs to really appreciate it. He watched the others dancing with reckless abandon. There was a group dealing in the corner, their faces pale against their black jackets. They glanced over at him and he looked quickly away. He looked longingly at the bar, but he knew he couldn't afford a drink and Katie couldn't either.

They danced for a while in an exaggerated way, taking the piss out of the others around them. Dave waved his hands in the air manically, mimicking the guy a few feet away from them, who was dancing on his own with an intense expression of concentration on his face. Katie laughed, and copied the move in an even more exaggerated fashion. The she started jumping up and down dementedly, in the style of a group on the other side of the dance floor.

Dave laughed. Nights out with Katie were always entertaining.

But then he started to sober up and began to lose his confidence, worried that one of the other dancers might take offence. They didn't look like the kind of people you'd want to get on the wrong side of.

They danced in a more serious way, and he found himself embarrassed by his clumsy movements, as if all the cokeheads around him might suddenly start laughing at him, instead of the other way round. But Katie was closer now; he could feel the warmth of her. He found himself kissing her. She tasted the same as she had always done: slightly sweet – strawberry lip balm with an aftertaste of stale wine. The moment took him back to all their previous kisses. Throughout their time at university when they had been between boyfriends or girlfriends (and even sometimes when they weren't), they had reverted to each other. It felt natural holding her in her arms. It was relaxed and nostalgic.

When they pulled apart they smiled at each other.

"Like old times," he said, suddenly feeling horny.

"Yeah," she said. "It's nice to remember."

They kissed again and Katie pulled away.

"I really need a drink," she said.

"I can't afford one."

"No, me neither."

"We could go back to mine."

"Yeah, that would be good." She nodded, and Dave felt a tugging in his jeans. All of a sudden he couldn't wait to feel her again.

8

In the half-light of the bedroom, James tied his tie and checked his reflection in the mirror. He leant closer and peered at his face, noticing a spot of blood on his cheek where he must have cut himself shaving. He dabbed at it with a tissue and then stood back and surveyed himself. His shirt was well ironed and he looked professional and tidy. Ready for another day at the office.

He went over to the bed and bent over to kiss his sleeping wife. Then he tiptoed to the corner of the room and stared into the cot where Phoebe slept. She looked so peaceful. He reached out to touch his sleeping child and then stopped himself. After a fretful, sleepless night the bedroom was at peace, Meera and Phoebe both asleep. It wasn't worth waking Phoebe up just so James could kiss her goodbye. He would let them sleep.

He went downstairs and took his packed lunch out of the fridge. Fortunately the stresses and strains of motherhood had not lessened Meera's desire to look after James. The day after she returned from hospital, James had got up early, expecting to have to make his own lunch. Instead, he had found his packed lunch sitting on the middle shelf of the fridge, just like it always was. Of course, he shouldn't have expected anything less from Meera. She had spent the weeks before Phoebe's birth filling the freezer up with her cooking, to ensure that he would be well fed if she had to stay in hospital longer than expected.

He had been feeling guilty about not taking paternity leave, but the continued presence of the packed lunch had reassured him; Meera had communicated through her actions that she didn't mind, that she could cope.

They had met when Meera had been part of the team of accountants that had come to audit James's firm a few years before. James had been impressed by her cool, calm attitude and her unwillingness to take bullshit from anyone. As her team neared the end of the audit and their inevitable departure, James had made the effort to find time to take lunch, and had approached her in the staff canteen and insisted on joining her. It had soon become a habit, and although at first they only talked about work, they soon moved on to other topics. When James found out that Meera had never been skiing, he invited her on a trip with him and some friends. A year later they were married.

James picked up his briefcase and pulled out his Evian bottle. He went into the cupboard under the sink and reached right to the back behind the bleach and dishwasher tablets. He pulled out the larger plastic bottle that contained the vodka. He wasn't quite sure why he'd felt the need to pour the Smirnoff into a washed-out bottle of orange squash and put it behind the bleach. He supposed he had thought that if Meera found it she would assume it was some kind of cleaning material.

It wasn't that he even needed to hide the vodka from her. She didn't mind him drinking. He had just decided to transfer the vodka into a more innocuous bottle one day. It was supposed to be his "emergency supply" for when he had particularly bad days at work. But his emergency supply often ran low and he got into the habit of topping up the plastic bottle under the sink from supplies he bought on his way home from work and stashed in other strategic locations around the house. Of course, after a short time this had raised the problem of what to do with the empties. They couldn't appear in the recycling bin if no one in the house had been drinking vodka. So James stored them in the boot of his car and would often stop at Sainsbury's on his way to work to dispose of them in the green bins in the car-park.

He was aware that, to an outsider, it might seem like an unnecessary level of deceit. But Meera didn't drink, so she wouldn't understand. It was best not to worry her. Especially with a new baby.

James held the Evian bottle over the sink as he poured the contents of the larger bottle into the smaller bottle. He screwed the lid on tight and put the small bottle back in his briefcase.

Right. Did he have everything? He checked his pockets: house keys and wallet. He checked his briefcase: water bottle and phone. Whistling to himself, he picked up his car-keys from the side and went out the front door to the car to make his way to work.

9

Katie reached sleepily for the phone on her bedside table and checked the time. Ten thirty a.m. She must have fallen back to sleep.

The smell of a cooked breakfast wafted up from downstairs, and she could hear the clanking of cutlery and the lull of voices in the kitchen. Her grandfather would be up having breakfast with the carer who came on weekdays to look after him, while her mother was at work.

She rolled over lazily. She should get out of bed, but the sheets were so soft, enveloping her body in a warm cocoon. By the time she went downstairs breakfast would be over and she would be greeted with a pointed look at the watch from her grandfather. It was like being a child again.

Staring at the ceiling, she thought about what she should do today. She really needed to find a job. Any job. Her mother's patience was starting to run out. She also needed to go to the supermarket and do the weekly shop and run some other errands that her mother had mentioned last night. Perhaps she could search for a job while she was in town. The thought reminded her of when she'd been sixteen and had wandered round town going into each shop to see if there had been any vacancies. She had landed in Superdrug, ich had several. Which wasn't surprising, as they paid £2.16 an hour.

At least they had a minimum wage now. And she should be able to get something clerical, or maybe even some teaching work. People always wanted after-school tutors for their children, didn't they? She had lots of experience. Maybe she could put an ad in the local paper.

The thought tired her, but she forced herself to roll out of bed, and went to have a shower. When she came back she checked her phone again. Still no text from Dave.

She sighed. It was a week since the reunion and he still hadn't contacted her. It was just sex, then, she supposed. Again. Nothing had changed.

This time she had thought it might be different. They were both older. They were supposed to be grown up. She'd thought he'd have matured enough to want more than casual sex. She'd thought that this time it might have meant something.

She had gone through her entire time at university thinking the same thing. As Dave had flitted from girlfriend to girlfriend, Katie had always been there. He had told her frequently that she was one of his greatest friends, an ally. He had kept coming back to her, kept sleeping with her. She had thought it meant something. But when they left university he was with a girlfriend of six months. Katie had gracefully detached herself from it all and told herself to cut her losses. Three months later Dave and his girlfriend split up, but by the time Dave called her to meet for sex Katie was already teaching in Japan. When she'd received the drunken call she had felt simultaneous longing for his affection and relief that she was so far away that she couldn't succumb to his whims.

Since the reunion, she had been wondering if there was a future for them. Maybe, just maybe, men took longer to catch up with what was right for them. Maybe, after six years apart, something would click in Dave's brain and he would finally see Katie as someone he could spend romantic time with, rather than just someone to hang around and have sex with. It wasn't like she was even that bothered about the romance. After all, most relationships were just friendship and sex. All they needed was the monogamy on top. Was that too much to ask?

It probably was. He hadn't called, had he? If he'd wanted anything from her, then he'd have called. But then again, she hadn't called him either. Had she ever, at any point during their time at university, told him she liked him? No. Perhaps he didn't know.

Of course he knew. She'd made it obvious, hadn't she? By always being there, ready and available.

But what if he didn't?

Fully dressed, she sat down heavily on the bed and picked up her phone again. Perhaps she should just call him, once and for all. She could ask him out.

She used to know Dave's number off by heart, but she had forgotten it. She found the number on the phone and stared at the familiar digits.

Right, she thought, and pressed call before she could stop herself.

She listened to the ringing on the other end and then suddenly prayed for an answer-phone message so that she wouldn't have to talk to him. She hadn't thought about what to say. She wasn't prepared.

The phone kept ringing, and she forced herself to keep holding it to her ear.

"Hello," Dave answered gruffly. She could hear the TV in the background.

"Hi, it's me, Katie."

"Hi."

"Umm . . . How are you?"

"Yeah, good."

She wanted desperately to hang up. Instead, she tried inane conversation.

"What are you up to?"

"Nothing much."

"Oh." Now or never.

"Do you fancy doing something?" She really should be doing the shopping this afternoon, but she had to ask.

"What – today?"

Katie cringed. Was this too desperate? Or too casual?

"Yeah."

"Urgghh . . . I kind of have plans."

"What plans?" What had made her ask that question? Why couldn't she just accept?

"The football's on this afternoon; it's a qualifier for the cup"

"Oh, right. Yeah, of course."

There was a pause, and the only sound she could hear was the murmur of the TV from the other end of the phone.

"Maybe another time then," she said.

"Yeah. Nice to talk to you, Katie." He hung up and Katie threw the phone down on the floor.

10

Steve surveyed the shopping centre. Caroline had insisted they meet in a public, crowded place. At first, Steve had been taken aback. Since she'd first sent the friend request on Facebook they had emailed each other so often that he no longer thought of her as a stranger. But when he thought about it, he understood her concerns. People lied about who they were online all the time and this would be the first time Steve and Caroline had met in person. It had been on the news just the other day: a paedophile had been arrested for targeting under-aged girls on Facebook.

He was early, and he'd already walked past Topshop three times to see if she was there waiting for him. She wasn't yet. Gaggles of girls walked in and out of the store giggling. Teenagers dragged their boyfriends into the shop and became lost in the racks of clothes. No Caroline.

Maybe she had been past already, spotted him scanning the entrance and changed her mind. Maybe he was wearing the wrong thing or she thought he wasn't as attractive in real life as in his profile picture. Or maybe she'd decided not to turn up at all. Maybe she was at home right now, watching TV and wondering why she ever suggested they meet in the first place.

Perhaps he should leave. He could do with getting some

work done. With Harry gone, Steve had to work harder than ever. He couldn't trust the rest of the sales team with Harry's accounts, so he was managing them himself. But sales were still falling. He had studied the figures, and his outgoings now far exceeded his revenues. A few more bad months for the firm and there would be serious consequences. He was pinning all his hopes on a proposal for one of his biggest clients. If he could just land that project, then the company would have enough to keep going with the existing staff for another six months. Steve thought guiltily back to the proposal that he'd left abandoned on his laptop to come and meet Caroline. He could finish it tomorrow.

His productivity hadn't been helped by the fact that he had been so distracted by Caroline herself. He would turn on his laptop at home after dinner and find himself spending all his time on Facebook, either emailing Caroline, or impatiently checking for her response. Over the last few weeks their online relationship had escalated and they were now exchanging up to twenty messages an evening. It got to the point where there was nothing left to do but meet up. Steve dithered over asking her out, and in the end she had taken the initiative herself and suggested their date today.

Steve hadn't known what to wear for the meeting. Although he always tried to dress well and had a collection of interchangeable designer shirts for social events, he had been baffled by the prospect of meeting in a shopping centre. He had wondered what Caroline would be wearing, and had browsed through her photos on Facebook to try and guess; the photos ranged from her in low-cut tops clubbing, to jeans and T-shirt at a theme park. In the end he had settled on designer jeans and his best polo shirt. Presumably they'd move on from the shopping centre, going for dinner and then drinks and maybe back to his later. He smiled at the thought. He needed to be dressed for all possibilities.

He had thought about bringing some kind of present for her. A rose had seemed too much, perhaps even a bit sinister, but then some girls really liked flowers. But Caroline had never mentioned flowers, so he decided against it. He'd thought about a CD or a book. They had talked about music a lot and he knew her favourite bands. But what if he bought her something she hated? Or something she already had? Did she even own a CD player? Or did she just have an iPod?

So he had brought nothing. Now he wondered if that was a mistake. He looked at his watch, then looked at Topshop. It was five past six and she still wasn't there.

Steve had tried internet dating a couple of years before, but he didn't remember it being this stressful. He hadn't remembered the nerves that came with waiting for someone who you weren't quite sure you'd recognise.

He'd go over there and wait nearer the shop. He walked over slowly, ambling as if he hadn't a care in the world. He pretended to look at some of the clothes in the window. Then he turned again and looked for her. She wasn't there. He went in the shop and looked at the clothes near the doorway. They were women's clothes, but people would assume he was shopping for his girlfriend. Did men shop for their girlfriends?

He hadn't had much luck with internet dating. He seemed to attract the wrong type of people. He had even tried one of the "high-class" dating agencies with a minimum income level. He'd only set up one date and the woman had insisted they went to one of the most expensive restaurants in London. She then proceeded to spend the entire meal checking emails on her BlackBerry. When they moved on to dessert, Steve had felt like he was at a job interview as she threw question after question at him, before promptly declaring he was unsuitable for her and leaving him with the bill.

By comparison Caroline was a breath of fresh air. She was beautiful, interesting, fun and straightforward. She wasn't afraid to state her opinions about politics, or music, or religion. She was happy to talk about anything and everything, from the Iraq war to Lindsay Lohan. Steve had never really followed celebrity gossip, and sometimes he had to go to Wikipedia to look up the celebrities she was talking about.

When he used to go internet dating, he used to have to rehearse the details of his dates before he arrived: age, profession, hair colour, eye colour. But with Caroline he knew it all off by heart: twenty-two, aspiring actress, dark hair, blue eyes.

In the shop across the mall, a gang of girls were bustling around and looking out of the window towards Topshop. Steve put his head down. Maybe it was weird to be looking at women's clothes like this. He went outside the shop and stood there once more, scanning the crowds for Caroline. The crowd ebbed and flowed around him. He thought he spotted her from a distance: a girl with long dark hair was walking purposefully towards him. He started to smile, and his smile grew as she walked towards him. But she walked straight past, not meeting his eyes. He slouched against the window, embarrassed. He took out his phone and checked it to see if she'd texted him. She hadn't. He played with the phone a bit, checking Facebook to see if he had any messages from her; perhaps she had cancelled. He checked his emails. Nothing there either.

A girl broke away from the group of girls that stood outside the shop opposite. The others laughed and she glanced back at them and then walked towards Steve. Was that her? She had the right dark hair. He watched her as she got closer. She was probably just going into the shop. She looked like a Topshop sort of girl, young and well dressed. He went back to playing with his phone.

"Steve."

He looked up. It was her.

"Hi," he said.

He took her in: the heavy make-up, skinny jeans and sparkly top. She looked marginally less pretty than in the photo on Facebook, but only marginally.

She leaned forward and pecked him on the check. Steve noticed that behind her the gaggle of girls had got closer. The girls stared as Steve leaned in and returned her peck on the cheek.

"Hi," she said.

They smiled at each other, suddenly shy.

"So we finally meet," he said.

"Yeah."

She took his hand and started leading him away from the shop. "Let's get away from here."

"OK."

Steve let her lead him down the bright, open corridors of the shopping centre. He turned his attention to the gang of girls that seemed to be following them.

"You brought your friends?"

"Ignore them."

"You must be *really* worried I'm an axe murderer or something."

She laughed. "I've decided you can't be."

"Why?"

"A murderer would be sleazy. They'd bring a rose or something. They'd try to persuade me to go back home with them immediately."

Her friends were still there. In their large group, with their hoodies, they looked like a group of aggressive teenagers.

"Are they going to follow us all night?"

She turned round and walked a few steps to talk to them. Steve watched as she talked and they listened, as if in awe of her. She gestured at him and they laughed. He wondered what they were saying. Was the whole thing a joke to her? Was she coming back or was she just going to go off with her friends?

A minute later she was back beside him. She took his hand.

He looked round and saw her friends sloping away.

"What do you want to do?" he asked.

"Shopping?"

The last thing he wanted to do was go shopping. He'd already spent enough time in the shopping centre waiting for her.

"Sure," he said.

They went round the shops together hand in hand, to River Island, then New Look, then Oasis. In each shop she would pick something up and ask what he thought. His opinion would be required again when she went to try it on. He never really knew what to say, so he just said she looked nice. She did look good. The dresses she tried on hugged her figure, and the tops brought out the blue of her eyes.

She didn't buy anything though. Each time she found something she liked, she would scrutinise the price tag and then declare that she couldn't afford it. It had been a long time since Steve had had to think before buying an item of clothing because he wasn't sure if he could afford it. He supposed Caroline didn't earn much from small acting roles in TV ads. He'd make sure he paid for dinner.

The shops started to shut their doors at seven, and Steve was relieved. They left the shopping centre and went out into the high street.

"Dinner?" he said.

She smiled up at him. "OK."

They went to a small Italian that he used to frequent a few years before with an ex-girlfriend. He was embarrassed to discover that the proprietor remembered him, and he batted away his questions about why he hadn't been back for so long.

The place was romantic; small and cosy, with candles on every table. The light was low, and when they were shown to their table and were seated, Steve wondered if perhaps it was too romantic. Perhaps it wasn't appropriate for a first date.

The waiter brought the wine list over and Steve went for an expensive bottle. As Caroline studied the menu, her legs shook nervously under the table and Steve put his hand on her leg to steady her. She looked at the list of food intently.

"Do you need help deciding?" he asked.

"No," she said. "Thanks."

Perhaps he had sounded like a male chauvinist. Of course she could decide on her food herself.

The wine came and the waiter poured a bit into Caroline's glass for her to taste. She looked at it and then glugged it down in one gulp. She looked at Steve, confused.

"Why don't they pour a whole glass?"

He smiled at her. She obviously didn't eat out much. "Do you like the wine?"

"Sure, it's nice"

Steve nodded to the waiter, and reached out across the table to hold Caroline's hand.

The waiter poured the wine and then left them alone for two minutes, before returning with a notepad. He stood expectantly at the edge of their table.

"Are you ready to order?" Steve asked Caroline.

"Yeah," she said.

She ordered a salad, but nothing else. The salad was usually a side dish. Maybe she was trying to save money. That might explain her reticence about the wine.

"I'm going to get this, so order what you like," Steve said.

"I want a salad."

Steve glanced at the waiter, who was frowning into his notepad.

"A salad's usually a side; are you sure you don't want a main course to go with it?" Steve asked.

"I'm fine," she said, fidgeting in her seat.

"I'm paying," he said, to clarify.

She looked down at the floor. "I just want a salad."

Steve smiled, embarrassed that their evident miscommunication had been witnessed by the waiter. "I'll have the risotto and the roasted vegetables," he said quickly.

"Very good, sir."

The waiter recapped their order and then left.

Steve tried to recapture the conversation. "I feel like I know all about you."

"Me too."

There was a silence as she took a gulp of her wine. She seemed so nervous. No wonder she had brought so many friends with her. He tried to make her feel at ease.

"Is this your first blind date?"

"Yeah."

"It feels strange at first."

"Yeah."

She grinned at him.

"Have you been on lots of blind dates then?"

"Not too many, but a few." Suddenly Steve felt shy.

"So you don't pick young girls up on the internet all the time?"

She grinned at him cheekily, but it seemed like she was hiding her nerves. "You're not that much younger than me," he teased. "I feel eighteen inside."

She laughed, and the atmosphere lightened. They laughed together and talked about everything from reality TV to politics. It felt good to be talking about something other than work for once.

The food came and the waiter set the risotto in front of him, and the salad and vegetables in the middle. The salad was plain; just tomatoes, lettuce and cucumber. It looked unappetising, and she stared at it.

He laughed. "It's what you ordered."

"I know." She grimaced. "It doesn't look very nice though."

"You can have some of mine." He took a spoonful of the

risotto and held it up to her. She laughed and opened her mouth and he slid the spoon slowly in.

"Ah! It's hot." She swallowed quickly.

He withdrew the spoon and she took a gulp of her wine. He laughed and topped her glass up.

He offered her the vegetables and more risotto and they shared all the food between them. When he asked if she wanted to order more she declined.

She drank quickly, and the wine bottle was nearly empty when they had finished eating. They sat and sipped the remainder of the wine, and he surveyed her. She was gorgeous.

When the waiter came with the bill, Steve paid up while Caroline went to freshen up. When she came back he looked at her appreciatively.

"You look nice."

She smiled slightly. "Thanks, but I have to go now."

She got up to leave and Steve felt a shiver of disappointment. He stood up and put his arm round her as they left the restaurant. "Do you want me to walk you somewhere?"

"No, I'm OK."

Outside the restaurant, she stretched upwards and gave him a quick peck on the lips. "I'll see you around."

She turned away from him and walked briskly down the street towards the Underground station. He watched her until she disappeared out of sight, and then started his own walk home.

11

"Renée, I don't think I can do this anymore."

Renée glanced up from the television and looked at Andy. His shoulders were tense as he stared at the screen. It was part two of the X-Factor. On the screen a sixteen-year-old girl was crying as she begged the judges to save her. Renée forced herself to stare at the television, and pretended she hadn't heard. The girl continued to beg, as the judges ummed and ahhed.

What did he mean? She couldn't concentrate, and she realised she was holding her breath as she waited for Andy's next words.

"Renée, did you hear me?"

"Hmm," she said noncommittally, her ears pricked up to what he might say next, her body tense.

"I think we need a break from each other."

Renée swallowed. "Andy, it's late." She shifted her weight, trying to find a more comfortable position on the sofa.

"I know," he said.

On screen, the contestants waited for the judges to tell them their fate. No one spoke.

Andy stood up.

"Where are you going?"

"To pack some things."

Renée stood up too.

She couldn't pretend this wasn't happening. This was real. Andy was thinking of leaving. She had to stop him.

"Andy, can't this wait until the morning? You need to think this through." Renée heard her voice crack, despite her efforts to sound reasonable.

"I'm been thinking about it."

"Not for long enough."

"Really? Because I've been thinking about it for a long time." He sounded irritated now, and she heard a quiver in his voice.

"Why didn't you mention it then?"

"I can't talk to you, Renée." He reached out as if to touch her shoulder, but she stepped back and pushed his hand away.

"You haven't tried to talk to me."

"Well, I can't."

"Why?"

He didn't answer, and she saw he was fighting back tears himself. "It's not working."

What? What wasn't working?

"It's working for me," she said, as if that just might be enough. OK. Things weren't great, they weren't perfect, but wasn't that what marriage was about, give and take?

Andy walked towards the door of the living room and Renée ran round and stood in front of him. "Don't," she pleaded.

He put his hands on her shoulders and tried to move her gently out of the way. "It's only a break, Renée."

"You'll be back?"

"We'll see how it goes . . ."

"But you'll be back?" She needed him to say it.

"Maybe."

"Probably?"

"Yeah, maybe."

He moved her to the side and she heard him go into their bedroom. She didn't know what to do. Cheers rose from the TV. One of the contestants was through to the final. The other was not. The girl on stage sobbed openly. Renée sat back down to watch the end of the programme.

From the next room she heard a bag unzip and cupboard doors open and close.

How could Andy do this to her? How could he be so ungrateful? They'd built their lives together, and yes, sometimes it was hard, sometimes it was boring, but he couldn't just tear it all apart. This was their future.

The sound of muffled sobs, and then footsteps. Noise in the hall. He couldn't be leaving already could he? No. He'd need to say goodbye.

The front door shut.

Something in Renée was certain he hadn't left. He couldn't have. She watched the end of the X-Factor with the sound on low, listening for other sounds in the flat. It was silent.

When it finished she left the living room. She poured a glass of wine to calm her nerves. She walked into the kitchen first. As she left it: washing-up still in the sink. She walked into hallway, then the spare room. Then finally their bedroom. No Andy. She went to the window. His car wasn't in the parking space. He'd left.

She surveyed the bedroom. It didn't look any different. She opened the cupboards. The only visible difference was the empty space in the bottom corner, beside their tennis racquets. He must have packed his sports bag. Everything else looked the same. There were still rows of shirts and pairs of jeans hanging neatly in the cupboard. Renée managed a tense smile. He wouldn't be gone for long, then.

She picked her wine back up from the bedside table and took a sip. She walked to the window again. Then back to the bed in the middle of the room. She sat down for a second with her wine, then got up and went to the kitchen. The washing-up taunted her. She went to the living room and sat on the sofa and flicked through the channels.

She needed to get out. She grabbed her car keys from the side. She was OK to drive. She had hardly touched her wine.

*

Renée drove down the motorway, tears streaming down her face. She wanted to drive recklessly, faster than usual. But instead she concentrated on driving slowly and carefully, as she knew she was distracted. Why did she have to been so sensible, even in times like this? Why couldn't she react like a normal person, and speed? She cried harder, angry at herself.

Perhaps she would have an accident. Then Andy would be sorry. He'd come to identify her mangled body and realise the mistake he had made.

What did he mean by a break, anyway? How long was a break? A week? A month? What would happen at the end of it?

She felt more hopeful. It was just a break. He'd soon realise how much he missed her, and they'd get back together. Years later they'd probably laugh about it. Except that she wouldn't laugh very hard, as Andy was really screwing her over. He hadn't said anything about a break before. He had seemed a bit down, a bit distant, maybe, but he hadn't said anything was wrong. How could you just decide one day that you needed a break from your wife? How could he announce it so coldly, so unexpectedly, when she was watching the TV?

It felt like it had come out of nowhere. Yes, they had the normal ups and downs of any relationship, but not the kind of problems that needed to be fixed with a break.

She glanced up at the road-sign. She had driven halfway to her parents' house in Kent without even realising it. She gulped down tears. She couldn't go there. She couldn't admit to them that she and Andy were going through a tough patch. They'd expect better from her. And they'd ask questions that she wouldn't be able to answer. Like what had happened. If she told them what had happened, that Andy had left for no reason, they would probably hold it against him forever. She thought ahead to uncomfortable family meals with her father staring across the table accusingly at Andy, unable to forgive him this one transgression. It was easier not to tell them. Pretend everything was normal.

But she still wanted company. Could she go to a friend's house? No. She couldn't cope with their sympathy right now. She didn't want them expressing their surprise, their pity. Worse, they might accept the situation as inevitable and tell her they never liked him anyway. They'd blow it out of proportion. They'd see her turning up tear-stained at their door in the middle of the night, and draw their own conclusions. She didn't need that. This was just a blip. She and Andy would get back together in a week or two anyway, and it would be like nothing had ever happened. There was no point in telling anyone.

And there was nowhere to go except back home. Renée turned on the radio and opened the car windows wide, letting the cold wind blow her hair and start to dry her tears. At the next junction, she pulled off the motorway and turned around.

12

James and Meera eased themselves off the sofa and James turned off the lights in the living room. As he checked that the front door was locked, he heard Meera's leaden footsteps going up the stairs. They were both exhausted.

James sighed contentedly as he wandered into the kitchen to fix himself a nightcap. He and Meera had been out all day with Phoebe, first at the park and then the shops. He hadn't wanted the day to end. The last two hours in front of the TV watching X-Factor with Meera seemed like the first time they'd spent together sitting down and relaxing in ages. Phoebe had been asleep and the house had been quiet, but James hadn't even switched his laptop on to check his work emails.

He blinked as a pool of light filled the kitchen and a car pulled up slowly onto the drive. Someone must have taken a wrong turn and was using their driveway to turn around. He took the plastic bottle of vodka from under the kitchen sink, and started to pour his drink.

The doorbell rang. Upstairs, Phoebe started crying.

James downed his drink and went to the door. He unlocked it cautiously and then opened it to see Andy, his shirt untucked and his hair all over the place.

"Andy?"

"Err . . . Hi, James . . ."

It was late, and Andy hadn't visited before. Something must be wrong. James would have to invite him in.

"Are you OK? Do you want to come in?" He struggled to recall whether he had left the plastic bottle of vodka on the side in the kitchen. He was usually careful about things like that, but as Meera had already gone to bed, he might have been lax.

"Is this a good time? I mean I know it's not the best time . . . But, yeah, I'll come in, if that's OK."

James held the door and escorted Andy to the living room. He turned the light back on and indicated the sofa.

"Sit down; you look like you need a drink. What do you want?"

"No, it's OK. It's late. You've got work tomorrow. I don't need anything."

"It's fine. I'll join you. Beer? Or something stronger?"

"A beer's fine."

He was grateful for the excuse to go back to the kitchen. Phoebe was still crying upstairs, but he knew Meera would be down soon to see who was at the door. He opened the cupboard under the sink to check the vodka. Still there. Nothing to worry about.

He opened the fridge and pulled out two beers and then opened them expertly with the bottle opener magnet that was stuck to the fridge door.

He returned to the living room to find Andy idly flicking through a car magazine. He handed him the beer and sat down. Upstairs, Phoebe's crying stopped.

"What's up, mate?"

"I left Renée." Andy stared at the floor as he spoke.

"Why?"

"I just couldn't do it anymore, James. I know it sounds crap, but I couldn't."

This sounded like it could be a long conversation. James

suddenly felt fully aware that it was Sunday night and it was not long until work on Monday. He wanted to curl up in the duvet beside Meera and fall asleep.

"Do you need somewhere to stay?"

"Yeah. I mean if that's OK? I didn't know who else to come to."

James thought back to the reunion and regretted being quite so encouraging about people visiting his house. He remembered stressing that there was more than enough room for people to stay over. Andy had obviously taken it at face value.

"No worries," James said. "I'll go and prepare the spare room. You stay here."

He crept quietly upstairs, and went into the bedroom, where Meera was getting changed for bed. He explained the situation. She was as understanding as always, despite not having had a full night's sleep in days. She offered to make up the spare room, and James suddenly panicked.

"No, you go to bed. I'll do it." He forced a smile and looked at his watch. He estimated that Andy could finish his beer in fifteen minutes. James didn't have long to check everything. He hurried to the spare room and opened the chest of drawers beside the bed, where he kept old clothes. He rummaged around until his hand gripped the cold, reassuring glass of the half-full bottle of vodka. He paused for a moment, uncertain. He opened the bottle and took a swig and then went downstairs to the kitchen to get some empty plastic bags. In the living room, Andy had turned on the television.

"Best to have the door shut. Phoebe's asleep," James explained to Andy as he closed the door.

He went back upstairs and placed the vodka in one of the plastic bags. In the top of the cupboard in the spare room there were spare duvets and blankets that he and Meera never used. Behind them he had stored two bottles of whisky and a bottle of vodka. He had to stand on a chair to reach them, so there was no chance Meera would find them by mistake. But Andy was taller than him, and there was a possibility he might open the cupboard looking for a spare blanket or pillow.

James pulled the bottles from the back of the cupboard, leaned over on the chair, and placed them on the carpet one by one. Then he got off the chair carefully.

"What are you doing?" Meera stood in her nightdress at the doorway, watching him as he returned the chair to the corner. James's breath caught in his throat. How long had she been there?

"I'm just fixing up the spare room for Andy."

He tried not to glance at the row of bottles at his feet, blocked from Meera's sight by the bed.

"The spare towels are in airing cupboard, you know, not the cupboard here," she said.

"Ah." He smiled sheepishly at her.

He walked over to her and stroked her hair. She watched as he went to the airing cupboard in the hall and put some fresh towels on the bed in the spare room. What did she want from him?

"How long will Andy be staying for?" she asked.

That explained it. She didn't want Andy under her feet for too long. "Only a few days," he said. They were interrupted by Phoebe's cries, and Meera left the room.

Relieved, James returned to the spare room and shut the door behind him. He put the glass bottles into the plastic bags, trying not to clink them together. He waited for a minute, listening. Phoebe was still crying, so Meera would still be with her. He picked up the bags of bottles and carefully carried them out of the room, aware of the gentle clinking sounds they made with each step. He hummed noisily in a futile attempt to disguise the sound.

He went downstairs and unlocked the back door. He stopped humming and carried the bottles over to the shed, watching his step in the pitch black. He turned the key in the padlock and went inside. He would have to turn the light on to see what he was doing. There was no choice. He flicked the switch and surveyed the contents of the shed.

Only he used the shed now. Meera used to be a keen gardener, but she'd hardly been into the garden since Phoebe had been born. Sometimes she still talked about the garden, but wistfully, nostalgically. The shed was now James's territory. He moved the lawnmower slightly towards him and stuffed the bottles behind it. The plastic bags looked a little odd, but if Meera saw them she would probably just assume they contained petrol or oil. There would be no reason for her to look inside them . . . Unless she'd misplaced something. But that was unlikely. Anyway, there was no better place to put them now that Andy was in the spare room. James was the only one who would go to the shed, so the bottles were safe.

He turned the light off, padlocked the door and made his way back inside the warm, welcoming house. He had a strange desire to go upstairs and see Meera, to check whether she had seen the light on in the shed. What possible reason could he give her? He was relieved to hear Phoebe's cries still reverberating through the house. Meera would still be distracted.

He paced the kitchen. Had he forgotten anything in his preparations? If Andy found anything . . . Again he checked the plastic bottle under the sink that contained his supply of vodka. It all looked fine. There was nothing suspicious.

He stood still for a moment, trying to calm down. Everything would be fine. He took a deep breath and went back into the living room. Andy was sitting on the sofa, exactly as James had left him.

"I'll show you your room," he said.

13

Dave reached behind the sofa cushion, in search of the remote control. His hand touched a small collection of coins and he pulled them out hopefully: three pennies, one with a hair attached, and two foreign coins from his flatmate Charles's latest holiday. He reached down again, and felt something sticky, which might have been gum. He hoped it was gum. Last weekend, Charles's friends had stayed over and slept on this sofa, keeping Dave awake with their unmistakeable grunts and groans.

He didn't investigate further, instead twisting his body so that he could reach right over to the other side of the sofa without having to actually stand up and lift up the cushions. A biro. He left it where it was. Still no remote. Bloody hell.

His eyes scanned the room. The opening bars of the theme tune for Loose Women were starting to hum insistently from the television, and the need to turn over quickly was getting more urgent. But nothing on the tables; and only a plate with his half-eaten toast resting precariously on Charles's DVD rack. As the camera scanned the faces of the four women on the television, Dave stood up and went to the other sofa. He lifted the cushions up with some aggression. No remote control. Empty condom wrapper. He put the cushions back and scanned the room.

Where else could it be? He couldn't have taken it into the kitchen with him when he made breakfast, could he? He went into the kitchen: last night's takeaway boxes, a few dirty pots and pans, but no sign of the control.

He sighed and returned to the living room and sat down on the sofa. Last weekend's Sunday Sport lay open on the floor, from when he'd been reading it over breakfast. He lifted it up and there was the remote. He flicked over to Sky Sports and settled back into the sofa. He looked at his watch: 11:15. Soon it would be time for lunch. And after lunch the dreaded but inevitable trip to the job centre.

When the redundancy money had first hit his bank account, it had shifted it out of its permanent position in the red. For the first time in his life he'd felt like he was rich, and he had pictured the money in a cartoon-like pile of coins and notes, voluptuous and inviting. He'd bought a new phone, a new computer, and went out clubbing during the week. Just because he could.

But now his redundancy money had gone and he was struggling to pay the rent. None of the job applications had met with any success, so there was only one option left. Charles had made it pretty clear that he'd have to move out if he couldn't afford the rent.

*

As he entered the job centre, Dave was greeted by a waiting room of people in dirty jeans. He looked around the room self-consciously, fully aware of his new suit, and selected the chair furthest away from any other human beings, wiping the seat before he sat down.

The harsh fluorescent lighting wasn't doing anyone any favours. Across the aisle from him, a grey man hunched over on his seat and shook, tell-tale bruises on his inner arms. There was an overpowering stench of booze from the other side of the room, and Dave tried to hold his breath. Another man came in and sat opposite him. Dave tried to look at him out of the corner of his eye. It was possible that he could be normal. He wore the same regulation jeans as the others, but they had splashes of paint on. Perhaps he was a decorator. Still, it was best not to make eye-contact.

Was Dave really one of them now? He supposed it was possible. He was, after all, unemployed. And he had settled into unemployment alarmingly easily. It hadn't been as awful as he imagined. His first week of unemployment had been a flurry of activity; using the tube without fear of being crushed, buying cheap afternoon cinema tickets and drinking in afternoon happy hours. He'd even been to some museums. But now he felt too tired to get out and do anything. His days were taken up watching TV while he conducted half-hearted job searches.

When he was first made redundant he'd thought about all the things he could do, all the things he could be. He didn't have to spend all day in the office anymore; he could train to be a chef, join the navy, become a writer. But it wasn't working out. After watching too many cookery programmes on the TV, he'd concluded that Jamie Oliver and Gordon Ramsay were only interested in training schoolchildren and celebrities. He'd written one paragraph of a comic novel about a man who was made unemployed. After a while, he had decided that he had quite liked life in an office after all.

At first Dave had been confident that he could easily get another job in an office. He was a graduate. He had been employed before. How hard could it be? He'd sent his CV off to five different head-hunters. A lot of the job adverts they sent him were a bit below him, but he had taken the time to apply for a couple of them, bashing out targeted covering letters to accompany his CV and sending them out immediately. He'd thought that he could always work his way back up to the level he'd been at his previous job. But he still hadn't heard back from any of the companies. And now, signing up for Jobseeker's Allowance seemed like the most sensible thing to do.

Across the room, a man let out a big chesty cough. Dave looked at him; his stained jeans, his unshaven face. Dave had shaved this morning for the first time in a week. Perhaps it wouldn't take him that long to truly become one of them.

"Dave Young."

He stood up and followed the woman through the double doors and down the corridor to the interview room. As he did so, he realised that he kind of missed work. He missed the people, the banter. He missed having something to do with his time. And he missed going to the pub in the evening. Apart from the occasional text, he hadn't seen or heard from any of his former colleagues since he'd been made redundant.

14

Sam hummed to herself as she got ready to go out. She had been preparing for this day all week. She was finally meeting Patrick's work colleagues.

She had been shopping with her mother the previous weekend and had spent a whole day in search of the perfect outfit. Her mother didn't like most of the clothes Sam tried on, dismissing each garment as either too slutty or else too boring. It had seemed that for her mother there was no middle ground between the two.

Eventually, after a break for lunch, they had found the perfect outfit: a blue trouser suit that showed off Sam's long legs and gentle curves. When Sam tried it on in the mirror she knew immediately it was right, and she was surprised when her mother agreed. She also found a matching sea-blue necklace and earrings in Accessorize, and bought those too, despite her mother's evident disapproval of the extra spending. Sam had seen pictures of the women Patrick worked with. They were always immaculately dressed, with matching shoes, bags and jewellery. She wanted to be the same. She wanted to show them she was good enough for him.

She put on the suit and surveyed herself in the mirror. She looked a lot better than she used to, but she was starting to suspect she was putting weight back on. The jacket of the suit stretched slightly where it did up at her waist, even though it was a size twelve.

She looked smart though. She should fit in with Patrick's work colleagues, who would be coming straight from the office. She wanted to impress them and have fun. She didn't want to be the Sam she had been at university, who had stood on the edges of conversations and laughed in all the wrong places.

There had been an office party a few months back that she hadn't been invited too. That night she had had to sleep in her bed at her mum's house, staring at the pink floral wallpaper while she imagined Patrick having fun. Patrick had reluctantly shown her the pictures of the party on Facebook. Sam had seen picture after picture of pretty, well-dressed girls. As the evening wore on the pictures got more blurry, as people got more and more drunk. There were pictures of Patrick with his arm round one girl, Patrick pinching someone's arse and Patrick squeezing someone's breast.

"Boys will be boys," he had said, and Sam couldn't tell if the tone had been apologetic or matter-of-fact.

She hadn't minded though. He trusted her enough to show her the photos. And even if something had or was going on with one of the girls, it was Sam he was marrying.

She was more used to being second best. There had never been a time in her life when the man she had fancied or had been sleeping with hadn't fancied someone else a bit more than her. They had to accept they couldn't have the person they fancied, and Sam had to accept that she was going out with them as a result of that person rejecting them. So all in all, it wasn't so bad. She was the one who benefited.

With Patrick, though, she was first in line. She was the one he was marrying. She had never been happier.

She applied her make-up carefully in front of the mirror, following the guidelines in an old copy of *Cosmopolitan* which lay open on her dressing table. She wasn't used to wearing make-up, but she made the effort for Patrick. She put on foundation, then blusher, bright red lipstick, liquid eyeliner, eye shadow and mascara. She pushed her face closer to the mirror. She looked alright. She looked better when she took a step back.

She heard the door go and she knew it would be Patrick, coming to pick her up and take her out.

"Are you ready?" he called up the stairs.

"Nearly."

"Well, hurry up. The others are already getting the drinks in."

Patrick hated missing out. When he wasn't with Sam he was drinking with his colleagues. He had told Sam he was one of the most well-liked people in the office and Sam had been suitably impressed. At the library, she was just another member of staff, paling into insignificance amongst the chatter of the louder librarians. She'd always been impressed by Patrick's confidence. He always said what he thought, and people liked him for it. Sam was sure that if she said the same things she'd be regarded as rude and obnoxious.

"Just coming," she said, taking one final look in the mirror and sitting down on the bed to put her new shoes on. They were designed so that the material that held the buckle twisted round your leg first, and it took her a while to figure them out.

"Where are you?" Patrick shouted, impatient. "I don't want to come upstairs."

He sounded like her mother, and she laughed.

"I'm coming," she said, finishing doing up the buckle and making her way slowly down the stairs.

He was already standing by the open door. "Hurry up!"

She tried to hurry up, but nearly slipped and fell, grabbing at the banister to steady herself. He grunted at her as if disgusted, and started down the driveway.

When she caught up he was already in the car with the engine on. They drove to the pub in silence.

When they arrived, he pulled into the last remaining parking space. Sam looked at her watch. They were late, but only by about two minutes. Patrick hated to be late. He got out of the car and slammed the door. He walked round his silver BMW once and inspected the car-park. They'd be getting a taxi back later and Patrick was just checking that he was leaving the car somewhere where it wouldn't be damaged. It was only six months old and it was his pride and joy. Sam had offered to forgo drinking and drive them home, but he had declined, not trusting her with the car.

She eased herself out of the passenger seat, putting one high-heeled foot down tentatively at a time. She rose to her feet carefully, wobbled a little, then stood up straight and shut her door. Patrick was already halfway to the pub. When he heard the door shut he turned round quickly and clicked the key to lock the car. He strode on ahead of her as she tottered forward on her heels. She saw the pub door swing shut behind him. When she reached the door herself, she stopped and took a deep breath. She straightened her shirt and pushed open the door.

She spotted Patrick's work colleagues immediately, and her heart sank. Most of the girls were in skirts and tight tops and look much more casual than Sam had expected. No-one was in a suit. Either they didn't wear suits to work or else they'd changed between finishing work and going out. Why hadn't Patrick told her? Sam was the most smartly dressed of everyone.

She approached the table and perched herself on a bar stool, next to Patrick. He was deep in conversation and didn't stop to introduce her to his colleagues. She strained her ears to try and hear the conversation, and forced an interested smile.

The girl sitting next to her introduced herself and held out her hand. "So, your Patrick's girlfriend?"

"Fiancée," Sam said quickly, and then wished she hadn't.

"Right." The girl seemed to be struggling for conversation. "So, have you come straight from work?"

"Er . . . No."

The girl eyed her suit, bemused. "So what do you do then?"

"I'm a librarian."

"Oh."

The girl turned to speak to the person the other side of her. Sam wished she'd lied and made up a more exciting job. Although she loved her job, it was hard to make it sound interesting. The conversation around her had turned back to the work at Patrick's office. Sam knew nothing about the work or any of the people they were talking about. Patrick brought her a drink and then went to talk to the people at the other end of the table. Sam could only join in the conversation by asking questions, and after a while she got the impression that the others were getting fed up with pausing their conversation to fill her in on the background.

She watched Patrick talking animatedly at the other end of the table. She wished she could be more like him, and she hoped he wouldn't notice that she wasn't fitting in. She was trying her best, but she had no idea what anyone was talking about. She had held out so much hope for this evening, and yet it was the same as it always was. She took her phone out of her bag. She knew she wouldn't have any messages, but it was something to do. She unlocked the phone. No messages. She pretended to be engrossed as she checked her emails, although there was nothing more interesting than the announcement of an electronics sale at Tesco.

When someone went to get a round, no one offered her a drink, so she sipped the last dregs of her wine and then went up to the bar herself. The bar was a respite from the others, and she stood back, trying to avoid getting served to prolong the break.

She thought back to when she'd first met Patrick. She'd been on a train, on her way to a job interview. It was shortly after she'd completed her WeightWatchers programme, and with her newfound confidence she had found herself starting a conversation with the attractive man beside her. She had been surprised when he'd asked for her number. Men like Patrick weren't usually attracted to women like her.

She didn't get the job, and had resigned herself to working in the library forever and living with her mother, when Patrick called her unexpectedly. She had had to hold the phone tight to her ear to block out the sounds of her mother shouting at one of the characters in Coronation Street in the living room below her bedroom. She immediately said yes to the date.

He had taken her to an expensive restaurant in Covent Garden. Sam, shackled by the rules and regulations of WeightWatchers for so long, but now at her target weight, had practically gorged herself on all the food. Afterwards they had had mediocre sex back at Patrick's house. He had been a selfish lover, and Sam had reflected the fact that the better looking a man was the worse he was in bed. Like the phrase, "Fat girls make more effort," she thought. It had always offended her, but then maybe it was true. She had to have something to offer over and above the skinny girls.

Their relationship had unexpectedly continued, with the wine Patrick bought her getting cheaper and the sex getting better. She stopped assuming that the relationship would fizzle out, and began instead to think about a possible future together. She couldn't quite believe she was the girlfriend of someone as attractive and successful as Patrick. When he proposed, she was over the moon with shock and elation.

She looked over at him now, still not quite able to believe it. He sat at the end of the table nearest the bar and she watched the back of his head as she listened to him tell a long and rambling joke. He reached the punch-line, but no one laughed.

He quickly went into a less-than-complimentary impression of his boss. Sam watched his colleagues turn away from him and change the subject. He sat up straighter in his chair and just kept on talking.

Perhaps she and he weren't so different. But while she let her social status defeat her and sank into the corner, Patrick tried to talk through it, becoming louder with each slight.

*

In the taxi home, silence descended once again.

"It went well, didn't it?" she said. Patrick didn't reply.

Sam stared out the car window. She hoped Patrick wasn't angry with her. She hoped that when they got home his mood would lift. Perhaps sex would cheer him up. She didn't feel like it really; she was tired. But it would be worth it to lift his mood.

She smiled at him and reached for his hand. He pulled his hand away from her.

They arrived home and he got out of the taxi and walked to the door without waiting for her to follow. She shut her door and tottered towards the house, slipping on an icy patch on the driveway and falling down and grazing her knee.

Patrick was struggling to get his key in the lock and he turned round when he heard her fall. "Clumsy bitch," he said.

Sam got up and followed him into the house, her knee stinging as the blood rose to fill the tiny cuts. Patrick shut the door behind them and turned to her.

"What the fuck was that about?" he shouted, so close to her that her ears rang with the sound of his voice.

"What?" she said weakly.

"You! Showing me up. Turning up in that '80s suit and lipstick on your teeth."

Sam reached self-consciously to her mouth and rubbed her teeth with her fingers. She knew to be quiet when Patrick got like this.

"You know, don't you? You know that when I take you out you reflect on me? All I asked was that you made a fucking good impression. And what did you do? Just sat there like a fucking lump."

"Sorry," Sam whispered, knowing what was coming next.

Patrick reached out and slapped her so hard across the face that she fell against the wall, jarring her back. She stayed where she fell and looked up at him.

"You know what?" he said. "I'm embarrassed to be with you." He shook his head, regretfully. "I'm actually embarrassed to be with you."

He looked at her with contempt and then turned and went upstairs.

Sam sat still for a few moments, giving him the time to calm down. When he was like this, any noise disturbed him, even the sound of her standing up. She waited. She loved him, and so she could accept his flaws. She wasn't going to be like her mother. She had been just like Sam. Except once, when Sam's dad had beaten her up, she had asked him to leave. And Sam had never seen her dad again.

Sam was different from her mother. She believed in true love. When you loved someone, you loved them despite their flaws.

15

Renée applied the finishing touches to her make-up and considered herself in the mirror. The make-up covered her puffy eyes and bags and she actually looked alright – at least, a lot better than she had in the past few weeks.

Andy was coming back tonight to collect his things. Renée tried to stop herself getting her hopes up too high, but she saw this as her last chance to win him back so they could continue their lives as normal.

The flat was spotless and the kitchen surfaces were sparkling, a result of a trip to Sainsbury's that morning to buy cleaning fluids and then a four-hour cleaning spree. She had taken their wedding photo from the top of the bookcase in the spare room and put it proudly on display on the side table in the living room. She had filled any spare photo frame with pictures of her and Andy: on honeymoon; graduating from university; at a friend's wedding. They had lived so much of their lives together. When Andy saw the photos, she hoped he'd remember the good times and realise their relationship was worth saving.

When she had seen his name on her phone display the day before, she had answered it nervously. Since he left, he rarely answered her calls or replied to her texts. He had told her he needed space. But now he had taken the time to call her. When she had picked up the phone, just the sound of his voice made her heart leap. Recollections of their previous phone conversations echoed in her head: speaking for hours and hours in their university holidays, calling each other at work to ask what they wanted for dinner, calling just to say they loved each other.

When he'd told her he was coming round to pick up a few things, she hadn't really heard him properly. Her mind was entirely focused on the fact he was coming over. She would see him. She could talk to him. She could explain why they should get back together. She could show him she had changed.

She wandered round the flat once more, checking that everything was perfect. Maybe once he saw how clean and tidy it was, he'd forgive her. She'd tell him she'd be less selfish, that she would listen to him, whatever he wanted to say.

She was wearing her most flattering jeans and a smart-casual orange top which he had once told her suited her. Underneath was her best underwear. Hopefully tonight he would realise he didn't need to pick anything up and would decide to stay instead.

The flat's buzzer rang. Renée checked herself in the mirror one more time and smiled reassuringly at herself. By the time she got to the door, Andy was already unlocking it and letting himself into the flat.

"Hi," she said.

"Hi." He didn't look her in the eye, and took one step into the hallway. "I wasn't sure if you were in." He held up his key, apologising for letting himself in.

"It's still your flat." Renée smiled at him, tears already pricking her eyes. She had to control herself.

He glanced at her for half a second. "Looks like you're off out. Don't worry, I'll be quick. Or you can leave me to it if you like. If you've got somewhere to be."

"I can stay," she said quickly.

"Well, I need to be quick anyway. I've got plans tonight."

What plans? What was he doing without her? What friends was he going out with?

He stepped into the hallway and then went through into the bedroom, without taking off his shoes. Renée had spent four hours cleaning the house.

Andy saw her looking. "You want me to take my shoes off? I thought you didn't care about that kind of stuff."

"I've changed," Renée said, wrapping her arms around herself. She wouldn't cry.

"There's not much point me taking my shoes off and putting them back on again every time I go in and out of the house. It'll take ages that way."

"OK," she said. She followed him into the bedroom. Scattered on the bed were a few tops she had tried on earlier. On the desk, her make-up was similarly spread out. Messy. She should have cleared that up.

Andy was already at the wardrobe. He took a suitcase from the shelf at the top and began to load it up.

"You don't have to watch, you know."

Renée didn't know what to say. "Maybe I can help."

"I'd prefer to do it myself."

"Right." She stood and watched him, unsure what to say. He pulled shirts and trousers out of the wardrobe. When he'd finished, he put the suitcase on the floor of the bedroom.

"Do you have any other bags I could use?"

She went to the kitchen and brought back some Sainsbury's carrier bags from her shopping trip that morning. Andy frowned at them and then began to fill them up with his pants and socks.

"Andy."

"Yeah."

"Can we talk?"

"About what?"

She didn't know what to say to that. What did he think she would want to talk about? They were still technically on a break.

What did this all mean? The end of the break? A separation?

Renée's throat grew thick. "What does this mean?" She mumbled the words.

"I'm just collecting my stuff."

"I know . . . so . . . so the break is over?"

He continued to load the socks into the carrier bags. "Yeah, I guess so."

"Why?"

"You know, Renée, I don't want to talk about this. I'm tired."

She sat down heavily on the bed. She listened to him take the bags out into the hall, and heard him open the door and carry them down to the car. It was too awkward for him to carry them all, and he'd left a couple in the hallway. Renée picked them up and followed him to the car.

He was already loading his suitcase through the passenger doors. The back seats had been folded down to make more room. She realised just how much of their lives he planned to drive away with. He wasn't just taking a suitcase. He was planning to take as much as he could. She put the plastic bags carefully in the boot and returned to the flat. She wouldn't help him anymore.

She sat down in the living room and turned on the TV. She turned up the volume to block out the sound of Andy in the other room. What was he doing in there? After ten minutes she couldn't sit still anymore. She went to look and found him in the spare room taking the duvet and sheets from the bed.

He looked up apologetically.

"Do you mind if I take these? I don't have any. If I buy everything new it will cost me a fortune."

"OK then," Renée said. They had spare sheets in the chest of drawers anyway, but Andy had obviously forgotten. They didn't have a spare duvet. She supposed she'd have to buy a new one.

She went to the kitchen, thinking of pouring herself a glass of wine. But the wine in the fridge was an expensive one that she had planned to drink with Andy. She'd bought it that morning, imagining that he might stay for a drink. Thinking that they might talk. The tears threatened to come again, and instead she returned to the living room and sat back down.

She heard Andy go into the kitchen and start going through their pots and pans and glasses. She didn't have the energy to check on him.

When he finally came through to the living room, the first thing he seemed to spot was their wedding photo. He looked at her with a complete lack of comprehension. And in that one look, she knew it was over.

He leaned over the side table and turned it face down. "I'm sorry. I just can't look at it."

She started to sob.

He refused to look at her, instead going through their CD collection systematically and pulling out the CDs that were his.

It seemed to Renée that he was unpicking their lives piece by piece. Everything they had built and worked together for, he was untangling and taking away. Tables, pots and pans, chairs, anything that was his before they met was being loaded into his car.

"Do you use the stereo?" he asked.

"Yeah I do."

"Well, technically it's mine." When they'd moved into the house, they'd had two stereos, and as Renée's was very slightly older, they'd thrown hers away.

"Well, I don't have one."

"I suppose you can keep it for now. But we'll need to go through our joint things in more detail later. For now I'll just take the things I know are mine."

"OK."

As she watched Andy going through their DVDs one by one, as if he never planned to set foot in the flat again, she knew it must be over.

16

Steve looked at Caroline, drinking in the milk-white skin of her body. He couldn't believe his luck.

She pulled the cover over her, as if ashamed. He smiled at her and stroked her cheek. "That was great."

"Yeah," She smiled tentatively back at him, holding the duvet like a shield.

Steve lay back against the pillow. Didn't girls always want to talk after sex? Maybe she was different. She was always different. He leant over and kissed her on the lips, breathing in her smell.

It was only when she had bled that he had known it was her first time. Afterwards he had seen the spots of blood on the sheets, but he had said nothing.

It made sense now. He had thought she was losing interest. She always seemed to object to going back to his house, and they had never got beyond kissing and fondling in the depths of a club, or in a crowded bar. He had never really had her to himself. Until tonight.

He looked at her. She was beautiful. Her long dark hair highlighted her oval eyes, and her complexion was flawless.

She looked back at him.

"What?" she said, hugging the duvet closer.

"You're beautiful," he said, shifting closer to her.

She smiled and sat up, the duvet still encircling her. She felt around under the duvet until she found her pants, and put them on awkwardly under the covers. Her bra was on the floor and she kept the duvet round her as she reached for it and then put it on and did it up.

Her underwear was red and black; matching. When Steve had undressed her, he had felt a shiver run through him. She had not been like the others, reaching in desperation to unbuckle his belt. She had stood back as he had undressed her, taking off each item of clothing one by one.

She had laid back on his bed, complicit and silent, excitement and fear in her eyes. It was then he had suspected it was her first time, and a wave of excitement had flowed through him. He wanted to ask her if she was sure, but as she lay like a gift before him, he couldn't.

When he was inside her he had concentrated intently, determined not to come instantly and ruin it. She had uttered a sound like he had never heard before. The expression on her face had shifted from wincing to a forced smile, until he couldn't look at her anymore.

He hadn't been sure that she had been enjoying it, but he couldn't stop.

When he'd lifted himself off her, she had looked him in the eye and he had been unable to read her.

Now they lay side by side, together and apart.

He loved her, yet he didn't want to say it. The moment would be gone. The excitement and sense of possibility would be lost forever. She'd say it back or she wouldn't say it back. Whichever way, that would be that.

He felt a strange urge to talk to her, to get to the bottom of her, to understand her. He had felt like he had waited forever for this moment.

He turned to her now, wanted to absorb her, to know everything about her. "Are you tired?" he asked.

"No," she said.

"Do you want to do it again?" he grinned.

She looked worried. "Not now."

He turned away, desperately wanting to be close to her again, yet feeling denied. "In the morning?"

Her next words were a whisper, spoken as she looked into his eyes for affirmation. "I love you, Steve."

He stroked her hair. "I love you too."

She turned and curled up in the duvet and fell asleep next to him in his bed.

17

Renée sat in her living room staring out the window. It was a warm day, possibly warm enough for a lunch in a pub garden and then a lazy Saturday afternoon. But she had no one to share it with. Maybe she should eat at home. She walked restlessly into the kitchen, knowing what she would find when she looked in the fridge. She opened the door and her expectations were confirmed by the empty shelves. She would have to go to the supermarket or go out for lunch.

She flicked through her phone idly, her hand automatically hovering over Andy's number for a moment, before she quickly clicked cancel. Ringing Andy used to be so automatic, but now she had to stop herself. She dialled Katie's number instead and listened to the phone ring and ring. Then she flicked through the other names until she got to Dave. They'd got on well at the reunion. Why not see if he fancied lunch? She clicked "call" before she had thought about it properly.

To her surprise, he picked up. He said he was short of money and didn't fancy going out, but she was welcome to come over. Renée couldn't bear to stay in the empty flat any longer, and agreed. She could grab a sandwich on the way over.

An hour later, she was standing outside Dave's block of flats. It was a new-build, white, with clean lines and well-kept gardens, located in what appeared to be a prosperous street. She smiled. It was typical of Dave to understate his success. He didn't like to talk about his job, but it was clear from where he lived that things were going well. She rang the buzzer tentatively.

He answered, and she pushed her way through the door and into a maze of staircases. As she walked past a conveniently placed mirror, she checked her hair and make-up. Her white blouse accentuated her long dark hair, and her make-up covered the bags under her eyes. She looked OK.

When she reached the flat, Dave ushered her in and she took her shoes off and placed them by the skirting board.

"I brought some wine," she said, suddenly aware of the bottles she held awkwardly in her hands.

"Great," he said, taking it from her. "Do you want a glass?"

"Yes, thanks."

She followed him into the kitchen and watched as he got out two glasses from the dishwasher and poured the wine. "So, is this place yours?" she asked as she followed him into the living room to sit down.

"No, it belongs to my housemate."

She nodded. Perhaps he hadn't been so modest after all.

*

Dave watched Renée sit down on Charles's sofa, curling her legs under her. She looked fragile, small against the large white cushions. Her long dark hair cascaded over her shoulders.

"Andy and I have split up," she said abruptly.

He watched her face as she made the declaration. He had heard this already from Katie, but now that Renée was telling him face to face it was hard to tell if this kind of news justified a hug. To hug her would be very deliberate. He'd have to put his wineglass down, get up and go over to her. And she'd have to stand up too, to accept the hug, otherwise he would just end up looking stupid.

She was looking at him now, expecting some kind of response.

"I'm sorry." It was the best he could manage.

"He's moved out – taken all his stuff."

"Oh."

She was silent, but only for a moment. "What should I do, Dave?"

He was confused. What could she do? "I don't know."

The distance between them on the sofas now seemed too much. He leant forward to listen to her.

"I just don't know what to do. I can't believe he said he wanted to end it. I mean – Why? What's wrong with me?"

He saw the tears in her eyes and felt a flicker of sympathy. Even when she was upset she was still beautiful.

"What should I do, Dave?" she repeated.

The question was still unanswerable. "I don't know."

Tears were running down her face now. He scanned the room for tissues, but there weren't any.

He put his wineglass down, got up and went to the bathroom and returned with a roll of toilet paper. He sat down beside her and offered it to her. Then he gave her an awkward hug. She gripped onto him for a moment, like she was gripping onto life itself. Then she let go, but her head remained on his shoulder. He put his arm round her. She felt soft and warm, and he relaxed a bit, rubbing her back as she cried. He felt a flicker of excitement shoot through him as he wondered where this would lead.

"I just don't know what to do. I can't believe he's ended it." Her voice was muffled by tears, and he held her for a moment.

He saw that Renée's glass was empty, and he used it as an excuse to extract himself from their embrace and went back to the kitchen. He filled up her glass and topped up his own for good measure.

He sat back down beside her and handed her another tissue. It was weird; just the two of them. Renée had always been so unattainable at university, but now here she was, right here beside him, on his sofa.

"So have you seen any of the old crowd since the reunion?"

"Yeah, I've seen Katie."

Dave thought guiltily about the phone-calls with Katie he'd avoided. It wasn't that he didn't want to see her, he just couldn't afford to go all the way to her house and he knew she wouldn't be able to afford to come and see him either. It was pointless.

Renée wasn't interested in this line of conversation anyway. She turned the conversation back to Andy.

"I don't need him."

"Right."

"Dave . . . I am attractive, aren't I?"

"Of course," he said, subconsciously sliding closer towards her on the sofa. He reached out and stroked her hair. He could feel his erection pushing against his trousers. He topped up her wine.

She leant in to kiss him.

*

Renée pulled away from the kiss. What was she doing? It wasn't that Dave was unattractive, it was just that surely this was a bad idea.

She frowned, her thoughts struggling to connect through the wine haze. She wasn't betraying anyone, was she? There was no one to betray anymore. This was OK.

She finished her glass of wine and looked across at Dave. He hadn't shaved for a few days and the stubble grew over his face like a rash. She felt the weight of his arm on her shoulder.

She reached in to kiss him again and tasted the acid of the wine in his mouth. The kiss lacked the familiarity of kissing Andy, and yet it didn't feel that exciting either. Suddenly she felt more sober and she wondered if she should just go home, but that felt foolish. She had come all the way over here, and she'd started something. She would continue.

As they kissed, she reached to unbuckle his belt and her thoughts turned to Andy. What would he think if he could see her doing this? Would he finally realise that she was attractive to other men and know he'd made a mistake? Even his friends wanted to sleep with her. Would he feel betrayed? She felt a shiver of guilt, followed by a vindictive pleasure. He deserved it.

She wasn't really enjoying this, but she continued anyway, imagining Andy watching, imagining his face. She thought of him finding out afterwards. The jealousy he'd feel, the betrayal.

She smiled at Dave. "Let's go to your room."

His room was a mess, but he cleared a space on the bed for her. She tried to block out her surroundings and concentrate. Then she thought of Andy and had the sudden worry that he might be doing the same thing; he might be sleeping with other people too. She felt sick, but continued.

It was over quickly, and Dave rolled off her with a sigh. She wondered why she had done it. At no time in the whole proceedings had she felt good about herself. Dave hadn't even made her feel attractive. Now he was pulling on his jeans as if the whole process had been purely functional. Andy always used to cuddle her after sex, and they'd fall asleep in each other's arms.

She waited for Dave to leave the room and then began to dress herself. She went into the bathroom, took the hairbrush from her handbag and brushed her hair. She stared at herself in the mirror. What kind of a person was she? For so long she had defined herself by her relationship, her happy marriage to Andy, her neatly planned future. Who was she now that she had slept with Dave? What would happen next? Where would her life take her?

She didn't like the questions, and she returned quickly to

the living room, sat down and took a gulp of her wine. She needed to know she was valued. She needed Dave to tell her she was important to him.

He sat sipping his wine on the sofa. The TV had been switched on and Renée could see that a football game had just started. Dave made no effort to make conversation, and Renée realised she didn't want to stay there any longer.

"I'm off," she said.

"Are you sure?"

"Yes."

"You're welcome to stay and watch the football."

"No, it's OK."

"OK," he said awkwardly. He got up and followed her to the door.

"We should meet up again sometime," she said, searching for validation, for meaning above and beyond the sex.

"Yeah," he said. There was a cheer from the TV and Dave strained his neck to try and see the goal.

Renée tried to smile, but she felt tears forming. She let herself out and walked quickly away down the corridor.

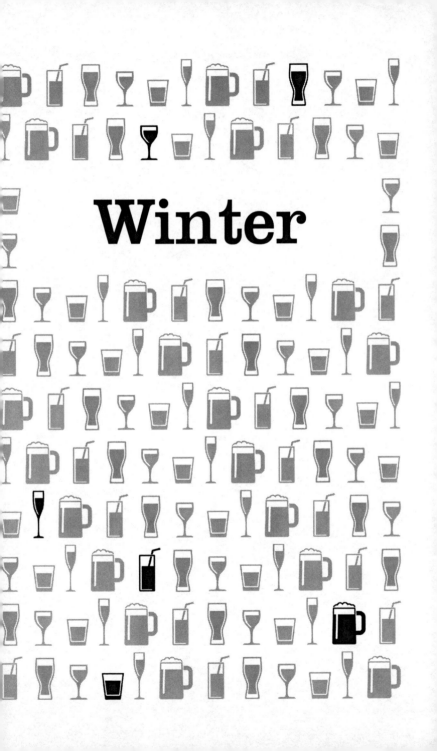

Winter

18

James woke up at six a.m. to the ringing alarm. Meera rolled over in her sleep and reached impotently across him towards the sound. James quickly turned the alarm off and got straight out of bed, to avoid disturbing Meera any more than necessary.

He stretched, went into the bathroom and turned on the shower to the hottest setting. He looked at himself in the mirror and observed the bags under his eyes. Staying up late with Andy, working all day, looking after Phoebe in the evenings and then getting up early the next day was starting to take its toll.

He stepped under the steaming shower and let the water wash over him. This was his favourite time of the day. The time when he could think. Or these days it was the time when he could worry.

He had expected Andy to have left long ago, either to go back to Renée or to a new place of his own. When Andy had told James and Meera that he and Renée were finished, they had encouraged him to go back to his and Renée's flat and clear out the rest of his possessions. Meera had thought that if he collected his things from his old flat, it would dawn on him that he needed to find his own place. That hadn't happened. Instead, their spare room and James's study were full with boxes and plastic carrier bags. Everything from CDs to duvets was crammed into their house.

Meera was losing patience rapidly, and the week before James had finally cracked and asked Andy to move out. Andy had responded graciously and had taken the week off work to look for flats. But he seemed to be treating the time off more like a holiday than a serious search. He'd look at a couple of places during the day, but when it got to the evening he wasn't tired and wanted to stay up late into the night, drinking and watching TV with James.

The previous night James and Meera had argued for the first time in ages. Meera hated having Andy around the house in the day, getting under her feet. Yesterday Phoebe had finally gone to sleep for her afternoon nap, but had then been woken up by the sound of the TV from the living room below. Meera had taken it out on James.

It wasn't just Andy. Meera thought James was working too hard, and the six a.m. starts hadn't been helping. When she had first met him, she hadn't minded his long hours and had supported him fully. But since Phoebe had been born there had been a subtle change in their relationship. She still supported him on the surface, but there were murmurs about what he might miss out on: Phoebe's first word, first steps, first tooth. It seemed like she thought he might somehow miss out on Phoebe herself. It worried James too. He loved being with Phoebe. He loved seeing her smile, he loved it when her little hand grasped his finger, and he loved watching her intelligent eyes roam back and forth over the room. He didn't want to miss out. Sometimes he would go days without seeing her awake. He worried that one day he'd come home from work and they she'd be all grown up, dressed in a mini-skirt and ready to go out. Her childhood would have somehow passed him by.

The six a.m. starts had become necessary since Andy had

arrived. Andy got up on the dot of six thirty every day regardless of how late he went to bed the night before. At first, Andy's early starts had meant that James hadn't been able to go through his usual morning routine. Andy would sit at the kitchen table, munching his toast, and for the first few days James had had to abandon the vodka under the sink and buy some on the way to work. This had led to some very undignified situations in the supermarket in the morning, as he stood over the boot of his car, carefully transferring the vodka into a water bottle, in preparation for the day. So he had started getting up at six, on the pretence of going into work early.

Once James got back to his daily routine he felt better: a shot or two of vodka in the morning to keep him going, then an extensive teeth clean, followed by two rounds of Listerine. He made sure he filled up his water bottle with vodka before he left for work. He felt at little more at ease, although it was hard to hide his lifestyle, with Andy omnipresent.

James didn't remember things being this hard before. When they had been at university, drinking had somehow seemed more acceptable. He would go out with Dave, Andy and Steve and they would drink all afternoon and all night. Then they would drink again at lunchtime. He couldn't do that now. No one else wanted to do that anymore. They restricted themselves to sensible drinking; perhaps a few beers with the football, a bottle of wine with dinner.

When James had first started work they had had a "work hard, play hard" culture among the new recruits and he had gone out drinking with them every night. He had drunk all of them under the table. He would stay out until four in the morning and then be at his desk at eight, feeling fine. But the new recruits quickly became old hands, and the heavy drinking sessions went from a daily occurrence to a weekly Friday-night binge. Around the same time, James had met Meera. She didn't drink, and when he took her out to restaurants he would make his way through a bottle of wine and she would have soft drinks.

She didn't mind him drinking in front of her, but he had a feeling of emptiness left in him. He missed the nights out he used to have, but not for the company. He missed the drink. He thought nostalgically about when it was the done thing to get bladdered and then spend most of the next day in bed with a hangover. Although James himself had rarely had hangovers. His alcohol tolerance had been much higher than the others', and while they were nursing their hangovers, he had been known to go for a five mile run.

Now, when he and Andy stayed up and drank they talked about the glory days of university when they had no commitments and nothing to get up in the morning for. They talked about the times they went out on the town and drank until they were unconscious. For Andy it was all in the past: a nostalgic memory. But for James, the only thing that had changed was that he now drank on his own.

He had got so used to his lifestyle that he never questioned it. He was fine. He performed well at work and was a loving father and husband. He was probably only drinking about the same as he had done when he went for regular nights out with his work colleagues.

He knew he could stop any time he wanted to. He just didn't want to.

But having Andy staying was starting to scare him. Andy used to drink just as much as James at university, but now there was no contest, even *without* James's alcohol stash. Whenever they drank together, James drank at least twice as much as Andy. Andy had even started to comment. He had no right. Andy was staying in *his* house, and he should just be grateful that he'd offered him a place to stay.

He got out of the shower and went to the bedroom to dry himself and get dressed. He crept around quietly in the dark so as not to disturb Meera and Phoebe. He wanted to be in bed with Meera, curled around her warm body.

No chance of that. Not with Andy here.

He glanced one more time at her, and went downstairs. He went to the cupboard under the sink and poured himself half a glass of vodka. He gulped it down, feeling the satisfying sting on the back of his throat. He washed the glass up and put it back in the cupboard. He surveyed the row of cereal boxes. He didn't really feel like breakfast. He went upstairs and cleaned his teeth. He smiled at himself in the mirror. Almost ready for another day in the office.

Downstairs, he poured the vodka from under the sink into his small water bottle, noticing that the larger bottle was nearly empty. He would have to pop into the supermarket tonight and pick up some more.

He went out the door and got into the car. He put the water bottle in the cup holder and loosened the lid so he could have some on the way to work. In the boot of the car he heard the clunk of empty bottles. When was the last time he had dropped them off at the bottle bank? With Andy staying, he was so tired that he was forgetting to do everything. What if Meera had driven his car at the weekend and heard the clinking of empty bottles? He had to pull himself together.

19

Steve sat back on the park bench beside Caroline. Her eyes were closed against the warmth of the winter sun. On the lake in Hyde Park, the ducks navigated round fragments of ice. He reached for Caroline's hand and then let his own eyes close.

When Caroline had suggested a picnic, at first he'd objected. It seemed like a crazy idea, in November. But she kept talking about it until he finally gave in. He was glad he had. It was the perfect afternoon.

He'd prepared the picnic the night before and met her outside Marble Arch station, old-fashioned wicker picnic basket in his hand. They walked hand in hand through the underpass to the park and found a spot by the lake. The pigeons watched as he unpacked the basket: champagne, smoked salmon, quiche, crisps. The champagne opened with a pop, its cork flying across the park behind them. They declared it irretrievable and finished the bottle before they touched any of the food.

Caroline didn't eat much. She took a few bites of the salmon and a few crisps, and Steve fed the rest to the ducks and pigeons. They must have been the best fed birds in the park, with a diet of smoked salmon and M&S sausage rolls.

"I love this," Caroline murmured.

"Me too." Steve opened his eyes and looked at her. She

was wrapped up tight in her thick winter coat, a scarf, and multicoloured fingerless gloves. Her face was flushed, and an image of her in his bed flickered through Steve's mind.

Time with Caroline provided a welcome distraction from the stress of work. Steve had spent the last week going through the books. He was going to need to find further investment, or else make some of the staff redundant. Unless he sold the company. The thought pained him. He'd dedicated the last eight years of his life to setting it up. But things weren't looking good, and at least if he sold the company there was a chance it would keep going and the staff would keep their jobs. Last week he'd heard from one of his clients that Harry had set up a rival company and had taken some of his customers with him. When Steve heard that, he knew that he was already on the slippery slope. He remembered the memory sticks of data Harry had taken with him when he'd left, and wished he'd stopped him.

He found himself escaping to Caroline often. It was like they fitted together implicitly. When he was with her he felt like he was living again, instead of spending every hour of every day cooped up in his office. They did everything together and they spoke every day. Even when Steve was at work he would find himself checking her Facebook page continually, looking at her updates, reading her wall-posts and browsing the photos she uploaded. Their emails were now even more frequent, and rarely strayed from the subject of sex and all the things they wanted to do together. Their exchanges about music and culture had diminished to a slow trickle.

Despite this, for a while their real sex life had been nonexistent. They lived in their heads. They went shopping and Steve bought her dress after dress. They went to the cinema. They went out for meals and to bars. They did everything except have sex. He had been sure something was wrong. Caroline had told him about her ultra-conservative religious housemates, and he wondered if they'd been influencing her.

Just when he had been on the verge of bringing it up, they had gone out to a bar and she had thrown herself at him, insisting he take her home. It had been two weeks since the first time, and Steve had been aching for her.

He watched Caroline now as she sat peacefully on the bench, and thought about her in his bed. Suddenly her eyes flicked open and she turned to him.

"Am I the only one?" she asked, searching his eyes.

He smiled at her. The question had come out of nowhere. "Of course," he said. "I love you."

"You're not meeting loads of girls on Facebook then?"

"No." He grinned at her. "I've never met anyone on Facebook other than you."

He turned towards her, suddenly curious. "Have you met anyone on Facebook before?"

"Yes."

"Not as good as me?" He laughed, nervously.

"No." She leaned over the side of the bench, pulled a blade of grass out of the dry soil and played with it, splitting it in two between her thumb and forefinger. She tore it into smaller pieces and let them flutter towards the ground.

"He was forty, but he said he was twenty-five. I told him to piss off."

She let her words hang in the air as she plucked another blade of grass.

"Oh." It was all he could think of to say.

She shifted her position on the bench, moving closer. She seemed to be studying him for a reaction, squinting into the light.

He said nothing, and she changed the subject. "When will I meet your friends?"

"When I meet yours."

"You've met them."

"Watching them follow us around doesn't count."

At the beginning of their relationship, Caroline's friends

had escorted her to their dates and watched them from the shadows for a while before sloping off. Steve had joked that they were her bodyguards. But he'd never been formally introduced to them.

"I'm going to a friend's birthday party after Christmas. You could come with me," she said.

"Which friend is it?"

"Actually it's more of a family friend. Her parents are friends of my parents. She's turning sixteen. She wants some older people there to make her look cooler."

"Where is it?" he asked, feigning interest.

"At the cricket club."

"Sounds good," he said, even though it really didn't sound good at all. Perhaps he could meet her friends another way. A sixteenth birthday party didn't sound like much fun. Would there even be any alcohol?

But she was beaming at him. "Great. I'll tell them you're coming. Everyone's dying to meet you!"

Perhaps he'd overplayed the enthusiasm. It seemed too late to talk himself out of it and he didn't want to disappoint Caroline. Besides, if he went with Caroline it was bound to be fun.

"So . . ." she said, fiddling with her hair. ". . . I've done my bit. When am I going to meet your friends?"

He hesitated. He loved Caroline, but at twenty-two she was a few years younger than him and he wasn't sure what his friends would think of her, or what she'd think of them.

"I could organise a dinner party I suppose."

But who would he invite? His closest friends had been at work, but since Harry's firing he was not the most popular person. He'd been locked in his office for the last few months and had hardly spoken to anyone in the open-plan area.

"That sounds great," she said, smiling.

Perhaps he could introduce her to his university friends.

James and Dave were easy enough to get along with, and not too judgemental. She could meet them first, and then the rest of the group later.

He'd work something out; but for the moment he would just focus on having Caroline all to himself. He leaned in to kiss her and she responded hungrily. All in all, life was good.

20

Renée followed the landlord up the stairs. The smell of urine infiltrated her senses and she kept her mouth closed to avoid the sour taste of it. Her heels clacked against the metal stairs, and she could hear Katie's footsteps echoing a few steps behind.

Since Andy had stopped paying his half of the mortgage, living in the flat in Wimbledon had become financially untenable and Renée had had to accept that she needed to move out. It hadn't been difficult to find people to rent the flat, and a freshly married young couple from Newcastle would now be living in the flat where she had thought she and Andy had been happy. Now she only had two weeks before the couple moved in.

She'd started her flat search in central London, thinking she needed a fresh start, far away from the suburbs and their daily reminders of family life. But prices in central London were so expensive, and she soon accepted that she wouldn't be able to live in the style she had become accustomed to in Wimbledon. Even by her lowered standards, the flat she was visiting now wasn't looking promising. It had been advertised as a "well presented flat in Notting Hill". It might be nice on the inside, but Renée was not sure that she'd be able to complete the walk home safely in the dark, even at the end of a working day. Even now, in the middle of day with Katie beside her, she had felt ill at ease walking through the estate.

"It's a nice area," said the landlord, two paces in front of her, on the never-ending staircase.

Behind her, Katie stifled a giggle.

"Hmm," Renée said, not wanting to agree with him, but not wanting to be rude either. She tried to think of something positive to say, but could find no inspiration in the grey concrete stairwell.

The flat was in a 1960s tower block, situated in a functional square of four identical blocks. Ex-council, she assumed, although some were clearly still occupied by the original tenants. In the centre of the square was a small, sad playground, complete with rusting climbing frame and guarded by surly teenagers. In one corner of the playground, three men leaned in towards each other, speaking conspiratorially and nodding sagely. As Renée and Katie had walked by, one of the teenagers wolf-whistled as he leaned against the playground fence. Renée had ignored him, but Katie had turned round and smiled. Renée pushed her along, checking her Google map to identify the right tower, and wondering if she should just give up and go home. The wind was vicious today and it screamed over the other sounds as it rushed through the man-made canyons between the blocks.

Renée could tell Katie was tiring of the viewings. Her initial eagerness to help had subsided, and now she followed Renée around like a shadow, evidently waiting for the promised drinks at the end of the day. Renée owed her a lot. After her initial, painful sympathy, she had helped her get organised. She had made her have a clear out, getting rid of all reminders of Andy, and then helped her find flats to view. Katie's pro-activity had shocked Renée back into action. She hated not to be in control, and she had started her flat hunt in earnest.

She had found this flat herself, and as such she felt an

irrational loyalty towards it. Although she had already known that she couldn't live here when she had pressed the sticky, faded buzzer, she had been determined to continue regardless. Plus, she didn't feel quite confident enough to turn back and walk straight back by the group of teenagers who they had just hurried past.

"I know all the neighbours; there's a family one side and an elderly couple the other. All very friendly."

"That's good to know," Renée said, wondering what floor the flat was on.

"Just here," he said as if hearing her thoughts. They came out of the stairwell and onto a long concrete balcony. Multicoloured washing littered the balcony, bed-sheets clinging to the railings, billowing in the breeze. The wind caught Renée's hair and she realised she had only ever seen housing like this in the gritty, low-budget films that she used to watch as a teenager. This could be a movie set, she thought, as a group of young children ran by her, chasing each other and shouting. She moved out of their way.

"See, it's a family area," the landlord said, as if trying to convince her.

Once inside, she recognised the flat from the pictures she had seen on the internet. It was newly decorated, with clean white walls and new leather sofas and a modern kitchen and bathroom. Yet even in the flat, the smell of urine seeped in from the corridor. It seemed to be embedded in the walls of the block and no amount of carefully sprayed perfume could disguise it.

The landlord appeared to be waiting for her to say something.

"It looks very nice," she said honestly.

The landlord seemed motivated by her compliment and began enthusiastically to tell her its merits.

"When I saw it I just couldn't resist it. It's great to have a Notting Hill address. You're so near central London. I can't imagine living anywhere else."

Katie had removed herself from the conversation and was staring out the window.

"So you'd be my housemate then?" Renée said to the landlord. The uninterested tone of her voice made it sound like she'd taken a dislike to him, but she had only intended to make conversation.

"Yes, Sarah's moving out." A girl Renée hadn't noticed previously lifted up her hand to wave from the sofa, where she sat watching a huge TV which covered the entire wall.

Renée followed the landlord round the flat politely, nodding appreciatively when he showed her the view of London and demonstrated the power shower. The tour didn't take long and she didn't even bother taking out her notebook.

When it was over she let the landlord take her number, although she knew already she wouldn't be taking the flat. They left, making their way down the stairs and then walking across the courtyard purposefully. The sun had moved round and the tower blocks now cast their shadows over the playground. The group of teenagers was gone, and she and Katie walked briskly past the other blocks and out onto the main road.

Once they were safely on the tube, Renée got out her notebook. That was the fifteenth flat she had seen in three days. Perhaps she was being too picky. She had another viewing in ten minutes, two train stops away. She reached into her handbag and got out the map she had printed off the internet, and tried to work out whether the area would be nice. There was no way of knowing. She sighed.

She studied the checklist she had written for her viewings: size of flat, size of room, number of housemates, number of bathrooms, living room, decor, messiness of house, dishwasher, tumble dryer, garden, length of contract. None of the flats she had seen had measured up to all her criteria.

She realised that Katie was looking at her expectantly.

"How many more?" she asked.

Renée looked at her list. There were three more scheduled for today. She sighed and looked at Katie.

"Let's just do the next one and then go for a drink."

*

An hour and a half later, Katie watched as Renée made her way through the crowds at the bar carrying a bottle of white wine in a wine cooler. She sighed with anticipation. It was so good to be back in the UK. It had been almost impossible to find white wine in India, and she had missed it. It was great to see Renée too and catch up. They had emailed a bit over the years, but because she had always been travelling they had only met up a couple of times a year since university. She realised she had missed Renée; it was so nice to have someone to share a bottle of wine with and have a gossip-filled chat. She was also glad to be out of the house. She'd started a part-time job in an office the previous week and had just received her first pay cheque, so she could finally justify going out drinking.

Renée put the wine on the table and poured it out into each of their glasses.

"It's so nice to have the chance for a proper catch up," Katie said.

"Yeah, I know. We should definitely do this more often, now you're back. Are you in London for good?"

Katie hadn't really thought about it, but she supposed she was. She knew she didn't want to go back to India, and she was kind of sick of travelling. It had been her life for so long and she had loved it, but now when she thought of the constant moving around and the sea of faces of her class at the school in India, it just made her feel tired. She didn't want to settle down exactly, but she didn't want to leave quite yet either. Perhaps she should get a full-time job. A career. The thought depressed her.

"Yeah," she said. She took another sip of wine. "At least for a bit."

"Well we should meet up again soon then . . . before you go away and desert me again."

"Yep," said Katie, hoping Renée meant just going to the pub, rather than meeting in one of the more expensive London bars.

"How about the week after next?" Renée asked, pulling out her diary.

Katie was used to making vague plans with friends which might or might not happen and which, in reality, usually didn't. She had forgotten the efficiency with which Renée managed her life.

"Yeah, sure."

"Wednesday?"

Every evening was the same to Katie. Her current focus was on creating an album of all her travelling photos and staying in touch with all the people she'd met when she was abroad.

"Sounds good," she said.

"Don't you want to write it down?" Renée said as she wrote it in her own diary.

Katie took the pen from her and wrote it on her hand. It was good to see Renée getting back to her organised self after the break-up with Andy. Katie knew it had come completely out of the blue for her, and as much as she tried to put a brave face on it, she was devastated.

"So, how are you doing?" she asked.

Renée smiled at her. "Better," she said.

"Did you see any flats you liked today?"

"Not really. But there were a few that were passable." Renée swirled her wine distractedly.

Katie smiled at her sympathetically. Renée had had it easy since university, living with Andy. She'd never had to live in a house-share. She broached her next question carefully.

"And how is Andy?"

"I haven't heard from him since he collected his stuff."

"Not at all?"

"No," Renée smiled, but Katie could see the tears forming at the corners of her eyes.

"Oh, Renée, I'm sorry." She would have put her arm round her, but Renée was sitting opposite her with her arms folded, as if she didn't want the attention.

"Don't be," she said. Renée sat up a bit straighter and forced a smile.

"Do you want to get back together?"

Renée contemplated her wine. "I don't know. I mean, I've started seeing other people, but it's complicated."

Renée's face flushed and Katie put her hand on her arm. "You know you can talk to me at any time," she said, wondering who she had started seeing so quickly. "I'm always at the end of the phone."

"I know," Renée said.

Katie could tell she didn't want to talk about it.

"So," Renée asked, with false cheer. "How's your love life?"

"Not that great." There wasn't even a glimmer of activity in Katie's love life. She hadn't heard from Dave in ages, and there was no one else on the scene. Besides, she'd never liked talking about relationships with Renée. At university she had always played second best to Renée, who was both prettier and more popular. Before Renée had got together with Andy, Dave had shown an unhealthy interest in her, and although Renée had known that Katie liked Dave, she had done nothing to discourage it. It wasn't until Renée and Andy had been together for six months that Dave had finally stopped looking at Renée and started to notice Katie.

But that was all water under the bridge. Perhaps Katie should tell her about her recent liaison with Dave. It would be good to talk to someone about it.

Renée looked impatient and topped up Katie's wine. "So, spill the beans. You've been distracted for ages; there must be something going on. Did you meet anyone on your travels?"

While travelling, she had had a string of flings with different men in different countries, but she hadn't told Renée about any of them. She took a deep breath. "No," she said. "Actually, it's Dave."

"As in the Dave I know – uni Dave?"

"I still like him . . . I suppose . . . I'm hoping that now I'm back something will happen."

Renée looked uncomfortable.

"We got on really well at the reunion," Katie added quickly. She didn't want Renée to think her interest was one-sided.

Renée was silent and played with her hair. "You still like him?"

Katie suddenly felt nervous. Maybe she was making a fool of herself. "Renée . . . something happened . . . after the reunion . . . I slept with him again."

"Oh my god," Renée said. But she didn't sound happy.

Katie gripped her wine glass harder and took a gulp of wine. Just because Renée wasn't having any luck with men anymore didn't mean she couldn't be happy for Katie. Katie liked Dave and it looked like something might happen for them. Renée should be pleased for her.

"What?" she asked Renée.

Renée stared at the floor. "Nothing," she said.

Katie felt her heart sink. She recognised the expression on Renée's face. It was the guilty expression she always had when she'd made a mistake. "Is there something I don't know?" Katie asked.

"I guess I should tell you," Renée said dejectedly.

"Tell me what?"

"I slept with Dave. I'm sorry, I didn't know you still liked him."

Katie sank into her seat. She had thought that there was still a chance with Dave. In the back of her mind, she had thought that, inevitably, one day, when Dave had got a bit older and calmed down, they would be together. She had believed it would just happen, eventually.

But now Renée had ruined it again. Nothing changed.

21

As they approached James's house, Caroline grabbed Steve's arm and stopped him on the path.

"Do I look OK?" she asked.

He turned to look at her. She was wearing four-inch heels, a silver mini-skirt, and an opaque black top which he'd bought her the previous week at Topshop.

"You look great."

She did look great, but her outfit was better suited to a night out clubbing than dinner at James and Meera's. He wondered what his friends would think of her. She was so different from his previous girlfriends.

When James had called the previous week and invited him for a pre-Christmas dinner, Steve had bitten the bullet and suggested that Caroline come too. She had been nagging him about meeting his friends for ages, and it seemed like a perfect opportunity. Andy was cooking the dinner as a thank-you to James and Meera for putting him up when he and Renée split up, and Dave would be there too. Caroline would be able to meet several of his friends in one go, in a relaxed environment.

Caroline reached for his hand and gripped it tightly as they neared the house. As Steve reached for the door knocker he felt his palms sweating. He really wanted them to like her.

He grinned nervously at her and knocked quickly. Meera opened the door, dressed in jeans and a T-shirt. There was unidentified wet dribble on her shoulder, presumably from the baby. Meera welcomed them in with smiles and hugs. Caroline dwarfed Meera in her heels, and she leant over her awkwardly for the embrace. Steve could almost feel the nerves radiating off her as she straightened her skirt.

"I'm about to change," Meera said. "I just put Phoebe to bed."

Meera disappeared upstairs and Steve and Caroline followed the sounds of chatter and laughter to the living room. When they reached the doorway the conversation paused and Dave, Andy and James looked up expectantly at Steve. Steve introduced everyone to Caroline and then Dave handed him a beer. Steve started to breathe properly again. First hurdle over. Caroline had met his friends. Why had he ever been worried? He reached out and put his arm around her protectively.

Steve surveyed the living room appreciatively as he sat down on the leather corner sofa. The room was tastefully decorated, with one wall covered in a black and white flower pattern and the others painted a pale cream. A decorative crystal lamp hung from the ceiling, and a couple of modern paintings adorned the walls. James had done well for himself.

On the sofa across from Steve, Andy sat sipping his beer and eyeing Caroline with open curiosity. "Where did you guys meet?" he asked conversationally.

Steve paused for a second. Why not tell them? "We met online."

"Internet dating?"

"Actually it was Facebook."

Caroline squirmed in her seat and Steve glanced at her reassuringly. Dave leaned in closer.

"How do you meet someone on Facebook?" Dave asked.

"Caroline's a friend of a friend. She added me and then one

thing led to another." He reached for Caroline's hand and she laughed nervously.

"I didn't realise you could meet someone like that; maybe I should try it." Andy laughed.

"Yeah, Andy, I'll just add one of your fit friends and then we'll just start dating, just like that." Dave laughed and looked at Steve for further explanation.

"That's it," Steve said. "That's how we really did meet."

There was an awkward silence as Dave studied Caroline, clearly trying to work her out. Caroline shifted in her seat and smiled nervously at him.

Steve changed the subject. Caroline was the first girlfriend he'd introduced them to for ages; he'd always been too preoccupied with work to dedicate any real time to his girlfriends, but with Caroline it was different. When he was with her he forgot about the stress of his work.

Steve's company was suffering more than ever, and without Caroline he wasn't sure how he'd cope. This week he'd lost another big client to Harry's firm, and he now knew the company stood no chance of survival unless it was bought out. He had spent the week in negotiations with a potential buyer, but he knew that all the buyer would be able to do was pay off the debts and leave Steve with a very nominal sum of money. Steve hadn't been drawing a salary for the past few months, so he could afford to continue to pay the other staff. Now he was behind on his mortgage repayments. Even if the deal did come off, the most likely scenario was that he would lose his house.

*

Dave watched as Meera helped Andy carry the plates from the kitchen and place them in front of their guests. Andy was apologetic about his cooking. It was the first time he'd cooked for so many. Dave murmured encouragement, trying to hide his growing impatience. He was starving and just wanted to get started on the food, but Andy was cradling each plate he carried like a child he might drop at any moment.

Finally all the food was on the table and they could dig in. Exercising considerable restraint, Dave offered Caroline the potatoes first, but she refused them and only took one bit of broccoli and a slice of turkey from all the food laid out in front of them.

Dave considered her. She wasn't Steve's usual type. Her make-up was plastered on and looked almost sluttish. It was hard to tell what she looked like underneath, but her features seemed youthful and fresh. How old was she again?

"So what do you do, Caroline?" he asked.

"I'm an actress."

"What have you acted in?"

She stared down at the piece of broccoli on her plate. "Just a few extra bits on TV, some commercials."

"Anything I would have seen?"

"No." She didn't elaborate, concentrating instead on cutting her food up into tiny pieces.

He tried again. "Did you do much drama at university?"

Caroline looked a little surprised. "Yes."

Dave chewed his food thoughtfully. If she'd only just left uni she'd be six years younger than them. Steve had done well for himself, but no doubt she'd soon move on. Was she just after him for him money? She'd need it if she was just doing extra-work and commercials.

Caroline reached over to the bowl of potatoes she had earlier refused, and reluctantly put one on her plate.

"What job do you do, Dave?" she asked innocently, trying to divert the attention away from herself.

Dave cringed. His visit to the job centre hadn't paid off. He'd had a couple of interviews, but they hadn't led to anything. He could no longer afford to pay his rent and Charles was losing patience with him.

"I'm an analyst," he said, unwilling to explain his situation to the others.

"Do you like it?"

"Yeah."

Steve rescued Dave unintentionally. "Let's not talk about our jobs. It's the weekend."

"Hear, hear," James said, raising his wineglass.

"How's Renée?" Meera asked, directing the question at Andy. Dave concentrated intently on pouring gravy over his food.

"I don't know," Andy replied.

For a while there was only the sound of knives scraping against plates. Andy held a forkful of food up to his mouth thoughtfully. "I don't miss her," he said.

Dave looked up, expecting him to continue, but he just pushed the food into his mouth and changed the subject. "Phoebe's lovely," he said.

Meera beamed. "Thanks."

"You're lucky, you know, that it's all worked out, I don't think me and Renée ever would have worked out really."

There was an awkward silence.

"We were going to have a baby, you know?"

Dave's fork paused in mid air and his full attention turned to Andy.

"I never realised," Meera said softly. The dining room was so still that Dave sensed that it might be rude to continue to eat.

"Renée was pregnant. But she miscarried."

"I'm sorry," Meera said. Dave saw tears gathering at the back of Andy's eyes.

"We hadn't told anyone. It was less than three months in, so there was no need to mention it. We just carried on."

"I'm sorry, mate," Dave said.

"And after, Renée just said it wasn't meant to be. And we didn't try anymore. Even though we'd always talked about having a child. It never came up again."

There was a silence as they all returned to eating their dinner.

"I'm sorry," Andy said. "That wasn't appropriate."

"It's OK," James and Meera said in awkward unison.

"I just needed to tell someone, you know. Because now me and Renée aren't together, well, there's no one to share the memory with anymore. I wanted someone else to know."

There was another silence. Dave scrambled to think of other topics of conversation, but his mind was blank.

"Has anyone seen her?" Andy asked.

Dave's breath caught in his throat as the image of her naked body flashed through his mind. He hadn't thought about Andy when he'd slept with Renée, but now guilt was starting to prick his conscience.

"Who?" Dave asked.

"Renée."

"Briefly, yes."

"How was she?"

"She seemed OK," said Dave. He didn't want to have this conversation. He didn't want to think about Renée's relationship with Andy. He didn't want to think about Renée at all. It had been a mistake to sleep with her when things were clearly still messed up with her and Andy.

"OK? Do think she's coping?"

"Well, obviously she's finding it tough without you, but I think she's coping," he said diplomatically.

He used the pause in the conversation to excuse himself and went upstairs to go to the toilet. He found himself in a queue behind Meera, who must have slipped away earlier. Ten minutes later they were still both waiting. Dave could hear the tap running full blast and he wondered if someone had passed out in there. Was it Caroline? He'd noticed her leave the table before him and seen her stumble as she made her way out of the room. She had had a lot to drink.

"Caroline?" Meera called tentatively through the door.

No answer.

"Caroline? Are you alright?"

Dave had come upstairs to escape but it seemed like he was just moving from one awkward situation to another.

"I'll knock and then open it up," Meera said "Check she's alright."

"Do you think we should get Steve?" Dave asked.

"No, no need to bother him."

Meera knocked and then unpicked the lock. Inside the bathroom the taps were running at full pressure. Then they heard the guttural sounds of Caroline throwing up in the toilet bowl.

"Are you OK?" Dave asked as he pushed open the door. Kneeling over the toilet bowl, Caroline turned her head in surprise, and pulled her fingers out of her throat.

*

Steve helped James clear the plates from the table while Andy tucked into the red wine.

"Caroline seems nice," James said.

"Yeah, she is, isn't she? Certainly helping to take my mind off things."

"Problems in your line of business?"

"You could say that. I'm going to lose the company." Steve tried to sound matter-of-fact, but saying it out loud somehow made it real and he started to feel queasy.

"Shit."

"Yep. We're being bought out as we speak."

"That's awful."

"I'll be on the dole soon." That was true too. His own words hit him like a punch in the stomach. How had he managed to get through the last months without thinking about his future?

James looked thoughtful. "You'll be looking for jobs?"

"Looks that way." Steve heard the quiver in his own voice.

Suddenly he felt extremely tired. He just wanted to go home, curl up on his bed with Caroline and go straight to sleep.

"Well, there might be something going at my place for a guy with your experience. I'll ask around."

"Thanks, James."

"It must be tough," James patted him on the back. "Hang in there."

"To be honest, being with Caroline makes it better; she helps me forget."

"She seems like a great girl," James said.

At that moment Meera and Dave entered the kitchen with Caroline, and the conversation was over.

"You'd better take her home," said Meera. "I think she's had too much to drink."

22

Dave took one final glance round the flat. It didn't feel like his anymore. Charles's friend John had already started to move his stuff in, and it sat in boxes behind the sofa, ready and waiting to occupy Dave's room as soon as he was gone.

Charles hadn't even bothered to hang around to say goodbye to Dave. Not paying rent for a month can do bad things to a friendship, and he and Charles hadn't spoken for weeks. They'd stopped eating dinner together, and Dave had taken to cooking himself large portions of all Charles's favourite meals, eating them pointedly in front of him and then freezing the remainder. Charles had been choosing to eat out more and more often.

Dave supposed he had lost a friend. He'd lost a lot of friends lately. It seemed like everyone was transient, just passing through his life. His former work colleagues seemed to have forgotten him, Renée hadn't contacted him after they slept together, and the rest of his university friends seemed to have disappeared into the ether.

Except Katie. Katie was waiting outside in her mum's car, packed with all his boxes of stuff.

He smiled to himself. If she hadn't helped him move, he would have had to accept his dad's reluctant offer of help. It would have felt like being collected from university again, like he had never grown up. He hadn't wanted Charles to see him reduced to that.

Dave went back into his bedroom and lifted up the duvet to check that he hadn't left anything. He looked under the bed and in the wardrobe. In the bathroom he checked the shower and the sink. A half-empty bottle of shower gel was his. He didn't really want it, but he didn't want Charles to have it, so he took it.

He went back into the kitchen and saw his Liverpool FC mug in the sink. He gave it a quick rinse and dried it on the tea-towel and put it under his arm. In the cupboard, an open bag of spaghetti was his. He took a can of coke from the fridge that he knew belonged to Charles. That would show him. Then he saw the six-pack of beers that Charles had got in for that evening's drinking. Since Dave had stopped paying rent, Charles had stopped sharing his beers. He really was a tight bastard. Dave took a plastic bag from under the sink and pocketed the beers too.

Right. He was done. His eyes made one final sweep over the living room, and he was out the door. He locked it and posted his keys back through the letterbox. That was it. Done. His life in the flat was over.

*

Katie opened the window of the car to get a bit of air in. It was cold outside, but the car felt stuffy and she felt claustrophobic with all Dave's stuff piled up on the back seats. Dave had just gone back into the house for a final check.

They'd been there for two hours. Dave had packed up most things already, but there had still been a few bits and pieces to pile into boxes, and it had taken longer than either of them had expected.

At university, Katie had loved spending time in Dave's room, seeing how he lived, what things he had. Every time she had slept with him she had always had a quick look in the drawer of his bedside table when he was in the toilet, to see if there was anything revealing or interesting to be found. Invariably there wasn't; just the obligatory half-empty pack of condoms, old packets of paracetamol and some beer tops that he obviously couldn't be bothered to take downstairs to the bin.

When she first started sleeping with him, she used to count the condoms. When there were too many missing and she knew he had slept with someone else, she always felt a bleak sense of disappointment, although their relationship had always been open. On the occasions when there were no extra condoms missing, she would feel elated and would beam at him when he returned from the toilet. She had thought it was a sign that soon their relationship would develop into something more serious.

She had been naïve. And yet today she had suffered the same affliction, looking through the drawers in his room on the pretence of checking to see if he had left anything behind. This time when she saw the pack of condoms, she had thought of Renée. The last time Katie had seen Dave she had been in this bed, and since then Renée had been there too.

Dave came out of the block of flats and headed over to her car, and she waved casually. He opened the boot and stuffed his few remaining things in, then slammed it. He opened the passenger door and swung himself into the seat.

"Ready?" she said.

"I suppose so."

She turned the key in the ignition and pulled slowly away as Dave craned his neck to catch the final glimpse of the flats before she turned the corner.

Katie supposed that now was as good a time as any to bring up Renée. She needed to. She needed to know that Dave wasn't interested in her, so she could get on with her life. She had wasted a lot of time already.

"I feel like I'm always helping people move these days; first Renée, now you."

Dave was staring distractedly out of the window. He glanced back at her.

"Thank you," he said "I'm glad you came."

That was all it took for Katie's heart to leap and her mind to start extrapolating on a future together. She needed him to tell her he wasn't interested. She needed him to be clear.

*

Dave stared out the window as the houses rolled by them and they headed towards the M25. This was what his life had become. Returning home to his parents at twenty-seven. Jobless and alone.

At least he had Katie with him to make the journey. She was always there for him, whatever happened. When he thought about it, she was probably one of his closest friends. She was the only one who'd been there for him through everything; from when his grandfather died of cancer, to his graduation, to now. Girlfriends had come and gone, but Katie had always stuck by him. The sex was good too. Their friendship was the best kind of friendship: free, supportive and uncomplicated by emotion.

"I really mean it Katie," he said. "Thanks."

She frowned a little as she looked at the road ahead. "So, how are things?" she said "In your love life?"

It was unlike her to be this direct. "Have you been counting the condoms?" he said.

Her face flushed. She pretended to be concentrating on the roundabout. "I saw you doing it once when I came back from the bathroom. I watched from the door."

"Oh."

"Then sometimes I'd take extra ones out just to wind you up." He smiled, laughing. Katie had always been so easy to wind up. It was cute, in a way.

She was silent.

"Hey, don't worry about it. I know you'd never do that now." He didn't want to upset her. He hadn't seen her properly since the reunion, because he'd been too broke, but he didn't want to lose her as a friend. She was one of his best friends. One of his *only* friends, now that his old friends from work had deserted him.

"Renée told me about the two of you," she said.

"Oh. Renée." It was Dave's turn to colour a little, as he remembered that awkward night.

"I guess your love life's going well then?"

"It's alright." He didn't want to lose Katie. She had never minded him sleeping with other people, or having girlfriends, but Renée was her friend. He hadn't thought about it before, but perhaps that made it different. Still, he wasn't going to apologise to her. He had nothing to apologise for.

*

Katie felt a wave of sadness wash over her and she bit down hard on her lip to try and control her emotions. That was it, then, wasn't it? Ten years since she'd started university and met Dave, and he still wasn't interested. Surely she was old enough now to get the message?

He had said something, but she hadn't caught it.

"So, how's your love life?" he said, as if they were just friends, having a normal conversation.

"Good," she said. "It's good."

"Really? Is there any gossip then? Anyone I should know about?"

Katie had always made it a rule never to tell Dave about other men. At university there had been very few; a couple of one-night stands, and a fling, but nothing serious. When she had been travelling there had been a couple more, but she had never mentioned them. She'd had enough other news to share with him, about the countries she'd visited, and she hadn't felt the need to share the details of her love life too. So he probably thought she'd never had a serious boyfriend. She should put him straight.

"Actually there is someone," she said.

"Who?" he asked. "Anyone I know?"

"No," she said. She wondered why she'd started this falsity, but didn't know how to end it.

"So tell me about him," Dave said.

"I can't tell you much really," she said. "It's all a bit hush-hush."

"Married?"

"Yeah." Katie hoped that would conclude the conversation.

"I see," Dave said knowingly, and then stared out the window, lost in thought.

23

Sam picked up the book from the trolley and studied its cover. It showed a hand-drawn picture of a young couple clenched in an embrace, Mills and Boon style. The book was bigger than usual, a large print edition, and Sam knew it was popular because the plastic cover was slightly tacky to touch; the combined effect of too many people using it as a placemat for their coffee cups. The large print section was one of the most popular in the library, but then pensioners were their biggest customers, at least since Sam had started at the library. Some of the librarians who'd been at the library over twenty years would laugh as they remembered the days when teenagers used to actually come in the library to look at the videos and even sometimes the books, but they didn't remember them nostalgically. They had been pleased to see them go, and were glad to have the pensioners instead, whose offences were restricted only to talking too loudly when they'd forgotten to put their hearing aids in.

Sam always lingered over her shelf-stacking, taking the opportunity to look through the books. No one really minded; they all did it. Sam had worked at the library six years full time and three years as a temporary member of staff in her university holidays, so she was as much part of the furniture as anyone, and therefore entitled to snatched moments of pleasure amongst the books. She pushed the other books down the shelf to make space, and slid the book in. She ran her hands over the neat row of covers, lost in thought.

She liked the near-silence of the library. It suited her. No one ever came into the library to cause trouble. But of course the silence was in some ways a problem. There was a chance that the cuts to the local library budgets would affect them. She hoped not, but then again it wasn't difficult to see that they weren't busy. She felt guilty for thinking it, but they could easily get by with less staff. Maybe if they asked for voluntary redundancies she would volunteer, so that the others wouldn't have to. Although she had been working there nine years, aside from the Saturday girl she was still the youngest, and it would be easier for her to find another job. The others had been there so long that they didn't know any other way.

She'd thought about other jobs before, even applied for a few. But that was all before she met Patrick and she'd put her plans on the back-burner. She liked this job, and it was close to Patrick's house and only a few tube stops from her mother's. If she took a job in the city, she'd have to commute for an hour. Besides, the library had generous maternity leave, and she and Patrick had already started planning children.

A tap on the shoulder distracted her. She turned to see one of the older librarians. "Accident in the children's section," she whispered theatrically. Accidents did happen, especially in the under-fives storytelling session on Mondays, and Sam hoped it was of the liquid rather than the solid variety. She abandoned her trolley and went over to the storage cupboard to get a mop and bucket. The other librarian went back and continued reading to the other children, to distract them. As Sam approached with the mop, she saw that the little boy was crying, his Thomas the Tank engine T-shirt wet with tears and dribble.

"Come on," she said brightly. "Let's get you cleaned up." She reached out her hand and the boy took it. His trousers were completely soaked through. "What's your name?"

"Ken."

"Where's your mummy, Ken?" she asked.

"She left." He stared at his feet. It was usual for the mothers to leave their children at the library for storytime while they did a quick bit of shopping.

"Never mind," she said. "I'll just clear this up. Then we can go and explore the secret part of the library. Would you like that?"

"Yeah," the boy said.

Sam mopped up the mess and then took the boy round the back to the staff room. He was still snivelling, and she wanted to distract him. He was a lovely child, quiet and attentive as she read to him from various picture books. She stared into his huge blue eyes and wondered what her children would be like. Hopefully they'd inherit Patrick's looks.

After ten minutes there was a knock at the door and a man appeared in a suit. Sam was a bit taken aback. She had expected it to be another librarian or a pensioner. He smiled at her, and then looked down at the boy.

"I'm so sorry," he said.

"Oh, you must be Ken's father."

"Yeah, I am. I'm sorry. We've potty-trained him, but he's never really got the hang of it." He smiled apologetically, and then turned to his son, who was still sitting on a plastic chair, which Sam planned to wipe down afterwards.

"Say sorry to the nice lady, Ken."

Ken just stared up at him and didn't move.

"There's no need for him to apologise. It happens all the time."

"It doesn't happen with my son."

"Well, no."

"Say sorry to the lady."

Ken started to cry again.

"Say sorry."

The child sniffled and managed to get out the word. "Sorry."

Sam rubbed his shoulders. "Not to worry. We hope to see you again."

"Only if he can behave himself."

The man reached out and picked his son gingerly off the chair and left the room. Sam watched as they walked out the double doors of the library. She went back to the staff room, saw the bins were getting full, and went out the back into the car-park to empty them.

The boy and his father were on the other side of the car-park. Sam held up her hand to wave, but they didn't notice. The man was too busy shouting at his son, although Sam couldn't quite make out the words. She felt sorry for him, cowering by the car. Then his father reached up and whacked him hard on the side of the head. Sam gasped and shouted over.

"Hey!" she said, the strength of her voice surprising her. She dropped the bin-bags and went over to the car. By now the man had put his son in the back and was getting into the front.

"You can't do that," she said, overcome by anger. It hadn't been a little smack. He'd hit him like he intended to hurt him.

The man stood up out of the car and Sam noticed how tall he was.

"Can't do what?"

"You can't hit him."

"And what are you going to do about it?" the man asked Sam, stepping towards her.

The passenger door of the car opened and a woman stepped out. She must have seen what happened too.

"Please leave us alone," she said softly to Sam.

Sam was shocked. She noticed the woman was almost completely covered up in a polo-neck jumper, gloves and a scarf, even though she had been sitting in the warmth of the car. There was a round bruise on her neck which was only half covered by her long hair and her scarf. Sam looked from the woman to the man and then back again.

"Mummy, can we go now?" a voice called from the car.

"We're just coming, Ken," she said. She glared at Sam. "Please leave my family alone."

Sam could think of nothing to say. They slammed the car doors and started to reverse. Sam side-stepped out of the way. On the back of the land ranger, a "child on board" sign swung ironically over a "PETA" sticker.

24

Renée looked at the overflowing plate of food in front of her and forced a smile for her mother, who sat across the table. She knew her mother was trying hard to please her, but Renée didn't feel up to eating the huge meal. It was Christmas Eve and Renée had driven down from her new house-share that morning. Her mother had insisted on cooking a special Christmas Eve lunch to celebrate her return, even though they would all be eating too much the next day.

Renée pushed her food around her plate. Since she and Andy split up, she had been comfort-eating, and she had started to notice that her trousers and bras felt a lot tighter than usual. She was determined not to let herself go, and in the last few weeks she had started dieting again. She used to be so careful when she was with Andy, living on salads and grilled chicken, but now she had started to eat what she liked when she liked. At first she didn't put on weight. It must have been the stress, but she had thought it had meant she could continue to eat whatever she liked without consequences. Now her jeans were a little tighter, she realised she needed to change her diet.

It didn't help that she'd been to at least three different Christmas meals at work. She was glad to get away from it all and come to see her parents, but it seemed like her mother was intent on feeding her even more. Renée picked up her knife and fork tentatively, and cut a small piece of her lamb chop.

"Are you alright?" her mother asked, surveying Renée's full plate critically.

Across the table, her father paused as he lifted his final forkful of potato to his mouth, and looked at her expectantly.

"I'm fine." She forced the piece of lamb down her throat. Lamb chops had been one of her favourite foods as a child, but it the last few years she had tried to avoid red meat. She couldn't quite remember why, but she vaguely remembered reading somewhere that it was bad for you. Plus she wasn't even hungry today. She had a slightly nauseous feeling in her stomach, and she wasn't sure if she was ill or if it was the overwhelming sense of Christmas in the house. The smell of mulled wine from the kitchen was making her feel slightly queasy, and the garish decorations in the dining room just made her feel depressed. Her mother had gone all out this year to make it a special Christmas for her, and Renée knew she was being unappreciative. She put another forkful of lamb into her mouth as she watched her mother finish off her own meal.

"Will you be wanting pudding?" her mother asked, looking at Renée's plate doubtfully.

"No, thanks."

"That's a shame, it's your favourite."

"Maybe I can have it tomorrow then." Renée tried to force a smile, but when she did she felt a wave of nausea wash over her and she rushed to the toilet.

*

She stood up, closed the toilet lid and held down the flush. She got a bit of toilet paper and wiped up some specks of vomit that had made it onto the floor. When the toilet finished flushing, she wiped the seat, chucked the paper in and flushed again. She took a deep breath and looked at herself in the mirror. She looked dishevelled and her eyes had deep bags under them. Since she had moved into her shared house, she hadn't been sleeping properly. She splashed water on her face, but she could still feel a coarseness in her throat and a stale taste in her mouth. She went upstairs to the guest room to get her toothbrush, and cleaned her teeth. When she was finished, she went back to the guest room and sank onto the bed.

She stared at the smooth white ceiling and looked round at the functional furniture. Her suitcase lay open on the floor. She should really unpack, but she felt weak and tired. Everything had been so stressful lately. She was working harder than ever, throwing herself into her life at the office to try to finally get the promotion she knew she deserved. But when she came home to her shared house it was always dirty and messy and noisy, and she would just retreat to her room. She didn't feel like she ever really relaxed.

She had been really looking forward to seeing her parents for Christmas. She was an only child, and she knew that they would spoil her. But now that she was here, their attention seemed overwhelming. She wasn't used to it. When she spoke to them on the phone she could keep the conversations short and pretend to be happy. But spending a whole week with them, it would be difficult to keep up the pretence.

She sighed. It wasn't their fault she was feeling sick. She had been feeling off-colour for a few weeks now. She knew she should see a doctor. The only problem was that deep down she thought she knew what might be wrong. The symptoms were exactly the same as last time.

She looked at the bedside clock. Three p.m. There was no time like the present. The pharmacy should still be open. She eased herself out of bed and stood still for a few moments. She waited for the nausea to hit her, but it didn't. She was fine. She wasn't going to throw up right now.

She tried to tread carefully on the stairs, so her parents weren't disturbed, but her mother must have heard something, because here she was, peering up from the hallway.

"Are you feeling better?"

"Yes, a bit, thanks."

"Do you need me to get you anything?"

"I'm fine. I was just going to nip out to the pharmacy."

"Do you want me to drive you?"

"No, I could use the fresh air." Renée forced a smile as she put on her winter coat. She pulled on her boots and opened the door. Her mother was still watching her.

"Are you sure you don't want me to take you?"

"No, I'm fine." Renée shut the door behind her.

*

When she returned, she went straight to her room and tipped the contents of the Boots bag onto the bed. She picked up the test kit, broke into the cellophane with her nails, opened the box and pulled out the test. She twirled it in her fingers for a moment, remembering when she and Andy . . . Back then, the stick in her hand had symbolised anticipation and excitement. She would feel a heady rush as she went to the bathroom to see what the results were. This time things were different. She just felt sick.

She tried not to think about what a baby would mean for her. Of course it had been what she wanted when she had been with Andy. But a baby would hardly fit in with her current lifestyle. She sighed. How could she have been so stupid? She hadn't used protection with Dave, because she never did with Andy. She was on the pill, but she knew that with the stress of her split she'd become a bit lax about taking it. She hadn't thought it mattered.

She listened hard for sounds outside her room, but couldn't hear anything. It didn't sound like there was anyone upstairs. She shoved the pregnancy test in her pocket, opened her bedroom door and crossed the hallway to the bathroom.

25

Steve parked his car right outside the main reception of James's offices. The roads had been icy, but he was still half an hour early. The car-park around him was empty and he stayed in the car and stared at the office building. Perhaps he was too early for his first day. Was it good etiquette to get in early, or should he give his new team the chance to make themselves cups of coffee and settle down before he made an appearance? It was a Monday morning in January and many people would still be on their Christmas holidays. He always used to get into his own office at least an hour before the other staff, but that was when he was in charge. Now things were different.

He watched as a few more cars entered the car-park. One pulled up beside him and Steve pretended to be absorbed in a text message on his phone. The man got out of the car without noticing Steve and walked towards the office.

A lot of things had changed lately. When he left the house this morning, a "for sale" sign was outside the property. The men had come at the weekend to put it up. He'd left to go shopping with Caroline in the morning, and by the time he returned it was there.

He hadn't known it would happen so soon. It felt odd to think that he wouldn't live there anymore. It had been a symbol of his success; everything he had worked for.

At the same time, he'd been surprised by his lack of emotion when he saw the sign. If anything he felt relief. After months and months of fighting to stay in the black, remortgaging the house repeatedly, it was no longer in his control. His business had been bought out for a nominal sum and he couldn't keep up the repayments on the mortgage. Recently the house had seemed more like a weight round his neck than a home.

At least he had Caroline. With her, it didn't matter about the house. He'd explained everything to her, and it seemed to make no difference to her at all. He was lucky. He'd found her just in time. Otherwise he might have gone off the rails.

Steve got out of his car and opened the back door. He took his jacket off the hook in the back of the car, shut the doors and then straightened his tie in the wing mirror.

New Year. New start. He could do this.

It occurred to him that he'd never had a first day before. Well, only for temping jobs, before he started his own company. That was over seven years ago. He hadn't even had an interview since. Could he do this? Could he work for someone else again?

He was lucky James had given him a chance. He strolled towards the building and the automatic doors slid open to welcome him. He spoke to the receptionist and asked her to call his new boss. He wasn't in yet and Steve sat down on the sofa in reception to wait. After a while he got bored of flicking through the magazines and decided to call James. He might be around already.

James picked up on the third ring. He sounded irritated at first, but when he realised it was Steve he invited him up to this office. Steve ascended the stairs quickly and stopped in front of the door plaque: *James Stephenson, Head of Strategy, UK and Ireland*. The door was shut and the blinds were down over the windows. It was much more private than the office Steve had had at his company.

He knocked twice. There was no answer, but James was expecting him, so he pushed the door open. James looked up from his desk, as if startled. He had been swigging from a bottle of water, as he stared at a mass of paperwork.

James's smile came too late to cover up his irritation, and Steve was concerned he'd done something to annoy him before he'd even started work. But he pretended he hadn't seen the frown. "How are you doing?"

"Good. Nice of you to pop by. Glad you've made a start."

There were no hugs or slaps on the back. Steve supposed that this was the formal style in which they would address each other from now on. They weren't at the pub anymore.

"Nice office," Steve said conversationally, as if James were a client. James had pictures of Meera and Phoebe on his otherwise messy desk.

"Thanks."

"How's Phoebe?"

"She's good." James stood up and took another sip of water. He placed the bottle back on his desk carefully.

"I've got some work I need to do before nine," James said, moving round his desk to touch Steve lightly on the shoulder and steer him towards the door. "How about we meet for lunch and we'll have a proper catch up then?"

"Sure." He let James guide him out the door.

*

Steve spent the morning in a flurry of meetings, and lunch came round quickly. At one, he went back to James's office. The door was closed, but this time a PA sat outside, eyeing Steve curiously.

"Is James around?"

"He's just in a meeting; he'll be back soon."

Steve hovered by her desk, unsure whether to stay or come back later, but at that moment James appeared and his decision was made.

James beamed. "Steve! Ready for lunch? I'm famished."

James put his briefcase away in his office and locked the door behind him. He seemed in a much better mood and was chatting animatedly as they walked to the car-park and got into his car. He accelerated out of the car-park before Steve had a chance to put his seatbelt on. Steve reached for the handle above the passenger door to steady himself as they took a corner sharply. There was a noise from the boot that sounded like glass clinking. He looked at James but he didn't seem to register the sound as he sped down the country lane. James braked sharply at a junction and the clinking got louder.

James registered it this time and glanced at him. "My golf clubs are in the boot," he said. Steve frowned, but decided not to comment.

A few minutes later they pulled into a pub car-park and got out of the car.

"Best pub for miles," James said.

They went inside and found a secluded table amongst the wood panelling. James went up to order food and get the drinks. Steve asked for a lemonade, but when James returned he was carrying two whisky and cokes.

"Surely you'll join me?" he said.

Steve couldn't refuse, yet he was worried about returning to work with the smell of whisky on his breath. They clinked their glasses together and waited for their food.

Out of the office the conversation flowed easily, and Steve began to relax. He thought he would like working with James.

They were in the pub for over an hour and James got through three whisky and cokes before they left. Steve sensibly declined all but the first one. On the way back to the car, Steve noticed James swaying slightly and offered to drive. James refused, and on the drive back Steve held the handle with an iron grip. James sipped from a bottle of water he had in the front of the car as he navigated them back to work.

Hopefully, Steve thought, the water would help James sober up. It was nice of him to take him out for lunch, but he didn't want James to risk his job for the sake of a boozy lunch.

26

Katie turned off the bath taps and checked the temperature of the water with her elbow. It seemed about right, it didn't scald her, and it didn't seem too cold either. But the most important thing was that it wasn't too hot, so she added a bit more cold water for good measure.

It was ten a.m. and she was an hour late giving her grandfather his bath, but she supposed it didn't really matter. It wasn't like he had much to do all day anyway. Surely he could wait an extra hour to watch television, especially as it was a Saturday and both he and Katie deserved a lie-in.

Her mother had left to go on a long holiday to Spain a week earlier. The holiday had been booked long before Katie's grandfather had moved in. Katie's mother had thought about cancelling, but Katie had persuaded her not to. Katie was more than happy to care for her grandfather. A carer came during the week, so it hadn't sounded like much work. She only needed to look after him in the evenings and on weekends.

But now the weekend had come round, she was starting to think of all the other things she could be doing. Instead of wheeling her grandfather to the park she could be going shopping. She could be going out with her friends tonight instead of being stuck in with the Saturday-night TV.

She went to the doorway of her old room, where her grandfather had taken up residence. There was a childish wooden sign on the door that still read "Katie". Katie knew if she had come back and been able to stay in her own room she would have removed the sign by now, but as it was it signified her previous ownership of the room, before her grandfather had taken it over.

He was only supposed to stay for two months while he recovered from his operation. It wasn't that she didn't want him there, it was just that she had been assured by her mother than he would soon be gone. She had graciously accepted his occupation of her room and professed that she didn't mind at all, on the grounds that it was temporary. When she arrived home from India, he had already been there a month, so there had only been a month to go. A month had seemed manageable.

But he hadn't got better. He could shuffle from room to room, but he couldn't manage the stairs. He could sit contentedly in front of the television, but he couldn't wash himself or cook for himself. He still needed constant care.

Katie knocked on the door.

"Yes." His gruff voice was hardly more than a whisper, and Katie only just heard.

"Time for your bath, Grandad," she said as cheerfully as possible, already picturing the indignity of her hands running the soap over his wrinkled skin.

She heard a grunt, and she took this as consent to enter the room.

Aside from the man in the bed, the room was almost exactly as she had left it when she had gone travelling. There was a bookshelf overflowing with fiction and travel guides and her files of university notes. There was her old stereo, a desk, and cupboards full of clothes. The only evidence that her grandfather now lived in the room was a battered suit-case on the floor, a large-print Agatha Christie novel on the bedside table, and a pile of neatly folded clothes on a chair in the corner.

"Let's get you out of bed," she said, suddenly understanding the false cheer of hospital staff.

"My bath was due an hour ago," he said.

"I know, Grandad, but it's Saturday."

"My programme started ten minutes ago."

"Well, you'll have to miss it this week."

He seemed to accept this, and she started to help him up, watching as he eased his legs over the edge of the bed and then offering him her arms to help him shift his weight onto his unsteady feet.

She let him lean on her, and took him across the hallway to the bathroom. He leant against the sink as she lifted the lid of the toilet.

"Are you OK to go on your own?" she asked. Of all the duties she had, helping him go to the toilet was the worst. After the first time she had helped, he insisted he could do it himself in future. Her mother had told her that she had to help him, but he didn't want her to. So she would help him pull down his trousers and pants and sit on the seat and then leave him to it. She would never go far, making sure she was in hearing distance in case he had an accident.

She went back to the bedroom and collected his towels. She waited until he called her through. When she went back to the bathroom there was a bit of soiled toilet paper on the floor that he hadn't managed to get into the bowl. He refused to meet her eyes.

She helped him off the toilet and pulled his pants and trousers up, although it seemed an unnecessary hassle, as he was about to get in the bath. But she couldn't leave him standing there with his pants round his ankles. It was too undignified.

She got another piece of toilet roll and used it to pick up

the dirty piece from the floor. She threw the whole wad into the toilet bowl and then flushed. She went through the routine of undressing him and easing him into the bath. He flinched, and complained it was too cold. When she felt it herself, she discovered he was right. She added some more hot water and mixed it in with her hands.

She was already looking forward to Monday, when she would be able to go to her part-time job, sit at a desk and relax without worrying that her grandfather was going to fall down the stairs or slip in the bathroom. The carer would be looking after him. Katie worked from Monday to Wednesday and spent Thursdays and Fridays at home. But it was always awkward when she and her grandfather's carer were in the house at the same time. She would try to have a lie-in, but would wake up to the sounds of clattering in the kitchen as the carer started to prepare her grandfather's mid-morning snack.

She would feel guilty, like she should be looking after him herself, rather than leaving it to a stranger. But she had never felt guilty enough to get out of bed and go down and help, listening instead to the murmur of activity and conversation below, until she heard the carer leave to take her grandfather out for some fresh air.

This week it had been different. She had been looking after her grandfather all week, so when the carer came she had felt justified in going down and chatting to him. They had discussed the best approach to bathing, why people didn't always step out of the way for wheelchairs, and how long it took people to recover from operations.

Despite their age difference, Katie had found herself laughing at his jokes, most of which were deeply inappropriate and politically incorrect. She supposed it was a generational thing, but she didn't think you could use the word "cripple" anymore. He was kind, though, and he looked after her grandfather well, always taking the time to talk to him and find out what he had been up to, even though all he did was watch TV all day.

Katie helped her grandfather dress, and then put him in the stair lift and pressed the button to take him down. She watched his slow progress from the top step, and found herself looking forward to Thursday, when she would see the carer again and would be able to engage in a normal conversation that wasn't about something on the TV or something that had happened fifty years ago.

It occurred to her that she didn't know the carer's name. They had passed in the corridors of the house on several occasions when her mother had been there and simply nodded at each other. And because of this degree of familiarity, they hadn't introduced themselves when they'd chatted the other day.

27

Steve pulled up in front of the cricket club. He had picked Caroline up from the corner of the road as usual. She had been shivering in her tiny dress, texting her mates on her mobile phone with one hand, her other arm wrapped tightly around her.

He had offered to pick her up from her house, but as usual she had refused his offer. He didn't want to push it, he would hate to argue with her. He had seen how intimidated she felt around his friends. He wanted to protect her and look after her. Besides, tonight was her night. They were going to meet some of her friends at her family friend's birthday party.

Steve smiled to himself. He'd never thought that at the age of twenty-seven he'd be going to the sixteenth birthday party of a girl he'd never met. You never knew what life held round the corner for you.

He got out of the car as Caroline checked her make-up in the mirror. All over the car-park, teenagers slammed car doors and made their way towards the cricket club, the boys loping in jeans and hoodies, the girls tottering in high heels. He could see their parents sitting watching from their cars, waiting until they saw their children go safely through the double doors before they revved their engines and drove off. He felt a bit parental himself; it felt wrong watching the young girls make their way inside, and he turned away.

He went round to the passenger side of his car and opened it. Caroline stepped out of the car carefully, her black sparkly dress straining over her thighs. She stood up slowly and smoothed down her dress. She looked beautiful. Steve shut the car door, took her hand and walked with her towards the cricket club.

As they headed to the doors a group of boys approached them.

"Hey Caroline! You're looking hot."

She ignored them, but they shouted after her.

"Why's your dad coming in with you?"

They went through the double doors to the sound of their laughter. Steve wasn't sure whether to be amused or disturbed. He was wearing chinos and his favourite designer shirt. Maybe the chinos made him look old.

"They're so immature," Caroline said, shaking her head sadly.

As Steve and Caroline went into the club, Steve scanned the room for the bar. It was all the way over on the other side of the room, and there was hardly any queue. Steve supposed that was one advantage of a sixteenth birthday party. They couldn't be seen to encourage underage drinking. At least it would be easy for him and Caroline to get a drink later.

A big group of girls approached them.

"Hi Caroline," screeched one of the girls.

"You brought Steve," squealed another. She stared up at him, wide-eyed beneath her false lashes, and Steve thought he recognised her from his first date with Caroline in the shopping mall.

"Hi Steve," a couple of the others chorused.

Steve held out his hand, but none of them took it. They all just laughed. They looked a lot younger than Caroline. Perhaps they were friends of the girl whose birthday it was.

"I'm Caroline's best friend," one of them whispered to him, conspiratorially. As she leant in, her large breasts threatened to liberate themselves from her tight red dress. Steve coughed. "Caroline said you might bring some of your mates."

He frowned. Caroline hadn't mentioned that to him. And he didn't think he had the powers of persuasion to convince any of his friends to attend a sixteenth birthday party. "Sorry, you'll have to make do with me," he said.

He glanced over towards Caroline, hoping she would rescue him, but she was deep in conversation with one of the other girls. Steve was left surrounded by the gaggle of her other friends.

"I'm single, you know," said the girl in the red dress. "Just in case you want to introduce me to your friends."

Steve laughed, unsure whether she was serious. Surely this wasn't really a close friend of Caroline's? "I'm going to the bar," he said.

The girls crowded in closer.

"Can you get me a drink?"

"I'll have a Smirnoff Ice."

"Me too."

"And me."

"I'll have a VK Apple."

He wondered if some of them were still sixteen.

"Are you all eighteen?" he asked carefully.

"Oh my god."

"I can't believe you just said that."

"We're friends with *Caroline.*" They said her name as if she was some kind of celebrity.

"OK, OK," he said, and backed away from them, heading towards the bar.

Now there was no queue at all. A man in his forties leant on the bar, sipping a beer.

"You felt the need to watch them too, did you?" he said, conversationally.

Steve wasn't quite sure what he meant, so he grunted and nodded, trying to get the attention of the barman, who was reading a book.

The man by the bar held his hand out to him. "I'm Stuart, father of the birthday girl." Steve realised that Stuart must think he was also a parent.

"I'm with Caroline," he said quickly, remembering that she was a friend of the family, and assuming Stuart would realise he couldn't possibly be her father.

"Right," said Stuart amicably. He hadn't seemed to register that Steve wasn't a parent, but Steve didn't feel like stressing the point.

The barman finally turned to them and raised his eyebrows at Steve.

"Three Smirnoff Ices, one Apple VK, a pint of Fosters and . . ." Steve tried to think what Caroline would want. She always drank wine when she was out with him, but maybe that was because they were always sharing a bottle. "And a glass of white wine," he finished.

As the barman got out the various drinks, Steve pulled out his wallet and pulled out a twenty.

"£22.50," the barman said.

Steve supposed that Smirnoff Ice must be an expensive drink. It wasn't something he normally ordered.

Caroline and the other girls suddenly appeared by his side. In seconds the Smirnoff Ices were gone. Steve collected his change and handed the glass of wine to Caroline. He could feel Stuart's eyes boring into the back of his head. Steve turned round to acknowledge him, but when he did Stuart looked deliberately away and muttered something to the barman under his breath.

Steve and Caroline went to try and find a seat. The tables and chairs had been pushed to the side of the room and each of the plastic seats seemed already occupied. Boys and girls sat in separate groups, occasionally looking over at each other and laughing.

Steve realised that Caroline's friends were still following them. He supposed he had to make an effort. After all, she had made an effort with his friends.

They eventually perched on the edge of the table. The music blared and Caroline moved her shoulders to the rhythm. She looked so comfortable and relaxed. Steve didn't recognise the music, and felt out of place among her friends.

A girl was perched on the table on the other side of him. She whispered in his ear. "So how's it going with you and Caroline?"

He didn't recognise this girl from earlier. "Hi," he said, holding out his hand. "I'm Steve."

She looked confused and asked the question again. "How's it going with you and Caroline?"

"Fine thanks," he said, and sipped his beer, keen to turn away and talk to Caroline.

"Are you going to get married?"

"Umm . . . I don't know."

"How old are you?"

"Twenty-seven."

"Wow, that's old."

"Not really," Steve said, irritated.

"Have you had sex?"

He laughed. "I don't think that's any of your business."

"It's just that Caroline said you had, and I didn't believe her, so I put a bet on with Claire that's it not true. I said I'd ask you so we know who's won." The girl spoke faster and faster and her face coloured. When she finished, she looked at him expectantly.

Steve laughed again, keen to escape the conversation. "I think I said it's none of your business." He turned back to Caroline, hoping the girl would go away. "Are you enjoying yourself?"

"Yeah." She beamed at him. "Can I have another drink?"

"Sure," he said, relieved to have a reason to escape from the girl the other side of him. He tried to creep away before her friends could follow him to the bar again. This time he succeeded and he bought back drinks for just him and Caroline.

He found that his perch on the edge of the table was taken, so he stood opposite Caroline for a few awkward moments, before she asked him if he wanted to dance. There was no one on the dance floor, and he felt awkward, but he saw the excitement in her eyes and didn't want to disappoint her. She took his hand and he followed her into the middle of the room.

Her dancing was a combination of sexy and manic enthusiasm, and he tried to hide his amusement at some of her moves. She looked so cute. She was gorgeous. They weren't dancing for long before others started to join them. Soon the floor was crowded and he longed to lean in and kiss her.

He looked around and saw that the teenagers were dancing self-consciously, circling round him and Caroline. No one was kissing on the dance floor. Would it be bad of them to be the first? He was sure they were up to all sorts out in the car-park. He glanced over to the bar and saw Stuart watching him.

He leaned in and whispered in Caroline's ear. "Do you want to go outside?" he asked.

"Yeah," she said.

Still aware of Stuart's eyes on him, Steve grabbed Caroline's hand pointedly and they walked outside together.

They sat on the steps looking out at the car-park. Caroline shivered and Steve put his arms around her and leant in to kiss her. The air was cold on his face and he felt goose-pimples on Caroline's arm.

A blast of warmth hit his back as the door from the cricket club opened. A group of lads came out, pulling packets of fags out of their pockets and looking for a quiet place to smoke.

Steve remembered being that age himself, and smiled.

One of the boys turned round to him and Caroline.

"Alright, Caroline?" he said.

Caroline didn't answer.

"What you doing with that paedo?"

Steve considered rising to it, but didn't. They were only young.

"Fuck off," Caroline said. Steve had never heard her swear before.

"You can tell us about the paedo's performance in Maths on Monday, slag."

Steve stood now and the boys ran away round the corner.

He turned back to Caroline and saw her face was red. He felt a tightening in his chest.

"Caroline." He was lost for words.

"I'm sorry," she said. "Don't leave me."

"You're at school?"

"Don't leave me. I love you."

"Caroline, I'm taking you home."

She cried harder, and he thought she was going to resist, but instead she nodded.

"OK."

He fancied her like crazy in her little dress, and wanted to comfort her. But he saw her for what she was: a schoolgirl in a woman's body.

Shit.

He reached out and helped her up, and then walked over to his car. She followed, struggling to walk in her heels. Oh god, she was drunk. He'd bought her drinks and now she was drunk. He'd bought them all drinks.

He opened the passenger door for her and she slid into the seat.

During the journey he could only hear the sound of her sniffling. He tried to focus on where he was going.

"Do you want to be dropped off on the corner?"

"OK."

"Or at your parents' house?"

"On the corner, please."

She cried harder, and it tore at him. When she got out at the corner and he watched her walk off, tears began to form in his own eyes.

Spring

28

On Thursday morning Katie woke to the sound of the bath running. The carer must already be here, she thought, irritated. Which meant that for the next hour she wouldn't be able to have a shower. She sighed and rolled over. It was a pain to have a stranger in the house in the mornings. She just wanted to wander round in her pyjamas, have a cup of tea, read the paper, then watch a bit of TV before she got dressed. But Monday to Wednesday she had to get up to go to work; on Thursday and Friday she was off, but the carer was there; and at weekends she had to care for her grandfather. She could never lounge around in the mornings.

She was counting down the days until her mother was back from Spain, but there was still another week to go. Katie had had a text from her the previous night, saying what a great time she was having, drinking outside in the sun. At the time, Katie had been watching a third rerun of the X-Factor with her grandfather. Somehow it felt like their lives had become mixed up. Katie should be the one drinking in Spain. But her mother deserved the holiday after caring for her grandfather for so many months, and Katie could hardly resent her for it after all the travelling she had done herself.

She lay still on her bed and listened as the taps were turned off and the carer walked over to her old room to get her grandfather out of bed. She was restless. She wanted to get up and do something with the day, but she couldn't think what. She picked up a book from the bedside table and tried to read, but she couldn't concentrate. She felt irritable just lying in bed as the day drifted by.

Maybe she should get up. After all, she shouldn't feel like she couldn't leave her own room in her own house. She'd never felt like this on her travels. She'd shared rooms and bathrooms all the time, with people her own age, older people, people who didn't speak English, people with poor standards of personal hygiene, girls who slept with their boyfriends when they thought everyone else was asleep. She had had no qualms or embarrassment about getting changed in front of people. So why did she feel like this now, in her own house? It was ridiculous.

Enough was enough. She was going to get up. She didn't care if he saw her in her old pyjamas. She slid herself out of bed and put her dressing gown on. She brushed her hair and checked her appearance in the mirror. She didn't look too awful.

She stood by her door for a moment and listened. She could hear the carer talking to her grandfather. They must both be in the bathroom. She could leave her room quickly and go downstairs to make breakfast without them seeing her.

She opened the door and shut it behind her firmly. She walked across the hallway confidently, as if she always did this.

"Good morning," the voice called from the bathroom.

She considered ignoring it, but decided she couldn't, and turned around. The bathroom door was open and the carer was standing over her grandfather in the bath, sponging his chest.

"Hi," Katie said, awkwardly.

His sleeves were rolled up and he lifted the sponge from the bathwater and squeezed it out. "Did you sleep well?" he asked.

She paused in the doorway. She didn't want to have a conversation with him while she was in her dressing gown and he bathed her grandfather. "Yeah, fine." She turned to leave.

"Don't go. We've never really introduced ourselves properly."

Now really wasn't the best time, but she forced a smile. "I'm Katie," she said.

"You're Tabitha's daughter?"

"Yes." Surely he knew that already. She'd been back six months and they'd had a long conversation just the other day.

"I'm Daniel." He reached for her grandfather's towel, dried his hands, and held out his right hand.

She shook his hand, using her left hand to ensure that her dressing gown was tightly wrapped around her. Her grandfather looked like he'd fallen asleep in the bath.

"So do you live here?"

"Yes," Katie said, surprised. Hadn't he noticed?

"I thought you might be at university."

"No, I left university years ago."

"Oh, right. I didn't go." He volunteered the information easily and without bitterness.

"Why not?" she asked, and realised how pretentious and young she sounded, as if she thought everyone went to university.

Daniel helped her grandfather to sit up and started to rub shampoo between his hands. He looked at Katie thoughtfully.

"I never wanted to. I always wanted to do this." He looked at her grandfather in the bath.

"Why?" Katie asked, unable to hide her puzzlement.

"I like looking after people," he said simply, as he started to wash the old man's hair.

"Oh."

His eyes were big and blue, and he smiled at her kindly, seeing that she didn't understand. "My brother was disabled.

My mother couldn't look after him, so I did. It was more rewarding than anything else I've ever done. Nothing else gave me the same satisfaction. And I was never very academic. And I suppose I never wanted to work in an office. I'm lucky. This is the perfect job for me."

Katie was taken aback with his straightforward, easy honesty. "What happened to your brother?" she asked.

"He died. But when he died I knew I'd given him the best life he could possibly have had. He'd been happy."

"How old was he?"

"Twenty-two."

Katie looked at Daniel. He must think she was so rude for asking him question after question. She didn't know how to end the conversation. "I'm sorry," she said.

"That's OK. I expect you'll be wanting your breakfast now?"

She realised he had deliberately offered her an escape, and she took it gratefully.

"Yes, I'm going to go downstairs. It was nice talking to you."

"You too, Katie."

*

At lunchtime she went into the kitchen and watched as Daniel prepared her grandfather's meal. Her grandfather couldn't chew well, so the food had to be easy to swallow, and Daniel was boiling sweet potato and roasting carrots in order to later convert them into the mush that her grandfather would then eat. When Katie was responsible for the dinner, she usually just fed him tinned soup. She admired the pride Daniel took in his work. It seemed so important to him that he got every detail just right.

He looked up at her when he felt her watching, and smiled, his big blue eyes sparkling in amusement.

"Seen a lot of you today, Katie," he said in an almost paternal fashion.

"Yeah," she said, and felt unexpectedly shy.

He took a plate out of the cupboard and prepared the cutlery. She watched, observing his full head of grey hair and the laughter lines around his eyes. He must be her father's age, if not older. She had never met anyone like him. All the men she knew who were that age were businessmen, and most had families.

She wondered if he had children. He hadn't mentioned it, but then they'd hardly spoken about anything personal. She scanned his fingers for a wedding ring, but found none.

They ate lunch together with her grandfather, and the conversation flowed easily between the three of them. Daniel was constantly aware of her grandfather, sensing when he wanted the salt passed before he even asked, and getting up to get him a second glass of water when it ran out.

They talked about everything: her grandfather talked about when he'd been younger and met her grandmother, Daniel talked of his own parents, and Katie told them about India and the colours and smells and noise. Daniel was impressed, but he thought that travel was not for him. He had never travelled outside the UK and had no desire to.

Afterwards, Katie and Daniel cleared away the dinner together and Daniel went upstairs to put her grandfather to bed for his nap. Katie wanted to say goodbye to him, so she waited for him on the sofa downstairs. When she heard his footsteps on the stairs, she went over to the door. He saw her waiting, and paused on the last stair. It wasn't until now that she noticed how tall he was. When they'd previously talked he's always been leaning over something; the bathtub, the cooker, the dining table. Now he stood at his full height and with the extra help of the stairs.

She felt unnaturally nervous and moved out of his way. He stared at her as he walked past.

"See you tomorrow," she said, but their eyes communicated to each other in a different language.

They leant into each other and kissed deeply. Katie's eyes widened in surprise at the intensity.

He pulled away first and spoke seriously. "Shall we go upstairs?"

She was shocked at his directness, and laughed nervously at the sincerity of his tone. He took her laughter as a no.

He looked crestfallen, and turned to leave.

"Yes," she said. "Yes."

They went to her brother's room, where she was staying. It was across the hall from where her grandfather was sleeping, and she worried that the sound would wake him. Daniel undressed her carefully as she tugged at his clothes clumsily. She felt scared, like she might be making a mistake, or that she might get into some kind of trouble, but she continued regardless.

Daniel was gentle, his hands soft. Afterwards, he kissed her lightly on the lips and began to dress.

"Thank you," he said, as Katie's eyes started to refocus on one of the pictures of some 90s popstar on her brother's wall.

"That's OK," she said.

He left her to get dressed alone, but when she came out of the room he was waiting for her. He smiled, and she smiled back, and then laughed. They looked at each other, indecisive, and then Daniel started down the stairs with her just a step behind him. At the doorway he kissed her passionately.

"See you tomorrow," he said.

Katie felt her heart leap.

29

Steve sat at his desk, staring out of the window at the people busy in the offices opposite. He watched a girl feed paper into a photocopier and stand by it as she waited for the documents to print, playing with her phone idly. The sounds of endeavour buzzed around him as his co-workers typed furiously and talked loudly on their phones. He knew he should be concentrating, trying to make a good impression, but he just couldn't focus. His first few weeks in the new job had gone really well and he couldn't slack off now. He needed to get back to work and stop staring into space.

He turned back to his desk. On a pad of paper next to it he had written his to-do list for today, but it was eleven a.m. and he hadn't started it yet. Every time he looked at his computer he thought of Caroline. He couldn't look at an Excel spreadsheet for more than thirty seconds, before her face appeared in his head to distract him.

How could he have been so stupid? How could he not have known that she was a schoolgirl? There had been so many hints: their first date at a shopping mall, the gaggle of girls that seemed to follow her everywhere, her lack of familiarity with different types of wine, her lack of experience in bed. Steve felt sick. He had taken her virginity.

The guilt brought the image of her naked on the bed back into his mind. Even now, despite himself, he still wanted her. What kind of a man did that make him?

All the things that had appealed to him about her – her naivety, her determination to be an actress, her simplistic political views – had merely been symptoms of youth.

He looked back at his to-do list and tried to focus. He was supposed to call three different clients today to chase up proposals he had written, and yet he didn't feel able to pick up the phone. He didn't think he could string a coherent sentence together, let alone talk to a client about a proposal he could hardly remember writing.

He picked up his mobile from his desk and swirled it round in his hand. He had switched it off this morning. He had received twenty-four missed calls from Caroline since Saturday night. Each time, he had wanted to answer it, to talk to her, but he had to stop himself. He couldn't get in any deeper.

He didn't know how to feel towards her. It was difficult to just switch off the love he had felt. He knew he had taken advantage of her, and he felt guilty. But she had taken advantage of him too. She had misled him. She had told him she was twenty-two and he had believed her. He had never questioned it. But what twenty-two-year-old sent a stranger a message on Facebook saying "you're fit?" And she was a stranger. She had said she'd known a friend of his, but he'd since realised that they had no friends in common. She had just found his picture somehow and decided to pursue him.

He knew he should be angry with her, but he couldn't find it in himself. He should have realised straightaway. He certainly should have realised before he slept with her.

He had scanned her Facebook profile the day after the party. He had been expecting to see something he had missed before; perhaps photos of her in school uniform, pictures of her parents, wall posts about Chemistry homework. But there was nothing. The only hint that he could possibly have picked up was that her friends looked so young. Her profile presented the image she wanted the world to see: the woman, not the schoolgirl. He played with the phone. She had left messages, but he hadn't listened to any of them. He wondered what she had said. How did she feel? Was she sorry? Did she regret it? Did she regret him? He didn't want her to regret him.

He turned the phone on. Seconds later the messages came through: three new ones since yesterday. He looked at the answer-phone screen. He had twelve new messages in total. Eleven were from Caroline. One was from a client.

He put the phone down and turned back to the spreadsheet on his computer.

He couldn't concentrate. He went to make himself a cup of tea. There was no one else in the kitchen, and the kettle seemed to take ages to boil. He paced restlessly.

When he had finished making his tea he couldn't face going back into his desk. He walked round the open-plan area, trying to engage his colleagues in conversation. But as they spoke he became distracted, and when they looked expectantly at him for a response, he found he hadn't been listening and could think of nothing to say.

He wandered over to the printer and pretended to be overly interested in the documents that had been left on the top. There were a couple of emails and someone's holiday booking form. He put the papers back and returned to his desk.

His mobile taunted him. He picked it up again. Surely it wouldn't do any harm to listen to her messages.

30

"And when you've finished making the tea, you can do the filing."

Dave's new "boss", Craig, made no attempt to hide the glee in his voice as he gave the instruction.

Dave gritted his teeth and went into the kitchen. He and Craig had history. When Dave was at school, Craig had joined his class in the middle of term. Craig had been put back a year, and thus was much bigger than the other kids, and Dave, a small, weedy kid, had found himself immediately replaced on the Under 14s football team. Dave arranged for some of his mates to fight Craig, but when Craig punched back in front of a teacher, it was Craig who was expelled. Dave wondered if he still blamed him, or if it was too long ago for him to remember.

Dave had forgotten all about Craig until he'd started this temping job at a local business near his parents' home. Despite leaving school with no qualifications, Craig was now office manager. He was fond of telling Dave and the other temp, Rachel, about his meteoric rise from lowly temp to his current position.

Dave switched on the kettle and got the teabags. He wanted to explain to the others in the office that he hadn't always been a temp. He'd been to uni. He'd had a good job. But there was no point. It would just draw attention to the fact that he was once successful and now he was just one of them. He needed to get himself in gear and find another job.

Craig was actually an alright boss, and somehow that made it worse. He was well-liked and he seemed happy with his place in the world. On Craig's desk there was a picture of a very attractive wife and two small children. When Craig had asked about Dave's family, Dave had had to mumble under his breath that he was living with his parents. Rachel had burst out laughing as Dave squirmed, but Craig had been irritatingly sympathetic, patting him on the back and telling him that he'd find someone some day.

Dave finished making the tea and took it back into the open plan office, putting a cup on each of the desks. Most of them didn't even say thank you. Craig always asked him to make the tea. He didn't think Rachel had made a single cup of tea since she had started temping herself – two weeks after him.

It was unusual for the office to have two temps, but he appreciated the company. Rachel had been employed because Craig and the admin assistant hadn't done any filing all year. They had saved it up, putting papers and files randomly in a big storeroom at the end of the office and leaving them there to gather dust. Now they were in a mild panic because the auditors were coming in.

For Rachel, the job was just for a few months. She was on a year out from university, and afterwards she would return to her life as it was before. Therefore she felt perfectly at ease looking at Craig and the other managers with complete disdain and sighing and rolling her eyes when they said something blindingly obvious. She had no fear of being fired. Dave wished he had her guts, but he was a more of a getting-on-with-it, anything-for-a-quiet-life type of man. Rachel said he was an arse-licker. Dave objected, but in his heart he knew it was true. He just didn't like confrontation. He had changed a bit from the small boy who'd ganged up on Craig at school.

"Do you want to help me with the filing?" he asked Rachel.

"Not really," she said, but she got up and they walked over to the filing room together.

Files were piled up on every surface. Dave had been in the room briefly earlier in the week to make a start, but since then he had managed to avoid the place completely, taking ages to complete other small, menial tasks instead. Now even those tasks had run out.

He surveyed the room. The piles had actually got bigger since he was last in there.

Rachel stood in the doorway, hand on hip. "Shit," she said.

Hadn't she been in here yet? Hadn't she been employed solely to do the filing? "Yeah," he said.

She picked up one of the piles of files and sat with them on the floor. She took charge. "Right. I'll read out the names on the file, then you can find the right place in the filing system and I'll hand you the file."

"OK." Dave thought her "system" created considerably more work for him than for her, but he appreciated the company and so remained silent.

For the next hour, she read out names from her position curled up on the floor. Dave would go round the filing cabinets and find the right place, then take the file from her and put it away.

After a while he had learnt the right places for all the files and was able to work quickly. He got bored, and started joking around for Rachel's amusement, running from one side of the room to the other, opening and closing the cabinets and pretending to be in a panic over the sheer volume of files.

It wasn't particularly funny, but instead of her usual expression of disdain, she started to laugh. Dave ran round a bit more, pretending to slip and slide on the files for comic effect.

Rachel laughed harder and harder, and he began to wonder if she was actually laughing at him messing around or at something else.

He paused. "Er . . . what are you laughing at?"

She grinned mischievously. "Your flies are undone."

Dave turned away from her and reached down, embarrassed. They weren't undone. He looked back at her to find her laughing harder than ever.

"Let's take a break," she said.

They went back to their desks and sat down. Everyone else in the office was in one of the meeting rooms. The temps were never invited to team meetings. They existed on the edges of the office.

Dave stretched. "I'm going to get some fresh air. Wanna come?"

Rachel glanced up from her computer. "Nah. I'll stay here."

"OK."

He got up and left the office, walking by the meeting room on his way out. He felt strangely disobedient, taking an unauthorised break, but he figured if anyone saw him they would think he was just going to the toilet.

He went down the corridor and took the lift to the ground floor. He went past the receptionists on the front desk and felt a rush of freedom.

He pushed open the double doors into the fresh air. It was raining. He stood for a moment in the drizzle. He considered walking once round the office block to get some exercise.

He shivered, and went back inside.

He retraced his steps to the open plan office. When he returned, Rachel wasn't at her desk. He looked round for her.

She was standing over one of the other desks rifling through a handbag. She pulled out a purse, looked through it quickly, pulled out a note and put it in her pocket.

Dave coughed and she turned round, startled.

"Hi Dave," she said.

"Hi Rachel."

She put the purse back in the bag. "I was just checking something for Harriet."

"In her purse?"

"Yes." Rachel grinned nervously. "You *saw*?"

"Yes."

"Oh."

There was a silence where he expected her to apologise, or offer an alternative explanation. She didn't.

"Do you fancy going to the pub later?" she asked.

Dave wanted to go. He was intrigued by what he had seen. Why not? "Sure," he said.

"My treat," she said, and her smile got even broader.

31

Renée approached her manager's desk, her hands trembling. "We have a meeting scheduled," she said.

Her manager seemed engrossed in her emails, and for a moment Renée thought she hadn't heard her. Then she glanced up, irritated.

"Give me five minutes."

"Sure."

Renée went back and sat at her desk. She stared at the computer screen and pressed the buttons on the mouse sporadically, switching from the BBC news site to her emails, to an Excel spreadsheet, and then back again. She didn't absorb any of the words on the screen.

She glanced nervously over at her boss. She was still utterly absorbed in her emails. The meeting between her and Renée had been rearranged three times already. Renée had requested it two weeks ago, and she was sick of waiting for it. But at the same time she had been relieved each time it had been put off.

"Right, I'm ready." Her boss suddenly stood up and started pouring herself a cup of water from the water filter. Renée stood up too and followed her silently to the meeting room.

Her boss sat down and Renée pulled out a seat across the

table from her. She realised she hadn't brought a notepad. Did that look unprofessional?

They stared at each other awkwardly for a moment. They had never had the best working relationship, always speaking at cross-purposes.

"So what's this about then?"

"Well . . ." Renée took a deep breath. Could she do this? Was this real? Or just a dream? She could just leave the room now and pretend that this wasn't her life. She fixed her eyes on a point in the middle of her boss's face, a technique she had learnt in the "communication skills" training that the council sent all new recruits on. "I wanted to ask you about maternity leave." She spoke clearly and slowly, despite her seeming inability to control her breathing, which was coming so fast she thought that soon it would soon descend into loud, embarrassing gasps.

"Oh right," her boss said, surprised. "I thought it would be about promotion again."

"Not this time." Renée smiled. Before Christmas she had been working all hours to try and secure a promotion. Before she'd realised she was pregnant she had talked to her boss about it. But now that seemed like a distant memory.

"So . . . Congratulations," her boss said. She paused for a moment, as if considering what to say next, and then got up and went over to Renée and gave her an awkward hug. "You must be so excited."

"Yes. I am." Excitement hadn't been an emotion she had experienced, but she understood that it was an appropriate response.

"I bet . . ." Her boss paused and Renée waited. "I bet . . . Andy's excited too," she said with relish, clearly pleased with herself for recalling Andy's name.

"Yeah, he's pleased," Renée said quickly, hoping there wouldn't be any more questions.

Her boss appeared to be studying Renée's stomach, and

Renée cleared her throat. Her boss glanced away quickly.

"When will you want to start your maternity leave?"

She hadn't really thought about it. Admitting she was pregnant was the first hurdle. Saying it out loud. She hadn't even told her friends. This woman, who hardly knew her, was one of the first to know. "I don't know yet. Can I let you know?"

"Of course."

Her boss looked at her thoughtfully. "So that's why you had all those sick days at the beginning of the year – morning sickness, was it?"

Her boss spoke as if she had figured out one of life's great mysteries. "You never usually have sick days."

Renée nodded weakly. She was feeling a bit nauseous.

"Actually I'm not feeling that well now." She stood up and ran to the toilet as a wave of nausea washed over her.

When she returned to her seat, the other girls were peering at her knowingly over their computer screens.

"Congratulations," the girl sitting opposite her said.

"Thanks." Renée wasn't sure if she was ready for all this attention.

"So, when's it due?"

"In the summer. August."

"Have you thought of names?"

"No."

"Are you still feeling sick?"

Renée couldn't stand the questioning any longer. "Yeah, I am actually. I think I might go home." She turned off her computer and shoved some papers in her bag. Ten minutes later she was on the tube, far away from the claustrophobic atmosphere of the office.

*

Back in her room in Shepherd's Bush, she stared blankly at the television. In the flat above her she could hear the distinctive sound of a bed creaking. Although initially she had been pleased to take the opportunity to go home, now she was alone with her thoughts she realised that she'd really rather be at work.

She lay in bed, unsure what to do. Since she and Andy had split up, work had been a welcome distraction and she tried to stay there as long as possible to avoid coming home to the dirty kitchen in her flatshare. Her housemates tended to cook, leave their pots and pans in the sink, and then go out. Renée spent most of her evenings alone in the flat. She tried not to think about her life, and to concentrate on the DIY programme on TV.

Nothing had gone to plan. Andy never returned her calls anymore. Her marriage was clearly over, and now she was pregnant and alone. She couldn't even talk to Katie about it. They hadn't spoken since she had confessed to sleeping with Dave. And now she was pregnant it would make things a hundred times worse.

Besides, telling her parents had been hard enough. They had asked if she was back with Andy and she had had to explain she wasn't. They had asked if she was in a relationship. Again she had had to say no. Silence followed. Even through the mobile phone waves she could feel the sting of her mother's disappointment.

Things had improved since then. Her mother's initial shock had morphed into sympathy and caring, and she phoned constantly to see how she was doing. Renée didn't have the energy to answer her calls anymore. She had such mixed feelings about the baby that anyone else's thoughts and feelings just felt like an extra load. She needed to get her own head in order before she dealt with her mother.

She knew she should call Andy and Dave and let them know about the baby, but she'd been putting it off. When they first split up, Andy hadn't returned her calls, but recently she had stopped trying to call him entirely. She didn't know how he'd react to her pregnancy, and she couldn't stand the thought that he might not care at all; he might be totally indifferent.

If she knew which of them was the father it would be easier. She knew she'd have to have a paternity test, but it was too risky before the baby was born. Her only previous knowledge of paternity tests had been from the Jeremy Kyle show, so she'd looked them up online and read that there was a risk of miscarriage if you had the test during pregnancy. She would have to wait until after the birth. Which meant she had to call both Andy and Dave to tell them she was pregnant.

She imagined their reactions. They might not be remotely interested, or they might want to be involved in the baby's upbringing. She felt a twinge of jealously. She already felt like she and the baby had gone through a lot together. When she'd seen its tiny arms and legs at the three-month scan it had felt like it belonged to her and her alone. The baby was a chance to take back control. *She* wanted to be the one who looked after it and planned its future. She didn't want to share it.

She picked up her phone and played with it idly, as she thought of the future. The baby would need to know who its father was. She stroked her stomach protectively and thought of all that was ahead.

She should just get it over with and call them. Perhaps the best thing to do was to leave a message that they could pick up later. Better for them to listen to it alone than for her to have to listen to their shocked reactions.

Right. She was going to do it now.

She took a sheet of paper from a notepad next to her bed and began to write out what she would say. Fifteen minutes later the page was covered in scribbled-out phrases. She sighed and started again. She was going to get this out of the way today. Then it wouldn't be hanging over her. She picked up the pen again. Eventually she came up with something she was happy with.

It was now or never. The best thing about phoning now was that it was three in the afternoon and the chances of either of them picking up were remote. She dialled Dave's number and then listened to the sound of it ringing and ringing.

"Hello."

Shit.

"Hi, it's Renée." She wanted desperately to hang up.

"How are you?"

"Yeah good."

"Ummm . . . I'm at work so can't really talk. Is it important?"

"Well, kind of, yes. It is important." She took a deep breath.

"Right. Well, now's not a good time. I'll call you later, right?"

"Sure," Renée said, and hung up quickly, throwing the phone onto the bed as if stung.

She knew he wouldn't call back.

She had been pacing her room while the phone was ringing, but now she sat back down on her bed. Tears pricked her eyes as she stared round her room.

In the past, when she was upset she would always turn to Andy. Whether it was work, or an old friendship, or she was just feeling a bit down, he had always been there to comfort her. She remembered when they were trying for a baby. Every night they would debate baby names and talk about where the best schools and parks were. When she had got pregnant the first time, she had signed up on the waiting list of the most popular local school immediately. Everything had been planned.

This time nothing was planned. She stared round the room. She couldn't bring up the baby in her house-share – but where else was she going to bring it up? She thought longingly of her old flat in Wimbledon, and the tears welled up again. She needed to talk to someone.

Without really thinking, she flicked through her mobile phone contacts, got to Andy and pressed "call". She'd get this out of the way now. She'd tell him, and maybe it wouldn't be as bad as she imagined.

Andy hadn't returned her calls for months, so she wasn't expecting him to pick up now.

"Hi." Just the sound of his voice made her heart leap. It was so familiar. Recollections of their previous phone conversations echoed in her head: speaking for hours and hours in their university holidays, calling each other at work to ask what they wanted for dinner, calling just to tell each other they loved each other. Tears filled her eyes again.

"Hi, it's Renée." She stumbled over the words.

"Hi. How are you?"

"Err . . . Good. How are you?"

"Good too, thanks."

There was silence while she tried to think of an excuse for calling. Despite herself, she started crying. She just wanted Andy to comfort her.

"What's wrong?" he asked.

"I'm pregnant." She heard her voice say the words, and felt sick. She suddenly realised that he was the wrong person to talk to. She'd have to tell him that she'd slept with someone else. He might be angry. He wouldn't help her. He didn't even love her.

He started to speak, but before she could hear what he was saying she stabbed at the red "end call" button. The line went reassuringly dead, and she sank back onto her bed.

32

Dave and Rachel sat in the pub across the table from each other. The pub was the closest one to work, and Dave had been surprised at her choice. If she was going to talk about her stealing, offer some kind of explanation, surely a pub frequented by their work colleagues was the wrong place to do it.

He had been thinking about it all afternoon. Had he really seen what he thought he had? It had certainly looked that way. She had been going through Harriet's bag, when everyone else was in a meeting. Why else would she have been looking in someone else's bag?

Anyway, she had as good as admitted it. She had said, "You saw." He had seen her stealing. She had acknowledged it. And yet now she seemed perfectly at ease.

She sipped her pint and contemplated him. He had bought the drinks in the end; it had seemed fairer. And he had felt uncomfortable when she'd pulled out the twenty pound note which he'd seen her take from Harriet's bag. So he paid for the round: a Carling for him and a Carlsberg for her. She didn't look like the type of girl who drank pints; she was too slim. It just went to show, you never really knew people.

Rachel leant forward. "So . . . Dave . . . What do you do?"

Dave shifted in his seat. "What do I do?"

She laughed. "Do you mean to tell me your temping job's your whole life and your dream is to one day become permanent and follow in Craig's footsteps and work your way up to the all-powerful position of office manager?"

Dave smiled. "I can only dream."

"So, what do you want to do?"

"I don't know."

"You still don't know. How old are you?" She smiled wryly.

"Twenty-seven."

"Twenty-seven." She rolled the number over her tongue incredulously. "I'm only twenty-three and I know what I want to do."

"And what's that?"

"Fuck the system."

She said it intently, staring hard at him. He started to laugh, but stopped when her expression didn't change.

"I think you'll find that difficult."

"You've got to have dreams, Dave."

She stroked her pint glass gently, as if it were a family pet. She looked up at him.

"What are your dreams?"

"Er . . . I don't really have any."

"So you're going to be satisfied doing a shitty job in a shitty town, and living with your parents?"

"I used to have a good job."

"Did you enjoy it?"

"No."

"Then it wasn't a good job."

Dave was getting irritated by the confrontational nature of the conversation, but at the same time he didn't want the evening to end. He was fascinated. Maybe they could just talk about something else. He noticed her pint glass was nearly empty. "Another drink?"

"I'll get these."

She got up and went to the bar.

Dave remained where he was. He didn't have a shitty life, did he? Yes, on paper it might look a bit shitty, but he was happy. He wasn't exactly going anywhere, but he was happy, and that was enough.

Rachel came back with the drinks. She set the pint down in front of him clumsily and froth ran down the sides of the glass and formed a puddle on the table. He put his lips to the glass and sipped the head, before lifting the pint from the table and taking his first proper gulp.

He turned to Rachel. "So how are you going to fuck the system?"

A smile played on her lips. "Maybe rob the rich and give to the poor. Amongst other things."

"Oh."

"Do you want to know how I did it?"

He hesitated. Did she mean the stealing?

He grunted noncommittally.

"It's not easy, you know."

"It looked pretty simply to me."

She frowned at him, visibly irritated. "Do you want to know how much I've made?"

"Go on then, how much?"

"£190."

He was surprised to find himself impressed. "How?"

"You want to know now, do you? You want some tips?"

She smiled at him and continued.

"You wait for them to go into one of their team meetings – you know, the ones that involve everyone in the office. Everyone thinks they're a complete waste of time, but they'll never tell the management that. Instead they'll just go to the meeting and nod and nod like those toy dogs, pretending they're interested."

Dave nodded himself, and then wondered if she thought

he was the same as the others. "Yeah," he said, to encourage her to continue.

"It doesn't always have to be the team meetings, there are other times when most people are out of the office on lunch and then the only person in will go to the toilet and leave their bag open under their desk."

Dave thought about earlier that day and his aborted walk.

"But that's all relatively simple. Do you know what the real secret is?"

"What?"

"It's to make them think they haven't had anything stolen. Have you heard any conversations in the office recently about money going missing?"

He thought for a second. "No."

"You haven't for a reason. It's because I always leave something in their wallets. If they've got £30 in their wallet, say a twenty and a ten, I'll just take the ten. They never notice. If they've got two twenties, I just take one. Then, when they go to pay for something, they have enough money. It's only a couple of days later that they run out and try and think how they spent so much so quickly. But then they just think that all the little expenses must have added up, and go straight to the cash machine to get more money. And sometimes they start getting more than they used to, because obviously they didn't get enough out last time."

She looked at him expectantly.

"What about if they've only got ten pounds in their wallet?"

She smiled triumphantly. "If there's only one note, you never take it, that's the rule of the game. You have to be disciplined. If there's one note left and you take it, they'll suspect in an instant."

Dave wasn't sure what to say. He felt a newfound respect for Rachel. He watched as she sipped her pint, a picture of the obedient, well-dressed office-worker.

33

Daniel opened the door of the terraced house and smiled.

"Katie," he said.

"Hi."

The house was full with the smell of roast pork, and Katie breathed in appreciatively.

"That smells nice," she said, sounding alarmingly like her mother.

"Thanks."

She followed him down the hallway, observing the faded flowered wallpaper, peeling slightly where it met the ceiling. The carpet was worn and stained, but everything was cleaned, polished and dusted to perfection. She imagined Daniel taking care over the house. He wasn't the kind of person who would just clean when someone was visiting. The house would be this clean and tidy all the time.

She followed him into the kitchen and he opened the oven and the smell of the crackling wafted out. She was starving. It was an hour and a half to get to his house on public transport, and she had got up too late to have breakfast.

"I brought some wine," she said as he lifted the roasting pan from the oven. He checked the meat and replaced the pan.

"Great." He took the bottle from her and studied the label.

"Looks good. We'll have it with lunch."

He went into another room and Katie wasn't sure whether or not she should follow. She heard the sound of the wine being placed on a table, and then he was back.

"I'll find some glasses," he said. He opened each cupboard one by one and rooted around at the back. He finally pulled out two small water glasses and smiled at her apologetically. "I don't think we have wine glasses. These will have to do."

"Sure, they're fine." She smiled back. Didn't he drink wine? Did he drink at all? She'd never thought to ask. She just assumed. He didn't seem religious or the teetotal type, but then she didn't know him that well.

"So how have things been?" he asked.

She had seen him the Thursday and Friday, and now it was Saturday, but she realised that when she had seen him during the week they hadn't really talked much about what was going on in their lives. They had had sex, as usual in her brother's room, but they hadn't really spoken.

She had started to apply for jobs teaching English to foreign students in London and she had an interview next week, but she had forgotten to mention it to Daniel.

"Good," she said. "Things are good." Why did she feel so reticent about telling him about her life? Did she think he wouldn't understand?

She felt awkward. She needed the wine to relax and loosen up. "How about you?" she asked.

"Well, after I saw your grandfather yesterday I had two more clients. I'm worried about one; she's deteriorating, and when I washed her I saw a rash. I'm trying to persuade her that she needs to go to the doctor. If I can persuade her, I'll take her next week"

"Ah," she said. "That's worrying." She felt out of place in this house, with him, with these conversations.

Daniel started to dish up the dinner and Katie wondered

why she had come over. It had seemed like a good idea. Daniel fascinated her. He was so selfless, so dedicated to his work, and so unlike anyone she had ever met. And the sex was good too. But the more she got to know him, the less interested she was becoming. His life was his daily routine of caring for others. She just couldn't muster enough interest in his work. She must be a very selfish person if she couldn't even care through Daniel, who was so passionate about what he did.

They walked through to the dining room, which contained a small plastic table and two wooden chairs. The wine was in the middle, and Katie stared at it as Daniel placed the steaming plates of food on the table. At least the food looked good, she thought. And then she kicked herself. Why was she so ungrateful? Couldn't she just appreciate Daniel taking care of her?

She was used to dates that involved going to dinner, drinking large amounts of wine and then going to bed. She could already see how Daniel expected this meal to go. They'd have a nice lunch, they'd chat a bit, and then perhaps have sex. The prospect of a long chat with Daniel wasn't remotely exciting. Katie sighed inwardly. If it wasn't exciting now, it wasn't going to get more exciting as their relationship progressed. She was going to have to just keep it to sex, or else end it. Why did her attempts at relationships always turn out like this?

Daniel poured a small portion of the red wine into each of their water glasses. "Cheers," he said.

"Cheers." She watched him sip his wine slowly, and resisted the urge to knock hers back.

They ate in silence for a while, and then were interrupted by the sound of a bell ringing. It didn't sound like a doorbell, it was more of an insistent, irregular ringing. Perhaps it was a ringtone. She looked over at him, expecting him to pull a phone from his pocket.

Daniel was already up and walking towards the doorway.

"Sorry," he said. "It's my mother. I just need to go upstairs and see what's wrong."

He left, and Katie stared at her food. She was starving, but she couldn't finish it while he wasn't there.

What man in his forties still lived with his mother? A mother who got his attention with a bell?

She felt disappointed. She had thought Daniel was so interesting, so different.

She decided it would be acceptable to eat her food if she ate it slowly, so she started to cut it into tiny chunks and chewed each carefully.

Daniel came back. "Sorry," he said and began to dig into his food.

Katie couldn't help herself. "You live with your mother?"

He heard her confrontational tone and raised his eyebrows. "She lives with me. It's my house. And don't you live with your mother?" It was the first time she'd seen Daniel look annoyed.

"But . . ." She wanted to say that he was too old for it. That it was OK for Katie because she was still young. But it sounded ridiculous, so she kept quiet.

"She needs care. I thought you'd understand that," Daniel said, his eyes dark.

34

Steve sat on his leather sofa reading the *Economist* with a glass of wine in his hand. He didn't know how much longer he would have the house, and he wanted to make the most of it while he still lived here. The house had had occasional viewers, but not that many, and no one had put in an offer yet. Since the house had gone on the market, he had started to spend more and more time at home, discovering little nooks and crannies he'd hardly realised were here. He'd never really used his three spare bedrooms, but recently he had found himself going in each one, sitting on the bed and then standing to look out the window at the view, as if he himself were a prospective buyer. He'd started alternating the rooms he slept in, just so he'd remember everything properly.

He had so much free time now. His new job didn't make the same demands on his time, and his evenings stretched out endlessly before him. But recently he had found he couldn't take the same pleasure from the things he enjoyed most in life: expensive dinners out, premium wine, entertaining clients. Everything he had once got joy from only seemed to have value as a distraction from his constant thoughts of Caroline.

He had listened to her latest answer-phone messages the previous day, and they had tugged at his heart. They had started simply, just asking him to call her back. But they had got more and more desperate, with her apologising in the next few messages, then getting increasingly aggressive and accusing him of taking advantage of her. She said she loved him and couldn't live without him.

As he listened to the messages, he saw two Carolines in his head: the girl he had loved and the desperate schoolgirl. The girl he had loved was reasonable in asking him to call her back, and reasonable in her apology. The schoolgirl was just blindly spitting out words in anger, in love with the idea of being in love, and nothing more. He knew that girl would grow up, and he hoped that instead of being angry she would look back on their relationship fondly as her first sexual experience. Perhaps she would wince at her first experience of believing she was in love. She might look back later from the comfort of a long-term relationship and see a little girl who had convinced herself of an everlasting romance with an older man.

Steve would not be able to look back in the same way. Over the past few weeks he had come to admit that he had genuinely loved her. It hadn't been that she had had him fooled. Well, not just that. He had loved who she was, not just who she said she was. He had loved the moments when she spoke her mind and said what she thought, he had loved her passion when she talked about acting, he had loved the way she looked. The fact he had thought she was twenty-two wasn't relevant.

Except it was relevant. Because it was illegal. But more than that: it wasn't fair. She wasn't old enough to know her mind like Steve did, and therefore he had taken advantage of her.

He longed to talk to her, but he couldn't. He couldn't return her calls or answer her messages. He couldn't let himself be sucked in again. He knew that soon she would lose interest and move on to someone else. And that was the right thing to do.

His Facebook wall was crowded with messages from her. He couldn't bear to read them. Recently lots of her friends had tried to add him as a friend, but he had turned them all down. It wasn't appropriate. They weren't his friends. But they still sent messages to his account. They told him that she still loved him, that as her friends they had to tell him. They told him she wanted him back. And when he didn't reply within twenty-four hours, they told him he was a bastard and what he'd done to her was illegal.

When he first realised Caroline was under-age, he'd been totally focused on the loss of his relationship with her, aware that he could no longer see her. But the comments from her friends had made him start to think about the legal side of things. What happened to men like him? Did they go to jail? All the articles he had read about this kind of thing in the papers painted the man as a predator, seeking out young girls on the internet to manipulate and sleep with.

There were bad people out there who did want to do horrific things. He just wasn't one of them.

He remembered the other kinds of stories in the tabloids: the teacher-pupil relationship stories. They were usually accompanied by a picture of a less-than-attractive man in his forties holding the hand of an average-looking schoolgirl. The pictures had always suggested to him a degree of compromise on both sides. Surely if the teacher was going to risk his job by sleeping with a pupil, he would have tried it on with the more attractive ones first? And had the girl been rejected by a boy her own age before she decided that an older, balding man would be sufficient?

He had read stories about some of these couples living happily ever after. Now he wished he'd paid more attention. He was sure there was one couple of whom the teacher went to jail and the student waited for him outside and then they resumed their relationship.

But there wasn't any point thinking about things like that. His relationship with Caroline was over.

He looked down at the *Economist* and realised he hadn't

absorbed any of the article. He went into the kitchen to pour himself some more wine.

There was a knock at his front door, and Steve looked at his watch, confused. He wasn't expecting anyone. Could it be Caroline? Would she have come to his house? He felt an involuntary shiver of excitement run through him.

A second knock. He'd have to answer it. He put his wine down and went to the door, checking his reflection as he passed the mirror in the hall.

He opened the door and found himself facing a short woman, in her late thirties, with cropped, dark hair.

"Hello?" he said, racking his brain. He didn't recognise her. He supposed she might have seen the "for sale" sign and wanted to view the house, but it seemed a little late for that. She wasn't carrying anything except a handbag, so she couldn't be collecting for charity.

She seemed surprised that he had answered the door, and she looked him up and down. "Steve?" she said uncertainly.

He smiled, bemused. "Yes."

"Ummm . . . can I come in?"

She saw his confusion and continued. "I'm Deena," she said, meeting his eyes. "Caroline's mother."

Steve's breath caught in his throat. He wasn't sure if he could cope with a confrontation tonight. What did she want from him?

"OK," he said. Maybe, if he was polite, she'd think more highly of him. He almost laughed at the thought. He'd slept with her fifteen-year-old daughter. She was more likely to try and hit him.

She followed him into the kitchen.

"Do you want to sit down?" he asked.

She shook her head. "How old are you?" she asked.

Steve felt a compulsion to lie, but stopped himself. There had been enough of that already. "I'm twenty-seven."

"Caroline's fifteen. Why did you do it?"

"I . . . I thought she was older."

"I don't believe you. She doesn't look older. She's a child; she looks fifteen."

She paused for the briefest moment, before resuming. "Did you sleep with her?"

Steve had no idea how to respond. This wasn't the kind of conversation you ever had with your girlfriend's mother.

"Did you sleep with her?" She was shouting now.

"Yes," Steve said.

"Oh God." Deena's voice cracked and she seemed to sink towards the floor. She reached for the table to steady herself. Steve, unable to do anything else, pulled out a kitchen chair for her. She swept her hand through the air, knocking the chair away and sending it clattering over onto the floor.

"Oh God," she said again. She was crying, sniffling and shuddering as she clutched the table. "Is she pregnant?"

"No. I mean, I don't think so. We used protection."

Steve just wanted this woman out of his house. He couldn't face the idea that her grief was due to his behaviour.

"I suppose you met her on the internet, did you?"

"Yes." Steve decided it was safer to stick to short, non-inflammatory answers.

"You're one of those men who stalks young girls on the internet." She stated it as a fact.

"No."

"I suppose you're going to tell me that you love her?"

"No." But he did.

She turned on him. "No? You do that to her – you take her virginity and you don't even love her – you don't even care for her?"

"I do care for her."

"How can you? She says you aren't answering any of her calls."

"How can I? She's under-age."

"She was always under-age. Now you've just used her and spat her out when you're bored. You're just like everyone else in her life."

"I . . . I didn't intend to do that. I just can't continue a relationship with a fifteen-year-old." Steve felt a strange sense of role reversal.

"You know her dad left us this year?"

"I didn't know."

"You don't even know anything about her. Yet you let her believe you cared for her. How can you do that to her? Her dad ran away this year. One day he was there. The next day he wasn't. No note. Nothing. And then you come along. Just when she's vulnerable. Just when she's looking for a father figure. You look a bit like him, you know. Did she tell you that?"

"No." Caroline hadn't talked much about her parents, and Steve had never thought to ask more than the most basic questions.

Her mother seemed to have run out of steam. She stood sobbing in the middle of Steve's kitchen. He brought her over a box of tissues and she took one and blew her nose loudly. She seemed unsure what to do next.

"Well, I've said what I came to say," she said, eventually.

She started walking towards the door. When she got there she put her hand on the latch and turned to him. "I just wanted you to know what you've done to us; what you've done to Caroline. It's not all about you, you know."

"OK," Steve said, feeling shaken and childlike in the face of her parental wrath.

She opened the door and turned once more. "I don't know what I was expecting from you. Someone less well-off perhaps, someone better looking. But I was expecting an apology. And you don't even have it in you to give me that."

With that, she walked out onto the street and slammed the door behind her so hard that the house shook.

35

Sam went to the pub early to set up for her hen night. She'd bought balloons in a party shop and spent the afternoon blowing them up in her living room. Patrick had laughed at her, but she didn't care.

She found the table she'd reserved, and began to tie the pink balloons to the chairs. She had too many and they kept slipping down the chair backs and coming to rest on the seats and on the floor. She realised she should have bought helium balloons, which would float towards the ceiling: a clear indication of a hen party. Her pink balloons looked limp and pathetic in comparison.

Never mind. Nothing would ruin her evening.

She got out her Tesco bag of other goodies. There were sashes and tiaras for each of them. Sam placed the sash that said "bride to be" at the head of the table and felt a flutter of excitement. That was her. She was the bride to be. She placed a tiara in front of each of the five chairs. Then she got out the confetti and spread it over the table.

She surveyed her work. It looked good.

The barmaid came over and raised her eyebrows at the confetti.

"What do you think you're doing?"

"It's for my hen night."

"That stuff's a devil to wipe up; I hope you'll clean up after yourself." She looked sharply at Sam.

"I will," Sam said. The barmaid grunted and ambled back to the bar. Nothing and no one would spoil Sam's mood. She was getting married.

She couldn't believe it had finally happened to her. *She was having a hen night.* She knew that usually the chief bridesmaid would conduct the preparations for a night like tonight, but she'd decided not to have bridesmaids, and besides, she had wanted to organise the night herself. It meant she could have it exactly how she wanted. And no strippers. She certainly didn't want a stripper. She just wanted a quiet night in a local pub. She was only glad the guests were coming: her mother, her aunt, and Estelle and Katie from university.

The pub was round the corner from her mother's. She always noticed it as she walked past on her way from the station to visit her. On the most miserable, grey day its windows would shine amber and inviting, and gusts of warmth would come from the door as the smokers drifted in and out. She had always thought it was the kind of pub that it would be difficult to leave, once you were settled in its cosy cocoon.

She had arrived an hour early to ensure that the table was reserved. It surprised her that it wasn't very busy on a Saturday afternoon. It seemed that others weren't similarly enamoured by its amber glow. There was a group of lads playing pool in the room the other side of the bar, and a couple sharing a bottle of wine and reading the papers, but that was it. It was good that it was empty. Sam hated to strain to hear over the noise of a busy pub, and she knew her mother did too.

She sat down in her seat at the head of the table. It was only half past five. It would be half an hour before anyone else showed up. She sat for a moment, straining to hear the couple's conversation a few tables away. She wasn't close enough to hear more than a few words. Perhaps she should have a drink while she waited. That was it. She would have a drink. You only had one hen night. She should treat herself.

*

Katie found the pub and ducked inside, out of the rain. She ran her hand over her wet, tangled hair. She had forgotten her umbrella and she knew she didn't look her best. Her jeans were soaked and her new top clung to her chest. She spotted the toilet sign and walked quickly towards it, hoping she'd get to the toilets before the others spotted her. She had been surprised to receive the invitation to Sam's hen night in her inbox. They'd been on the same course at university and they'd stayed in contact afterwards, but they hadn't seen each other since she had got back from India.

It would be good to catch up. Sam was the only one of her friends who'd seemed genuinely interested in what she was doing with her life. Renée had just seen her work abroad as a temporary holding position until she got a proper job. She had been so focused on her relationship with Andy and her job that she hadn't really had time for anyone else. She felt a tinge of pity. It must be really hard for Renée, now the life she had built for herself had fallen down around her. She would have to ring her soon and see how she was doing.

Katie checked her reflection in the mirror. Her brushed hair looked a bit better, but it was still sodden. She put the hairbrush away and walked out of the Ladies. She scanned the bar and soon spotted the table. Sam sat at its head. Two large, older women sat on her left, and a girl Katie vaguely recognised from university sat on her right. Everyone at the table was wearing a tiara. A sea of pink balloons surrounded their feet. Their shrivelled brothers and sisters hung limp from the chairs, where they had been popped as people moved in and out.

Sam smiled at her and waved enthusiastically, and Katie waved back, trying to mirror Sam's enthusiasm. She saw two bottles of wine in the centre of the table and observed that everyone's glasses were full. Sam and the older women were drinking wine, but the younger girl was drinking water. Out of politeness, Katie asked if anyone wanted a drink, and was relieved when they all shook their heads. Sam started to pour her a glass of wine from one of the bottles, and she sat down in the remaining seat.

"Mum, this is Katie," Sam said, turning to the woman immediately on her left. "She's the one I was telling you about; from university."

The older women appeared to look Katie up and down and find something disagreeable about her. "You're the traveller, are you?"

"Well, I suppose so, yeah, I've worked abroad a bit." She wasn't sure if this was the specific thing about her which Sam's mother disapproved of, and didn't want to expand in case it was. She was sick of people being condescending about teaching abroad. She smiled at Sam's mother to try and make her warm to her, but the woman just grunted at her.

Sam butted in quickly before the conversation could continue. "And this is my Aunt Liv. And you know Estelle."

Katie nodded at Liv, who seemed to be entirely focused on finishing her glass of wine. She smiled at Estelle. "We were at uni together, weren't we?"

"Yeah," said Estelle. "Different courses though."

"Yeah."

Katie took a sip of her wine. It felt like it could be a long evening. "So how are the wedding preparations going, Sam?"

"They're going well. I think everything's nearly sorted; the menus have been decided, we've chosen the flowers, the dress is nearly ready." Sam was almost shaking with excitement.

"That's great," said Katie, realising she knew very little about wedding planning, and didn't really care.

"They had to let out the dress a bit didn't they, Sam?" said Sam's mum.

"Well, yes. A bit," said Sam, turning bright red.

"You'll have to stop eating or you'll put all the weight back on and then Patrick won't be too pleased." Her mother laughed.

No one spoke, and Katie felt the need to say something.

"I don't think that will make a difference . . . I mean, they love each other."

"Have you met Patrick?" Sam's mother asked.

"Well, no."

"Then you can't comment, can you? "

Estelle began to fidget and swirl the water round in the bottom of her glass.

"I'm lucky to have met Patrick," Sam said.

"What's he like?" Katie said, eager to change the subject.

"He's tall, handsome, kind . . . perfect really." Sam giggled, as if the cliché she'd just come out with was an accurate description and had only ever applied to her.

Katie sipped her wine and started to wish the evening away.

*

Katie fidgeted in her seat. Surely she should have heard the bell for last orders by now. She looked at her watch. It was only ten p.m.; there was still another hour of the evening to go. She couldn't stand it much longer. Estelle had left a while ago, and now she was left alone with Sam, Sam's mum and Sam's aunt. She'd told herself she'd stay until the end, for Sam's sake, but now she really couldn't bring herself to.

"I'm going to have to head off soon," she said apologetically.

Sam seemed to accept this without question, not expecting an excuse.

Katie was tired of watching Sam's acceptance of her lot in life. She seemed to treat her mother and aunt with respect, despite the fact that they'd been goading her all evening. She couldn't imagine what it must be like to be Sam, to be resigned to the constant bullying, rather than feeling the anger and defiance Katie felt on her behalf, after being in their company for just a couple of hours.

"Before you go, I just wanted to ask you how the others are," Sam said hesitantly.

"The others?"

"Yeah, you know, the uni crowd. I was wondering if they'd got their invites."

They had discussed it at the pub at the reunion. To them it was an optional social event, but to Sam it was the most important day of her life.

"Yeah . . . I think so," Katie said. "Do you want me to check if they're coming?"

"Yeah, could you?"

"They were supposed to reply ages ago," Sam's mother chipped in. "We need to tell the caterers. Tell them they have three days to reply or we just won't cater for them."

"Er . . . OK," said Katie.

"Have you seen them lately?" Sam asked.

Katie didn't want to hurt her feelings by mentioning the reunion that she hadn't been invited to. "Yeah, some of them," she said vaguely.

"How are they? How are Renée and Andy?"

"Um . . . they've split up."

Sam's face fell. "Oh. That's awful."

Katie wasn't sure what to say. She didn't want to comment on their marriage. It seemed disloyal. "Yeah, it's sad."

Sam still seemed to be digesting the news. "But they seemed perfect together."

"Yeah." They had argued a lot too. And Renée had been so controlling.

"James and Steve are still the same as ever," Katie said, changing the subject.

"What about Dave?"

"He's good too."

Did they have to talk about Dave?

"I always thought you two might get together."

"Did you? Oh . . . Well, we didn't." Katie forced a smile.

Sam smiled back.

"Well, I'd really better go."

"It was great to see you," Sam said, with a genuine smile.

Katie left, feeling a strange mixture of emotions. She felt pity for Sam, and yet jealous of her contentment with her life, her ability to be satisfied whatever life threw at her.

36

James came out of a meeting and rushed to his desk. He had the feeling he was late for another meeting – he just need to check who it was with, and where. When he picked up his BlackBerry and saw the reminder, he breathed a sigh of relief. It was just a chat with Clive.

Clive was the Director of HR, and his approach to business was almost the opposite of James's. Whilst James was brutally efficient and ran his meetings to a tight agenda, Clive's were usually over a leisurely lunch or coffee and rarely had any obvious objectives.

Despite their differences, James enjoyed his meetings with Clive. They were a chance to relax and catch up on what was happening with the directors of the company. On some days, like today, James appreciated the time out from his busy schedule.

He made his way over to Clive's office. Predictably Clive was running late, and James sat on one of the sofas, getting a few emails sent from his BlackBerry. Clive was the only employee in the company who had sofas in his office, and James still wasn't quite sure how he had managed it. But he'd been there twenty years, working his way up from an HR administrator role, so James supposed he had a lot of favours he could call in.

Twenty minutes later Clive bustled in, apologising profusely.

"Shall we head out for coffee?" James asked, familiar with the routine of Clive's meetings, which served little purpose other than to offer Clive networking opportunities and satisfy his insatiable desire for caffeine.

"Yeah" said Clive. "Let's walk up the road." He grabbed his coat from the coat stand and took his wallet from his desk and pushed it into his pocket.

The wind whipped their faces as they walked side by side. Clive was unusually quiet, and James wondered if something was wrong. He had heard on the rumour-mill that Clive had been sleeping with his secretary, and James wondered whether his wife had found out.

James didn't fancy a coffee, but when they got to the coffee house he ordered two coffees anyway. It would have been poor form not to. Clive got out his wallet, but James insisted on paying and Clive accepted grudgingly.

They sat down and James pulled out his water bottle and put it onto the table. He took a few sips of coffee before taking a swig from the water bottle.

"So, how are things going?" Clive asked.

"Good, thanks," James said, taking another swig from the bottle. "I've just released our strategy for 2013 and I've got buy-in from all the other directors. It's been a good year."

Clive seemed uncomfortably and he gulped at his coffee.

"What's in the water bottle?" Clive asked.

James tensed. "Er . . . water?" he said. He tried to laugh as if it was a ridiculous question, but the laughter came out nervously. Clive was watching him carefully.

"I know it's not water, James."

James's shoulders were tight and his back straightened.

"Oh?"

He wondered if he should be laughing it off, or be indignant. By the time he had thought about it, it was too late. Clive had noted his shocked look, and his silence.

"It would make it easier if you would just tell me what's in the bottle. I don't want to have to reach over and smell it."

James felt a flush of heat rise through his body. He was one of the best performers in the company and he was well respected by the directors. Yet Clive was treating him like a child. On James's recommendation, Clive could probably be fired for his expensive lunches and laid-back attitude. Clive had no right to accuse him of anything.

"James?"

He wanted to get up and bolt through the door. It seemed there was no appropriate response. He needed to get away, back to Meera and Phoebe. He needed to tell them that everything was going to be alright.

He debated not saying anything and waiting it out, but Clive was still staring at him. He felt his life slipping through his hands. If he lost his job, he'd lose everything he'd worked for, then he'd lose the house, then Meera and Phoebe. Everything would crumble. Everything he'd worked for in the last six years would be gone.

Clive was still waiting.

"It's vodka," he said.

Clive sighed and looked directly at him. "This is going to be a difficult one to get out of, James."

37

Dave felt a hand on his shoulder, and jumped. He'd been concentrating on tidying up the online filing system for Craig, and had just clicked "cut" on a series of files, which he needed to paste in the right place immediately before they were lost for good.

"Hang on," he said, opening a series of folders and pasting the documents in. He checked he'd put them in the right place and then looked up. It was Rachel.

"Hey," he said.

She frowned, and he tried to work out what was bothering her. Sometimes he really couldn't read her.

"You're not very good at this."

"At what?"

"Seizing the opportunity."

Dave had no idea what she was talking about.

"You wanted to know how I did it? So I'm going to teach you. What do you notice about the office?"

Dave looked around. The office was deserted, but he'd been too engrossed in what he'd been doing to notice. The others must be in a meeting. "No one's here," he said tentatively.

"Right."

Rachel stared pointedly at the open handbag on the table opposite him. He hadn't even noticed that the woman opposite had left the office, but Rachel had obviously noticed immediately and had clocked her bag.

Rachel raised her eyebrows, and Dave stared at the bag. He liked the woman opposite him. She didn't talk much, but she was nice. She would offer to make him tea when she was making herself one, even though Dave was really supposed to make the tea.

Dave shook his head. "No, Rachel."

"Don't worry, I'm not going to steal anything."

Dave shrugged.

"*You're* going to do it."

"No, I'm not," Dave said, his attention now fixated on the handbag. Could he? Did he have the balls? Would he get away with it?

"The others are in a meeting. You'll be fine."

He kept staring at the bag. It would only take a moment to put his hand inside, pull out the purse, open it and take the money out. He stood up and walked across to the desk.

Rachel picked up a pile of papers from his desk and walked over to him and handed them to him. "Take these – that way, if someone comes out of the meeting to answer a call or something, you'll look like you're actually doing something."

He took the papers from her. He held them in one hand so that they would cover what he was doing with the other hand if anyone happened to walk by. He reached quickly into the bag for the purse. He felt around. Umbrella, tampons, glasses case, mobile phone . . . and finally his fingers closed around a purse. He pulled it to the top of the bag with one hand. He had to put the papers down to open the purse, so he placed them at the edge of the desk and used both hands to unzip it, keeping his hands in the bag. Rachel stood next to him, carrying her own papers and using her body to shield him from view if anyone glanced through the glass panelling of the meeting room.

Dave could feel his heart beating fast in his chest. He started to sweat, and he fumbled over the purse and it dropped back into the bag. Rachel coughed and he tried to move faster. He picked the purse back up and rifled through it. A twenty, a ten and some coins. He took the folded twenty out quickly and then realised he didn't have a pocket to put it in. He panicked for a second and then slid it between the papers on the desk. The water cooler gurgled, and he jumped. His ears were attuned to every sound, and he could hear the murmur of conversation from the meeting room. What if they were finishing up? He glanced over, but he saw they were all deep in conversation, engrossed in paperwork.

He zipped up the purse and put it back in the bag, shoving it to the bottom where he had found it. He checked that the twenty was still where he had left it, between the papers, and then picked them up and carried them across to his desk.

He put the papers down and sank into his chair. His whole body was tense and he felt sick. He could feel the adrenalin pumping through him and he didn't know how he would manage to sit still for the rest of the day.

Rachel grinned at him. "What did you take?"

"Twenty," Dave whispered.

"What was in there?"

"A ten and a twenty."

"I'd have gone for the ten. It's less noticeable. You might have broken into a ten when you bought a coffee, or got a mid-morning snack. It's less likely that you wouldn't remember spending a twenty. Still, it doesn't matter. Well done."

"Thanks."

The combination of adrenalin and guilt made Dave think he might actually throw up, and he hurried to the toilet. He went to a cubicle and retched into the bowl. He wasn't sick, but he felt a bit better. He put the lid of the toilet down and sat on the top of the seat. What had he just done?

38

Sam held her hand up to her forehead and felt the stickiness of blood. It was then the tears came. She needed to look beautiful on her wedding day. All the scars he'd left before could be covered up, but this couldn't. She would lift the veil and there it would be: a scabbed, bruised forehead. The tears felt hot on her face.

She knocked on the front door again. "Patrick – let me in!"

She could hear him pacing on the other side.

"Patrick!"

A light came on upstairs in the house next door, and Sam saw the silhouette of her neighbour at the window. She kept one hand on her head to cover her injury, and tried to wave cheerfully with the other. The neighbour didn't wave back, but the curtain closed and the light went off.

Sam turned her attention back to the door.

She lowered her voice and opened the letterbox. "Patrick," she whispered.

She could see his legs retreating into the kitchen. Through the letterbox, she heard him take a bottle off the shelf and pour himself a drink. She knew he'd had more than enough already. He had come home from a trip to the pub with his work colleagues, blind drunk. Sam had his dinner ready, but it needed reheating, as she hadn't been sure when he'd be home. When he saw it wasn't ready, he slammed his fist into the table and then swept the plates of food she was about to heat up in the microwave onto the floor.

He had been looking for a fight.

As she'd picked up the broken pieces of china and pasta off the floor he had berated her for putting on weight, for not earning much, for being unpopular. She'd confided in him about all her fears, and he knew exactly which buttons to push.

She knew she had to keep quiet and take it. This was just the side of him she had to put up with to see the other side: the loving, caring Patrick who looked after her. The man she would marry. It was the drink talking, not him.

But it wasn't always the drink talking. The other day she had forgotten to put the washing on and he had slapped her hard across the chest, even though he was stone cold sober. His acts of violence were becoming more unpredictable.

She knew he would apologise later. It was always the same in that way. You just had to wait it out until he had calmed down, and then he'd apologise.

She looked through the letterbox again. No sign of him. After he had screamed at her and she had finished clearing up the mess on the floor, she had stood up tentatively, not sure if it was over. That had been her mistake. She had stood up too quickly. As soon as she'd looked across at him she'd realised.

"You missed a bit," he said.

And as she'd bent down again to look, he hit her across the face. She fell back against the kitchen cupboards, catching her forehead on the corner of the granite work surface.

The instant Patrick saw he'd hurt her, his face changed. He couldn't look at her. He walked away.

When he left the room, she quickly cleaned up the remaining spot of mess and then took the plastic bag containing the broken plates and food outside to the bin. Her head hurt and she wasn't thinking straight. She heard the front door slam behind her. She didn't have her key.

She still couldn't see him through the letterbox. Perhaps he was still in the kitchen. She called out again, a bit louder.

No answer.

Had he passed out?

She tried ringing his mobile, and then the landline. He didn't answer either.

She tried again.

Still no answer.

She heard footsteps the other side of the door.

"Patrick?"

Through the letterbox, she saw him go through the hallway, switch the lights off and stumble up the stairs. He wasn't going to let her in.

She sat down on her doorstep. She wasn't sure if she could face sleeping here. A cold wind rattled the bins. She didn't have a coat.

She could always go to her mother's, but there would be too many questions if she turned up at this time of night, particularly with a head wound. She reached up to touch her head again and flinched as her fingers made contact. She needed to wash out the wound.

She looked back at her mobile. Who could she call?

She ran through the numbers until she got to Katie. She took a deep breath and rung the number.

Katie picked up.

"Sam?"

"Hi Katie."

"How are you?"

"Fine thanks," Sam automatically replied. "I've . . . been locked out of my house. "

"Oh no!"

"I was wondering if I could stay with you?"

"I live quite out in the sticks," Katie replied. "How will you get here?"

"Oh." Sam didn't have her handbag with her. She wouldn't be able to get the tube or a taxi. "I don't know," she said.

"Do you need me to come and pick you up?"

"You don't have to. I'll be fine." But she didn't know what to do.

"Have you got your purse with you?"

"No."

"Then I'm coming to collect you."

*

An hour later Katie pulled up on the driveway in her mother's car and saw Sam huddled in the doorway in jeans and a T-shirt. Sam got slowly to her feet when she saw the headlights.

As Sam came over to the car, Katie noticed the wound on her head. Katie opened her door and stepped out into the cold.

"Sam, you're bleeding. What happened?"

"I fell over," Sam said.

"On the driveway?" Was Sam drunk?

"Yeah," Sam said, moving away from the glare of the headlights.

Katie stepped closer to her. "Let me have a look."

She saw the wound wasn't too deep, just a nasty graze. There didn't seem to be any dirt in it, but it would be good to get it cleaned out. "Did you want me to take you to the hospital?" she asked.

"No," Sam said forcibly. "I just want to go to bed."

Katie was tired too. They could wash out Sam's wound when they got back to her house, then go to sleep and see if it was better in the morning.

"OK," she said.

They both got into the car. As they pulled out of the drive, a light came on in one of the upstairs windows. Katie stopped the car.

Sam looked over at her.

"There's a light on; someone's home." Katie searched Sam's face for answers, but Sam wouldn't meet her eyes.

"I must have left it on."

"No, it just came on."

Sam said nothing.

"Do you think it's an intruder?"

"I don't know."

"Shall we call the police?"

"No, no, I don't think so," said Sam, hurriedly. "Let's just leave."

Katie was about to protest, when she saw the desperate expression in Sam's eyes.

"*Please.*"

At the upstairs window, the silhouette of a man watched them.

"You've come all this way, Katie. Let's go."

She stared up at the man. Was it Patrick? Was Sam running away?

39

Renée stepped out of the tube carriage and made her way to the escalator. Her belly was prominent enough now to guarantee her a seat for her entire tube journey, yet she still felt hot and sweaty. She was dressed in a loose white cardigan, which diminished the roundness of her stomach and discouraged strangers from reaching out and touching her belly as if it was public property. She had thought about taking the cardigan off in the heat of the tube, but she valued its protection too much.

She swiped her Oyster card. As she exited the station she was relieved to catch sight of the sign for the pub where she was meeting Andy, about fifty metres up the road. When she pushed the door open and went inside she was surprised to see him sitting at a corner table, watching the door anxiously. She was early herself, so he must have got there even earlier. She eased her way round the tables by the bar as he stood to greet her.

He stared at her stomach, and instinctively she put her arm over it. She had prepared what she was wearing carefully, trying to look pretty and young, rather than motherly. She wanted to be the girlfriend he remembered. A part of her wanted him to regret splitting up with her.

She reached his table and he pulled out a seat for her.

"Maybe a pub's not the best place for this," he said nervously, nodding towards her stomach. "I didn't know what to suggest, I couldn't think."

"A pub's fine."

"Do you want a drink?"

"A lemonade, please."

"Right."

She watched as Andy made his way to the bar and waited to order. After a silence of few weeks, he had called her back and said he wanted to talk. She didn't know what to expect. Since he'd phoned, she'd thought of nothing but this meeting. She'd wondered if it was still possible for them to get back together, or if too much had happened.

Now she was here she felt confused. When she'd caught sight of him across the pub, she'd felt nothing except a vague sense of familiarity. It was almost as if he were a stranger.

She watched him at the bar as he politely let everyone else order before him. He had chosen to wear his favourite shirt, but it was one she secretly hated. It made him look ten years older than he was. His features were not quite as chiselled as she remembered.

He returned with the drinks and sat down opposite her.

"So, how are you doing?"

Suddenly Renée wanted to be anywhere but here. It felt like everything she'd remembered about him was wrong. She felt disappointed and confused. It felt like the Andy sitting in front of her was not the Andy of her memories, but an imposter.

"Good thanks. How about you?" So much had happened, yet Renée couldn't find the right words. So much had been left unsaid.

"I'm good too."

There was a pause, as they both searched for the right words.

"What have you been up to?"

"Not a lot." She didn't feel like sharing any of the details of her life with him, and she didn't feel like returning the question.

"Right."

There was an awkward silence. An eight-year relationship has come to this. They had nothing to say to each other.

"I guess we both know why we're here," Andy blurted it out.

"Yeah."

"I remember when we were trying for a baby." He spoke softly, about the one thing they had never discussed when they were living together.

Renée took a sharp breath.

"I remember how much I wanted it. How much you wanted it. How much I wanted to look after it; take it to Arsenal games if it was a boy. I had so many plans."

"So did I," she said quietly.

"I wanted to look after it with you. And now I suppose I just wanted to say, seeing you pregnant, I want the same. I want to help you. I want to help the baby." He reached out and touched her arm. She had to stop herself from pulling away from him.

"Oh," she said. She took a gulp of her lemonade.

"We can try and make it work again. You know, do all the things we planned. We can take it to the park together to feed the ducks. We can start again."

He painted images of a life she had longed for. She didn't know what to say. Perhaps it would work. And the child would need a father figure. She tried to remember the longings she knew she used to feel when she thought of bringing up a child with him, but she couldn't quite recapture them. It would be for the best for Andy to be involved in the child's life. If she tried hard enough, she was sure she would want him involved.

"Yeah," she said.

"Maybe we could move back into the flat? We could ask the tenants to move out . . ."

She thought about how much she hated her house-share, how there wasn't room for a baby in her single room, how much easier life had been with Andy. She thought about how pleased her parents would be if they got back together.

"Yeah, I could do, maybe," she said, still trying to compute what he was saying.

She thought of all the times she'd tried to call him since they'd split up. All the times he hadn't answered. All the hope which had been extinguished. Could they really try again? A month ago, she would have been overjoyed. But now the thought of it seemed like a weight, tying her to the past.

"Great," he said. "It's weird it happened this way, isn't it?" He laughed hollowly. "All that trying for a baby, and then, when we don't really want one anymore, suddenly we've got one."

Renée felt a wave of nausea. She needed to get away. She needed to think about what he'd said. Did she want to get back together? It seemed like the sensible thing to do. They could just pick up their lives where they had left them before they split up.

"Yeah," she said, distractedly.

"Do you want another drink?"

She looked down and saw that she had finished her lemonade. "No, I'm fine." She looked at her watch and saw that she had only been there half an hour. She smiled at him apologetically. "Actually, I've got to go. I'm meeting a friend."

She stood up and let him kiss her on the cheek. It felt overly formal, unnatural.

"We should meet up again soon," Andy said, before she left the table.

"Yeah," she said. "Are you still going to Sam's wedding?" Their invitation had been a joint one, and she wasn't sure whether Andy would still go if they weren't together.

"I hadn't thought about it. When is it?"

"Two weeks on Saturday."

"Well, if you're going to be there, then I'll go." He smiled at her.

"OK, well, I'd really better go now. See you at the wedding."

When she got out onto the street she saw it was raining. She didn't have an umbrella and she hurried to the tube. What did Andy want from her? Did he really want to get back together? Maybe it was for the best. Maybe it was the right thing to do.

Standing on the escalator, she passed an advert for a new type of baby formula. Something in her mind connected, and she jolted. Andy had assumed the baby was his. She hadn't thought to tell him it might not be.

She felt sick. She had a duty to tell him. And yet . . . If they did get back together, wouldn't it be for the best if she didn't mention it? They could slip back into their old lives easily, forget everything that had happened while they'd been apart. She didn't need to tell anyone that the baby might be Dave's – did she? Perhaps, the happy marriage and children that she had planned might still materialise with Andy. She tried to think positively, but for some reason she couldn't shake off an overwhelming feeling of sadness.

40

James's PA, Lyn, bustled into his office with a huge pile of papers. James had inherited Lyn from the previous Head of Strategy, and she was known for being ruthlessly efficient. He put his head in his hands involuntarily as he watched her approach his desk.

She put the papers down and pulled off the top sheet.

"Here's your diary for today."

He looked at it. There was a staff meeting with his own team, which he ran once a month. Aside from that, the page was blank. He felt a flicker of panic. Since his talk with Clive he had noticed his diary emptying as he was excluded from more and more of the important strategic meetings with the directors. He was sure there had been another meeting in his diary today when he looked last week.

"Isn't it the 2013 planning meeting today?"

Lyn was already going through the next pile of documents.

"Yes, it is. They called and said you weren't needed."

"Oh, right."

He would normally have done anything to avoid the long and tedious planning meetings, but his exclusion was a clear sign that he had a limited shelf-life in the company. He was Head of UK Strategy, and it was essential that the Head of Strategy attend all the planning meetings.

"It must be a relief for you," Lyn said. "You hate those meetings. And then you'll have a bit more time for lunch."

James turned to her sharply. Had she noticed his long lunches? He supposed she must have. It was now too risky have a water bottle of vodka at his desk, so he had to find other times to drink. At lunchtime he couldn't go out to the car and drink inconspicuously in the car park, so he had to drive out. Sometimes he drove half an hour to a country pub and sat drinking whiskies on his own. He didn't invite Steve on these lunchtime outings anymore. He didn't want to do anything that might suggest to anyone that the rumours were true. But even when the pub was miles away from the office, the fear of discovery was so intense that he couldn't enjoy the drinking. He would pick at his food and leave quickly.

"Actually, I've got that contract to work on," James said.

"The consultancy one? I thought you'd finished."

Why did she have to be so on the ball? "It just needs a few tweaks. In fact, I don't think I'll be able to run the staff meeting after all."

She frowned. "I think the staff have a lot of questions for you."

About what? Had the rumours about his drinking reached them?

"Oh?" James asked, keeping his voice level.

"About the corporate cuts. People are worried."

"Well, tell them I have an 'open-door policy'. He indicated the door. "They can knock any time and talk through their concerns personally." He knew that none of them would, because none of them would want to be identified as someone who moaned or was in any way dissatisfied.

"OK, I'll tell them."

"Is that all?"

"You just need to sign these papers and then I'll leave you to get on." She handed over the papers and then stood over his desk as he signed each document without reading it. He handed the papers back to her and she strode out of the office, without shutting the door.

"Can you shut the door please, Lyn?" he called.

She stuck her head back in. "What about the open-door policy?"

"It's a figure of speech. Shut the door."

She closed the door carefully. Through the glass partitions of his office, James saw her sit back at her desk and immediately pick up the phone. Was she gossiping about him? Was she telling the other PAs that he had been excluded from the planning meeting?

Perhaps he shouldn't have cancelled the team meeting. That wouldn't go down well with his staff. He was cancelling meetings more and more often since his talk with Clive. He preferred to be alone in his office, where he could try and control the shaking and the permanent headaches he was having these days.

It wasn't that he didn't care about his work. It was that he cared too much. Now that Clive knew about his drinking, it was only a matter of time before he lost his job. Clive had told him they would investigate and see what needed to be done. He had made it clear that he would look for the easiest option for James: he would look for a way out of it. But he had also made it clear that an investigation would be launched, and if the end result meant he had to fire James, then he would.

James had been surprised that, for the moment at least, he was allowed to keep coming into the office each day. He hadn't been suspended – yet – but he was sure his dismissal was being planned. It wasn't a lenient company. It wasn't willing to carry stragglers. He himself had had to let people go, for much less significant misdemeanours. He suspected that he was only being kept on while they found someone to replace him. He had relationships with a lot of their key clients; it would be bad for business if one day he just disappeared.

The evening after his talk with Clive, he had waited for everyone to go home and cleared out all the alcohol from his office and put it into the boot of his car. He had been late home to Meera and Phoebe. He had wanted Meera to berate him. This was all his own fault. But instead she had kissed him and told him she was worried about him; that he was working too hard. When they had sex that night he had only just managed to perform, trying not to communicate the overarching sadness that embraced his every moment. He needed to appreciate her. She and Phoebe would be gone once he lost the job and the house.

He looked back at his computer. He needed to get on, but he couldn't concentrate. It had been easier when he could pace his drinking throughout the day. Now he had to drink in short, sharp bursts, and even he could see the effects. He would drink nearly a whole water bottle of vodka before he arrived at work. When he got out of the car in the mornings he had to focus on walking straight across the car-park. His vision would blur a bit, and the daylight would hurt his eyes. Once inside, he would avoid saying good morning to anyone in case he slurred his words. He ignored the receptionist, he ignored his team, he ignored the directors. He just kept his head down and focused on getting inside his office and shutting the door. He felt anxious and shaky and unable to concentrate. All he could think of was lunchtime.

He tried to concentrate on the black and white type of the consultancy contract. Outside his office, he could see three of his staff talking at the water cooler. Were they talking about him? One of them glanced his way, and he turned his eyes back to the computer screen.

How far had the rumours spread? He assumed that the directors knew about the investigation. As a rising star in the company, James had frequently been invited round to their houses. But since the meeting with Clive there had been no dinner parties, no after-work drinks.

Did his staff know? Someone must have reported him at some point. Who was it? Had the rumour spread like wildfire through the office even before his meeting with Clive? He shivered. Perhaps his staff had even been asked to give evidence. He was sure he had noticed more of them peering as they walked by.

He needed a drink. He looked at his watch. Still two hours until lunch.

He walked over to the window of his office and stared out at the line of shiny BMWs and Mercs. That lifestyle wasn't for him anymore. He was nearing the end. All he could do was wait.

*

Steve had suggested meeting for a drink after work, and James found himself saying yes. Everything was already lost; he might as well go for a drink with Steve. And anyway, after work was OK. It was considered part of office life and wouldn't be frowned upon in the same way as lunchtime drinks.

Of course, he should really get back to Meera and Phoebe, but when he had texted Meera to see if she'd be OK on her own, she had encouraged him to go out and relax, away from the stresses of work.

When he entered the pub and saw Steve queuing at the bar, James felt a strange sense of release. He was in a pub with a friend after work, having a drink like a normal person. He could forget all his worries about losing his job and his house and Meera and Phoebe, and just have some drinks with an old mate.

He tapped Steve on the shoulder and Steve turned.

"What do you want to drink, mate?" Steve asked.

He tended to stick to spirits, as they left him feeling less bloated and could easily be mistaken for other drinks, and so were less conspicuous during the day. He saw that Steve had ordered a beer.

"I'll have a pint," James said. He thought he'd be able to

make a pint last longer than a spirit and mixer, and avoid the embarrassment of waiting, on edge, for Steve to catch up.

They sat down at a corner table and Steve took a glug of his pint. James looked at him closely. He looked exhausted. His eyes had huge bags under them, and his chin had broken out in spots. "How are you?" he asked.

"Alright mate. You?"

"Yeah, me too. How's the house sale going?"

"No offers as yet." Steve stared into his pint. "What did you think of Caroline?" he asked.

"She seemed nice." James remembered what Meera had told him about her throwing up in the toilet.

"Yeah, well she's not quite all she seems."

"Something happened, mate?" James felt a sinking feeling. He didn't have time for Steve's girlfriend troubles, and he had a feeling the whole evening would be dominated by them.

"She's a lot younger than me."

"I know," They'd discussed this at the dinner party. And anyway Meera was three years younger than him – it really didn't matter.

"Her mother came round the other day to speak to me."

"Don't worry. Meera's mother comes round all the time. You never lose the mother-in-law." James tried to laugh but he didn't feel like laughing. Steve's problems seemed so trivial compared to his own. He was going to lose his job and then his wife. He was drinking too much and he couldn't stop.

He frowned, wanting the thoughts to stop, and knocked back the final gulp of his pint. That felt better. He was so lost in his own thoughts that he nearly missed what Steve said next.

"She's fifteen."

"*What?*"

"Caroline's fifteen."

"Oh . . . she's at school?" James tried to picture Caroline clearly again, but he found he couldn't bring an image of her to his mind. But she had seemed young. He remembered Dave mentioning it after Steve and Caroline had left.

"Yeah."

James's knee was shaking under the table. What did you say to that?

"Do you want another pint?"

"Nah, not yet."

James squirmed in his seat.

"I'll get a drink for me." He went to the bar and returned quickly with a triple whisky and coke. There was no reason for Steve not to think it was a single. He sat back down and took a gulp. Steve was still staring dejectedly into his half-full pint.

"Do you love her?"

"Yeah . . . What should I do?" Steve said, picking at a splinter of wood that was starting to come away from the edge of the table.

"I don't know, mate"

For a moment James was desperate to get rid of the weight from his own shoulders, to tell Steve that his drinking had got out of control, that he was about to lose his job. But he knew Steve wouldn't be able to help him any more than he could help Steve.

He was lost.

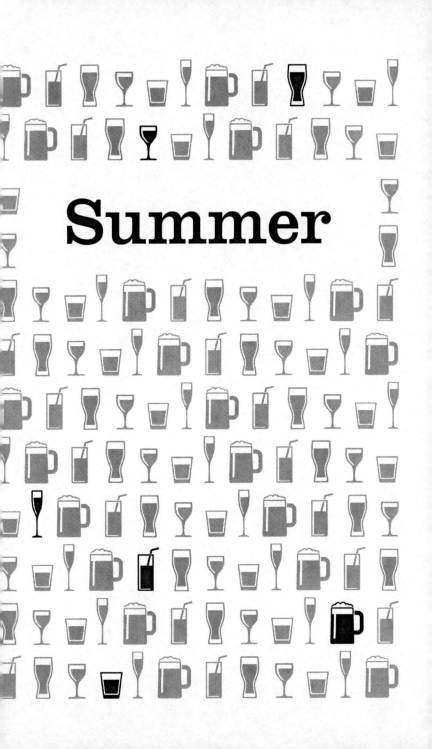

Summer

41

Katie folded the pale blue flowered dress she was planning to wear to Sam's wedding, and placed it on top of the other clothes and shoes in her overnight bag. She smoothed it down, and hoped that it wouldn't get creased on the train journey to the wedding. She'd have to keep her bag with her so that no one shoved their heavy luggage on top of it on the train.

She carefully zipped up the bag, put it over her shoulder and went downstairs. She was going to go into central London to do some shopping before she went over to St Pancras to catch the train.

Daniel and her grandfather were sitting at the kitchen table, chatting. Or rather, Daniel was chatting away and her grandfather was just sitting listening. Katie wondered if she'd be able to sneak out without saying goodbye. She'd been avoiding Daniel since the awkward lunch at his house. She'd left as soon as she'd finished her meal, and she'd hardly spoken to him since.

She had started to think there had been something sordid about having sex with a man twice her age in her brother's bedroom, watched by a picture of Anna Kournikova. Since she'd gone to dinner at his house, the mystique surrounding him had disappeared. She knew who he was and he no longer fascinated her. He was just Daniel, a nice, kind man. Nothing more. She couldn't kid herself that she was going to fall in love with him. There didn't seem much point in continuing the relationship.

Daniel caught sight of her on her way to the door and came over.

"Are you off?" he said.

"Yeah . . . I'm going to a wedding." She hadn't even mentioned the wedding to him.

"Right, well, have fun."

His eyes looked confused. She reached up and gave him a quick peck on the cheek. "Thanks," she said.

She felt guilty because she hadn't said goodbye to her grandfather, so she went into the kitchen and bent down to give him a quick kiss on the cheek. She had hardly spent any time with him since her mother had been back from holiday. In the evenings her mother took care of him. In the day time Katie found herself going out more and more, just to get away from Daniel. When she had been seeing Daniel, the three of them had used to eat together and chat. Now that she was avoiding him, her communication with her grandfather had all but stopped.

She'd have to rectify that when she got back from the wedding. Just because she and Daniel were no longer communicating didn't mean her relationship with her grandfather had to deteriorate.

*

Four hours later, she was settled into her seat on the train north, her overnight bag and her shopping bags crammed into the small space under the seat in front. She stared out of the window, watching the green hills and fields of crops whizz by. It was a Friday afternoon and she thought of other people working hard in offices as she relaxed on the train. For once she was appreciating her days off.

She was looking forward to meeting Renée and the others when she arrived at the hotel. She felt guilty about not contacting Renée since her admission about Dave. It wasn't that she didn't want to talk to her. She'd just been busy. As the only girls in their group, she and Renée would be sharing a room. They would have plenty of time to catch up then, and Renée would see that Katie didn't hold her relationship with Dave against her.

The fields changed into cul de sacs of semi-detached houses, and then again into blocks of flats, and then the retail units of a city centre. She was in Nottingham. It would still be another couple of hours before she arrived at the nearest town to the church where Sam's wedding was taking place.

She thought about the last time she had seen Sam, when she'd locked herself out of her house. Katie had meant to look at her head wound in the morning to check that it was OK, but by the time she got up, Sam had already left. The sheets were folded neatly on the sofa, and she'd left a note to thank Katie and let her know that she would reimburse her for any petrol at the wedding.

Katie had almost forgotten about that night, but now she remembered how odd it had been. Sam clearly hadn't been drunk, but had managed to fall over. And there had been other odd things too. A face at the window when they were driving off. Had that been Patrick?

She started to worry. Had the head wound really be the result of a fall? Why had Sam left in such a hurry the next day? Was it possible that Patrick had injured Sam?

Katie felt sick. It would make sense. Katie had seen for herself that Sam was incapable of sticking up for herself. At the hen night she had let her mother and her aunt walk all over her. If Patrick was hitting her, would she stand up to him, or try and protect him?

Sam calling her like that had been a cry for help; but she had been too distracted to realise it. She should have acted when she saw the head injury. Even though it was just a graze she shouldn't have left it. She should have asked questions. She should have helped Sam escape from Patrick.

But it was too late. She was going to their wedding. What was the right thing to do? Should she try and talk to Sam? Or should she leave things and let them run their own course?

She felt a rush of hatred for Patrick. How could he do that? Sam was so happy, so grateful, to be marrying him. How could he abuse her trust in that way?

*

By the time the train had left Nottingham and was back out in the countryside again, Katie had resolved to try and find Sam when she got to the village. She wasn't going to tell her not to marry Patrick. She was just going to be there in case she needed someone to talk to. And if she decided not to go through with the wedding, she could always stay with Katie if she wanted to.

Katie sighed. Why was she always so blind to things? She had been so jealous of Sam because she had appeared so happy and contented, but below the surface that hadn't been true at all.

She thought of Dave. She supposed they would never be together. She hadn't heard much from him since she had helped him move from his flat, although they had exchanged the occasional email. Things were back to how they'd always been: she was there for him when he needed her, but as soon as he didn't, he always forgot all about her. She was nothing more than a loyal friend.

She sighed. Despite herself, she was still looking forward to seeing him. And Renée too. All the stuff with Dave should be water under the bridge by now. It would be nice to see everyone and reminisce. She started to think about all the good times they had had when they were at uni: the picnics in the park, the drinks in Renée and Andy's room, the post-exam celebrations. She dozed off into a contented sleep.

42

Renée collected the room key from reception. She only had a small bag and it wasn't heavy, but she chose to take the lift up to the third floor because she felt too exhausted to take the stairs.

The hotel was pleasant, and would have been the ideal country retreat if she hadn't felt so tense. Steve had found it, and it was perfect for their needs: set a little outside the village, with views of an endless expanse of landscape, but still within walking distance of the church.

She opened the door to her room and found that the internal decor met the standards set by the hotel's exterior. Two neat single beds, dressers and two armchairs. Not too big but not too small. The bathroom was more functional, with a mouldy-looking shower overhanging a faded pink bath. She supposed you couldn't have everything. She put her bag next to one of the beds and stretched. Her back ached from the long journey.

Although she had had a seat, the motion of the train no longer seemed to agree with her. She had spent the journey racked with nerves. Usually she loved watching the countryside roll by, but today she was too scared of her own thoughts to gaze out of the window. She had been unable to concentrate on the book she had brought. Although she had read three chapters, she couldn't even recall what the book was about.

The receptionist had told her that Katie had not yet arrived, and Renée thought she would make the most of having the room to herself in the meantime. She noticed a small balcony, and fiddled with the doors to unlock them. They were stiff, and she had to put her weight behind them to force them open.

She was rewarded for her efforts: the view of the hills had been muted by the frosted glass, but once the doors were open she could see it was spectacular. It was a beautiful, cloudless day and the sun was high in the sky, shining down on the bright green fields.

Her ears were used to the constant noise and bustle of London, and she had to stand still for a while and strain in order to hear the very different sounds of the countryside. She heard birds, and the rustle of a light wind passing through the crops. In the near distance there was the occasional shout or laugh of a child. Idyllic. She smiled an ironic smile.

A year ago this was the kind of place she would have loved to have come with Andy, to talk about the future and make plans. But they had never got round to it. He would be there later, but they wouldn't be together. She'd thought a lot about what he'd said at the pub. When he'd offered her the images of a happy parenthood – the walks in the park, pushing the children on the swings – she'd been tempted. She'd wanted to believe they were real and not just pictures. But when she'd thought about it, she'd realised they were just that: pictures. What Andy was describing wasn't going to happen. She didn't love him anymore. He didn't love her either, and was only suggesting it for the sake of the baby. She'd have to tell him she couldn't move back in with him. She'd have to tell him the baby might not even be his.

She was dreading this evening: Andy, Dave and Katie all in the same place at the same time. Why hadn't she had the courage to tell Dave before?

She wondered what time Katie would arrive. They were

sharing a room, but hadn't spoken since their conversation about Dave. She hadn't been able to bring herself to tell Katie about the pregnancy. It felt like she had betrayed her friend all over again. She took her phone out of her handbag and considered calling her to see when she was arriving. She decided against it. There'd be plenty of time to catch up later. Katie would realise Renée was pregnant soon enough.

She felt her stomach tighten as she thought about the inevitable events of the evening ahead.

They were all going out to dinner later. Renée imagined the awkward, stilted conversations, and shivered. She came in from the balcony and locked the door. She took out her clothes for the wedding from her overnight bag and hung them up in the cupboard. Maybe she'd just read for a bit. She sat down on the bed and opened her book. She flicked through the pages, but couldn't remember where she was, and got frustrated. She couldn't concentrate. She felt claustrophobic. She needed to get out.

Outside, on the street, the quiet was even more apparent. She was alone on the walk down the single-track road to the village, and no cars passed her. She arrived to discover that there was one shop, two pubs, and the church. The shop was closed on Friday afternoon, so she occupied herself reading the adverts in the window. Several cleaners were advertised, a gardener, one car and a hi-fi. She hadn't thought that people used hi-fis anymore.

She kept going down the street and found herself at the church. It rose over the village green, foreboding against the bright blue sky. The grass was well cared for, but the graves were haphazard and crooked, as if put there by a child. She circled the church, reading the names on the graves and wondering about their lives. *Beloved daughter, beloved husband, beloved wife.* Everyone reduced to just a few generic words, defined by their family relationships. There was no one alone. No beloved friend, beloved businessman, or even beloved philanthropist. Just fathers and sons, mothers and daughters, husbands and wives. It was like the church was reinforcing its own teachings: the sanctity of marriage stayed with you beyond the grave.

One of the wooden double doors to the church was open, and she crept inside. The church seemed even more imposing on the inside, and it was cold despite the warmth outside. Line after line of neat pews led up to the altar. She looked up towards the distant beams of the roof, where the same neatness was replicated.

She wasn't sure what to do. She felt strangely calm here, but there was nothing to occupy her. She didn't want to return to the hotel, and the waiting, so she sat down in one of the pews.

She had married Andy five years ago, in a church much like this one. She had wanted the most glorious, impressive church to show off their love and impress their friends and family. The wedding had been magnificent. Everyone had said so. Perhaps she should feel sad, but the memories only made her feel wistful, for a time when she had been full of self-belief and so sure all the time that she was doing the right thing.

Tomorrow the church would be full of people and would take on a personality of its own.

*

Sam opened the door of the church and saw that someone had got there before her. A girl with long dark hair sat on one of the pews, staring at the altar. The girl didn't hear her, and Sam wasn't sure whether it would be politer to cough and interrupt her thoughts or to just let her be.

She had needed to get away from her family, and the church had been the only place she could think of. Patrick had decided they should follow tradition and spend the night before the wedding separately with their families, to amplify the moment when they caught sight of each other at the church. Although she had agreed, she was finding today, the day before the wedding, difficult. Her mother wouldn't leave her alone. She fussed over her constantly, kept checking that she was feeling OK and reminding her to stand up straight.

Sam felt like she was sitting on a divide between lives: a before and an after. So far in her life, everything had been more difficult than necessary; she had been fat, unpopular and unloved. Now she was thin, and from tomorrow she would be married. She would begin the happy-ever-after part of her life. Tomorrow would be her liberation from the ugly-duckling child.

She just wished her father could be there. He hadn't replied to her letter or her invitation. She didn't even know if he'd received them. A small part of her had thought he might turn up at the last moment. Even in her hotel she kept looking over her shoulder when she heard footsteps in the corridor, just in case it was him. She hadn't seen him for twenty years, and she wasn't certain she would recognise him. She found herself eyeing strangers in the hotel reception suspiciously, looking at the curve of their nose, the pitch of their cheekbones, and craning her neck to catch the colour of their eyes. Just in case one of them was him.

But she knew that there was little chance of him turning up. Her mother had drummed it into her, year after year, that he just didn't care. Maybe she was right.

She stared round the church and tried to imagine tomorrow: her white dress, Patrick in his kilt, a sea of faces watching them from the pews, acknowledging her big moment, her success. And then the confetti. And then the rests of their lives . . . Tomorrow everyone would watch and everyone would congratulate them. But then that would be it. She would be alone with Patrick. And no one would be watching anymore. Patrick would be her life.

She reached up to touch the bruise on her forehead. It was completely concealed by her make-up. But it was enough for her just to know it was there.

She remembered the little boy in the library. Perhaps she and Patrick would have children. Would they fear their father? Would he beat them too?

She didn't want to think about that, especially not now. She would wander up to the altar and think about the big moment, the exchange of rings. And then the kiss. She walked slowly up the aisle, head down, subconsciously rehearsing her steps for the next day.

She had forgotten about the girl in the pew, but as Sam passed her she looked up and Sam saw it was Renée.

Renée rose, and Sam saw the curve of her stomach and realised that she was pregnant.

"Hi," Renée said.

"Hi."

There was a pause while Sam wondered whether congratulations were appropriate. She had heard Renée and Andy had split up. Perhaps they had got back together. Perhaps they hadn't. "Congratulations," she said tentatively.

"Oh," Renée said, touching her stomach. "Thanks."

The silence was awkward, and then Renée sat back down and indicated the pew beside her. "Do you want to sit down?"

Sam sat, and they both stared at the vastness of the church in silence.

"So, tomorrow's the big day," Renée said, after a while.

"Yes," said Sam, and even she could hear that her voice didn't sound happy.

Renée seemed so calm and serene, sitting on the pew.

"Did you and Andy . . . did you get back together?" Sam asked, and then regretted it immediately, as she had only heard second-hand that they had split up.

"No," Renée answered. She touched her stomach protectively.

Sam stared round the church. Tomorrow her life would change. Marriage was supposed to mean everything. But here was Renée, who had been part of a fairytale relationship that Sam had always envied, and was now separated.

She turned to face Renée, and studied her face. She seemed calm, perhaps contented. "What's it like, being married?" she asked.

Renée shrugged. "I don't know really – I mean, the same, maybe – It wasn't that different. It wasn't bad and it wasn't like my life suddenly changed and things were amazing. It didn't fix anything. It was just life really. We just went through from day to day, living."

Sam nodded. That made sense. Things didn't change. People didn't change. "Thanks," she said.

"For what?"

"For being honest."

43

James sat in the back of Steve's car, staring out of the window and listening to the rise and fall of Steve and Andy's conversation. He couldn't make out all the words because of the music on the stereo, and he was tired of leaning forward to join in, so he just sank back in his seat and listened to the occasional word.

It was strange how sitting in the back of a car with two people in the front could make you feel childlike and excluded. Steve was politely asking Andy about his separation from Renée. Andy didn't seem to want to talk about it, and Steve moved on to talking about Caroline, explaining his problem in detail.

James didn't know why either of them was worried. Andy had decided to separate from a woman he no longer loved. That was a sensible thing to do, perhaps a brave thing, and now the worst was over, his life was improving. Steve, on the other hand, had been stupid enough to sleep with a fifteen-year-old. All he had to do was forget about it and get over her. It couldn't be that hard. What could he see in a fifteen-year-old?

James himself had serious problems, but neither Steve nor Andy seemed concerned about him. They just assumed he had the perfect life with his Meera and Phoebe, and never stopped to ask questions. It was like they looked at him but didn't see him. They assumed he was always happy. He stared out the window, his irritation growing as he listened to their self-indulgent conversation.

Steve's driving was painfully slow and it was probably going to be another hour before they arrived. James had brought one water bottle of vodka with him in the car and he had already finished it. His head was aching and he wanted some fresh air. The remainder of his vodka was in his overnight bag, and even if they stopped somewhere he wouldn't be able to get it out without Steve and Andy noticing. It would make no sense for him to be carrying bottles of water in his bag when he could buy it at a service station. It wasn't like he was short of money.

He wished he had driven, but when they had asked for volunteers he had deliberately not put himself forward. He was worried the others would notice the bottle of vodka. And he was worried about the quantity he might drink on a long-distance drive. His driving was becoming more and more erratic and a three-hour drive meant more drink, less concentration and more chance of an accident. He had had a couple of near misses lately on the way to work. Once he had nearly pulled out right in front of a lorry, and a second time he had hit his brakes a little too late when the car in front slowed down. But he hadn't felt the usual rush of relief you feel when you avoid disaster. Instead he'd felt a vague disappointment, and had a sinking realisation that it was only a matter of time before he did have an accident. His life was already over anyway.

He only drove to and from work these days. At weekends he always let Meera drive, as he didn't want to put her and Phoebe at risk. He had explained that he had had a near miss (which was true) and had become a more nervous driver (which wasn't), and she had accepted this in the way she always did.

He felt a surge of anger towards her. Why did she always accept everything he said? Why did she never question him? No matter how much he drank, she never seemed to notice. Why hadn't she found his alcohol stash? Why hadn't she punished him? Made him see sense? Why had she let it go this far?

He had always been proud of the way he was able to hide his drinking from everyone. It was a sign of immense self-control. It hadn't stopped him performing at work or having a happy marriage. He drank and he had had the perfect life. But now he couldn't help wishing that someone had found out. Someone who was stronger than him and could have told him to stop before it got to this stage.

What would Meera have done if she had found out? Would she have chucked him out of the house? Would she have sent him to rehab, or some awful religious organisation? He was sure he'd have had to apologise and change. But in the long run, would she have taken him back? Would he have kept his family?

He would never know. It was all too late to know.

In the front of the car, Andy was sympathising with Steve about his pathetic relationship with a schoolgirl. James felt like reaching forward and throttling both of them, causing the car to veer off the road and perhaps crash into a bridge. At least then it would all be over.

*

Steve pulled up to the service station, and Andy and James piled out of the car.

"Do you mind if I get something out of the boot?" James asked.

"No, go ahead. We'll see you inside."

Steve pulled his mobile phone out of his pocket as he and Andy walked across the car-park. Two messages. Both from Caroline. He sighed.

He wanted to listen to them away from Andy, so when Andy went to the toilet, he found a quiet corner under some stairs and played the messages.

"Steve, it's me. I know you don't want me back and I know you don't love me. But I can't live without you."

Caroline had left lots of messages for him when they had first split up, but he hadn't heard from her since he had been visited by her mother.

He listened to the second message.

"I just wanted you to know I've decided to kill myself. I hope you realise it's your fault. All I need is for you to tell me you love me."

He felt his heart wrench. But it wasn't the first time she'd threatened to kill herself since they had split up. It was just a way of getting his attention. She would never go through with it.

He stared at his phone, considering dialing her number just to check she really was OK. But there was nothing he could say to her to make her feel better. He did love her, but he couldn't tell her. He couldn't be with her, and they just needed to forget about each other.

"Alright mate?" Andy had come up behind him, and he jumped.

"Yeah, yeah, fine." He shoved his phone in his pocket.

"Have you seen James?"

"No. Maybe he's back at the car."

They began to walk back across the car-park. Steve decided he would phone Caroline when they arrived, from the privacy of the hotel. They were only half an hour or so away. He was sure she was fine, but he just wanted to check. Just in case.

44

Renée sat down on the sofa in the hotel reception and looked at her watch. They were supposed to be meeting for dinner at seven. She was five minutes early.

She had dressed carefully, but there was no longer any way of disguising her growing belly. She scratched at the skin of her inner arm nervously. It was surprisingly hot in reception and she felt sweaty and uncomfortable. As she sat alone, she thought about leaving, skipping dinner and spending the evening in her room. But that would only be putting off the inevitable.

She heard the sound of footsteps on the hotel stairs. Her heart sank as Andy appeared.

"Hi," he said.

"Hi."

"I was hoping I'd catch you alone." He grinned at her and looked round to confirm there was no one else in the room.

The sofa was so low that shifting her weight to rise would have been a real effort, and he leaned in to give her a clumsy kiss on the cheek. To outsiders they would have looked like mere acquaintances, but kissing on the lips would have been no less awkward. There was no right answer for them anymore.

Andy sat down on the sofa across from hers. "So, how are you feeling?" he asked.

"Good," she said. "How are you?"

"Good."

"I've been thinking about the baby," Andy said.

"So have I," Renée responded quickly. She stared down at her belly. She needed to tell Andy that she didn't want to move in with him, that she didn't see a future for them anymore; but the words were cold dry lumps in her throat.

"Steve and James were asking about you in the car and I didn't know what to say. I thought about telling them that we we're having a baby, but I wanted to speak to you first."

He reached out and touched her leg.

"Andy –"

"I've bought a present, you know, for the baby." He reached awkwardly into his rucksack and got out a plastic bag. Then he pulled a tiny red Arsenal kit from the bag. "It's important he knows who he is from day one," he grinned.

Renée couldn't smile back.

"Andy, I can't move in with you. I'm sorry."

The silence was long, and Renée looked up to see that his face was pale and his eyes confused.

"Why not?" he whispered.

"I don't know. I just . . . can't. I don't think I'm ready for all that again."

"But . . . but . . . all the phone calls you made to me. I thought you wanted to get back together?"

"I did." She paused, trying to understand her own feelings. "But now I suppose I've moved on. It's just . . . too late."

She took a deep breath. "And Andy . . . I'm not sure if the baby's yours."

Confusion shadowed Andy's face. He opened his mouth as if to speak.

*

Katie was late. She had missed her connecting bus and had had to get a taxi. She bustled into the reception, flushed and sweaty.

She caught sight of Renée sitting on a sofa and she rushed over, leaving her travel-bag by the door. "It's so good to see you . . . I'm sorry I'm late."

She leaned over to hug her and stopped.

Renée was pregnant.

Her mind was a jumble of thoughts as she tried to compute what it meant.

"Does Dave know?" she blurted out.

There was a gasp, and the scrape of a sofa being pushed back with force. And now she noticed Andy sitting on the opposite sofa, his face like thunder.

"*Dave*?" He turned to Renée, his voice loud with anger and muffled with emotion.

Katie tried to recover. "I just wondered. I mean, I wondered who else knew. As I didn't know, I wondered if Dave knew, or Steve, or James."

But Andy was staring directly at Renée, and her face gave everything away.

Katie felt momentarily sorry for him.

"You and *Dave*." Andy's voice was controlled, with only ripples of anger, barely audible on the surface.

"No, not *me and Dave*. We're not in a relationship." Renée was shockingly calm.

Katie looked at her. The facts were still sinking in for her too. Even though they weren't in a relationship, a baby would tie Renée and Dave together. It would connect them forever.

There was a silence that seemed deafening, and James appeared from the stairway and walked straight into the middle of it, oblivious.

"Are we going to dinner then?" he asked.

"Yes, of course," Katie said, taking charge. She looked round quickly, and saw it was only the four of them. "Where are Steve and Dave?"

"Steve had to go back. He had an urgent call," said James, "and Dave's going to join us at eight."

Renée hadn't moved from the sofa, and Andy was pacing up and down the lobby.

"Let's go," Katie said, keen to escape the claustrophobic atmosphere. She grabbed her overnight bag. She could take it with her to the restaurant and drop it back in her room later.

Renée and James followed her out of the hotel, with Andy deliberately lingering, following a few meters behind.

They walked to the pub in silence, each of them lost in their own thoughts.

45

Sam arrived back at her hotel two hours after she'd walked to the church. After Renée had left the church, she had sat alone contemplating her future. She had thought of the wedding and everything it meant to her. It had been planned for months. She'd hardly been able to sleep since Patrick had proposed. Tomorrow everything would be perfect: the flowers, the dresses, the car to take her to the ceremony. It would be a magical day.

She had tried to just think of the day and to hold back the thoughts of their life together. A life in which Patrick was more than likely to continue to beat her. And their children. Till death do us part.

She went into her hotel room and stared round it. It was plain, yet it represented the last time she would be alone, without Patrick. Her last night of freedom. Her last night without fear that something she did would set him off and he would hit her.

She went down the corridor and knocked on the door to her mother's and aunt's room. They welcomed her in and she watched them fussing over the preparations for the morning, checking their outfits in the mirror and debating which jewellery matched best. Sam felt detached from it all. She told them she was tired, and they encouraged her to get some rest. She agreed demurely. She knew what she had to do.

She left them preening in front of the hotel mirrors, went back to her room, gathered everything into a pile, and dropped it unceremoniously into her suitcase. She went to the bathroom and cleaned her teeth and then put her wash bag in her suitcase along with the rest of her stuff. She caught sight of her wedding dress hanging in the wardrobe. She stroked the soft white material one last time.

She smiled at herself in the mirror. She was strong. She could do this.

She zipped up the suitcase and walked out of the room. She took the lift to reception and walked past the front desk. With every step, she expected someone to confront her; but nobody did. The receptionist stared blankly ahead. Sam kept looking behind her, expecting to see her mother and her aunt in hot pursuit, begging her to stay. There was no one there.

No one would notice that she was gone until tomorrow, when the wedding car came to pick her up from the hairdresser. She was scheduled in for hair and make-up from eight until ten forty-five. Her mother and aunt would be busy doing their own make-up at the hotel. By the time her mother came to collect her in the wedding car and realised she was gone, it would be too late to do anything about it: she would be safely away, and no one would be trying to persuade her to come back.

She knew that the sensible thing would be to tell someone now. To save Patrick the heartache of standing, waiting for her. But she couldn't. They'd put it down to pre-wedding nerves, and then she'd have to go through with it. No. There was only one way forward.

Outside the hotel, she shivered despite the warmth as she hailed a taxi to the station. She was silent in the back of the cab, and for once the driver didn't make conversation.

At the station, a part of her still expected Patrick to have somehow read her mind and turn up and stop her getting on the train. She bought her ticket and waited on the platform.

The train came in, and she started to wonder if she was doing the right thing.

Then she took a deep breath and stepped up into the carriage and let the train carry her away, escaping the wedding she had spent the last year meticulously planning.

46

Dave felt a blast of warm air as he went through the door of the restaurant. He ignored the waitress approaching him, and searched for his friends' faces. He spotted them at a corner table.

The table was only for four people, so Dave asked for an extra chair and positioned himself at the end. "Hi," he said.

"Hi." They all replied in unison, and then returned to intently focusing on their food. Was something wrong? Were they annoyed with him for being late? He got a menu from the waitress and chose his food quickly. He hoped it would arrive before everyone started on dessert.

He turned back to the table. The silence was stifling. No one was meeting his eye. Katie was frowning into the middle distance, as if trying to work something out. Andy and James were eating their food intently, as if starved. Renée had hardly touched hers, and she stared at it miserably. She had put on a lot of weight since he'd last seen her. He stared at her for a moment. She'd always been so careful with her weight. Was she . . .? The table partially blocked his view of her stomach. She couldn't be . . . could she?

He glanced round the table. Katie had been watching him looking at Renée. He could tell from her face that he was right. Renée was pregnant. He felt himself flush.

He played with his fork as he waited for his food. Renée must have started a new relationship. She'd split up with Andy a while ago. It was hardly unheard of. Or perhaps they'd got back together. Andy was sitting diagonally across from her, as far away as was possible. He was stony-faced and silent. Perhaps not.

He looked again at Renée's stomach. She was lost in her own world and didn't seem to notice him staring. Her belly was rounded, big, more than noticeable. He had no idea how far gone she was. Three month, six months, eight? It could still be Andy's, if it was conceived before they split up.

Dave swallowed a lump that had suddenly appeared in his throat. Or it could be *his*. But then, she would have told him, wouldn't she?

He called the waiter and ordered a triple shot of vodka. James looked up from his food and ordered the same.

*

Katie and Renée returned to their room in silence. Renée started changing into her nightclothes immediately, and Katie tried not to stare at her new, fuller figure. How far gone was she? Could the baby be Dave's?

"Renée," she said tentatively.

"Yeah?"

"Are you OK?"

"Yeah."

"I'm sorry I didn't get in contact earlier. I was just . . . busy."

"That's OK." Renée sat on her bed and began to brush her hair.

"It wasn't because of Dave, you know – that wasn't your fault. I was just being immature."

Renée looked up at her. "Thanks," she said. "I wasn't sure. I thought you'd be angry." She indicated her belly. "I couldn't face anyone."

Katie saw that Renée's eyes were watery, and she went

and sat beside her on the bed. "I'm your friend first, you know. Before I'm anything else. You come first, not Dave, not anyone else. You."

She paused, and heard Renée sniffle.

"We always said at university we wouldn't let men get in the way," she went on.

"We didn't succeed though." Renée managed a rueful smile.

Katie thought of Dave and how his interest in Renée had nearly ruined their friendship at university. She thought about the times when she'd been travelling and needed someone to talk to about relationships. She'd never turned to Renée. Renée had been too obsessed with Andy.

"We can't succeed at everything," she said. She gave Renée a hug, and Renée started sobbing.

"I'm sorry," Renée said.

"About what?"

"I don't know. I don't think I've been a very good friend."

Katie touched her shoulder. "You have. Don't worry."

She held Renée until she calmed down. She swallowed. She still needed to know the answer to the only question going through her mind. "Renée . . . the baby . . . is it Dave's?"

Renée started to sniffle again. "I don't know."

"OK."

"It could be Dave's, or it could be Andy's."

"Right."

Dave might be having a baby with Renée. Katie started to feel a hotness behind her eyes and she thought she might cry too.

Her mobile went off, and she used it as an excuse to stand up. She found her handbag and rifled through it. She had a text from Dave.

Katie. I need a drink – Please come with me!! See you at the hotel bar x

She heard the bathroom taps. Peering in, she saw Renée cleaning her teeth.

"I'm going to bed," Renée said.

"Sure . . . In that case, do you mind if I go for a drink?"

"No, of course not."

Renée's eyes were still red.

"Are you sure?"

"Yeah, you go." Renée gestured towards the door with her free hand. Katie picked up her handbag and left quickly. She hadn't unpacked yet, but she could do that later.

*

The hotel bar was tiny, and contained only five armchairs positioned round a coal fire, which was unlit in the height of summer. Dave thought it was more like someone's living room than a bar. James was already there, sitting on the armchair in the furthest corner with a whisky, reading the day's papers. Dave ordered a whisky for himself and then sank into one of the comfortable chairs beside James. He hadn't expected anyone to be here. At least Andy wasn't in evidence. At the thought of Andy, he took a gulp of his drink. It burnt his throat.

James seemed lost in his own world. Dave coughed, and he looked up, startled.

"Oh, hi Dave," he said.

"How are you?"

"Good, thanks."

"Good."

A silence descended.

"How's your job going?" James asked.

Dave had never told James or Steve that he'd lost his job.

"Fine," he said, thinking of Rachel. Right now he almost wished he was at his temp job, away from everyone, away from the prospect of fatherhood. He wished he was being frivolous and irresponsible with Rachel.

James looked at him. "Don't want to talk about it, eh? Me neither. We're supposed to be getting away from it all." The comment was jokey, but somehow his voice didn't seem to match.

"Yeah," Dave said.

"Another one?" James said, looking at Dave's glass.

Dave looked down to see that he'd drained it already. "Yeah, sure."

While James was at the bar, Katie appeared. She sat down next to him. He grinned, gratefully. "You took a while. I thought the prospect of a drink would have you down here in seconds."

"Seconds! I'm not an alcoholic." She gave him a disapproving look.

"Really?" he grinned, glad to be teasing her; glad that some sense of normality had resumed.

"Actually I was talking to Renée," Katie said.

The light mood evaporated. "She's pregnant," Dave said, staring into his glass.

"Yeah."

"Did she . . ." He played with his empty glass, swirling the ice-cubes around in the bottom. "Did she say who the father was?"

"She doesn't know."

"What?"

"It might be Andy, and it might be you."

Dave felt sick. "I'm too young to be a father."

"You're twenty-seven."

"I know."

"James is a father, he's twenty-seven. If he can be, so can you."

"Shut up, Katie."

She looked hurt. At that moment James staggered towards them, drinks in hand, his shirt hanging out and his hair dishevelled. Dave looked at Katie knowingly, and they both began to laugh.

47

Steve pulled into the overflowing hospital car-park. The information on the website had suggested that he take public transport, but he had chosen to ignore it. He drove round in circles for about ten minutes, keeping his eye out for anyone leaving the hospital, but he wasn't in luck. A queue of cars built up behind him.

Luckily he was half an hour early. It was nine thirty a.m. and Caroline could have visitors from ten. He had tried to get here the night before, after a mad dash down the motorway, but visiting hours had been over and Caroline was asleep. The nurse had told him to go home.

When he had checked his phone when he arrived at the hotel with Andy and James the night before, he had seen that he had two more missed calls from Caroline's number. The second message had not been from Caroline, but her mother, informing him that Caroline had filled her stomach with paracetamol and was having it pumped at the hospital. She was asking to see him, and her mother had decided to ring him. Her voice had been bitter, and it was clear she blamed him and didn't expect him to turn up.

He had got back in his car immediately and headed back towards London.

Steve decided to give up on the hospital car-park, and drove back onto the main road and then into a warren of side-streets. He found a space in a residents' parking area, and decided to risk the fine. By now it was ten minutes before visiting hours started, and he didn't want to be late.

He got out of the car, grabbed the flowers and the pile of magazines from the back seat, and headed over to the main hospital building.

When he arrived at the ward, Caroline's mother, Deena, was at her bedside. She had big bags under her eyes, and her face looked older than it had when they'd last met.

Steve coughed. "Hi."

"Steve!" Caroline eased herself up in the bed. She looked tiny, her small body encased in white sheets. He wanted to go over and hug her, but he was over-aware of the heavy presence of her mother.

He nodded at her mother, who rose. "Thanks for coming."

Automatically, he shook her hand. Then he went over to Caroline and gave her a peck on the cheek. "Hi, Caroline."

She looked momentarily flustered. "If I'd known you were coming, I'd have put some make-up on."

Without her make-up, her skin was almost flawless. She looked a lot younger.

"I brought flowers and magazines."

"Thanks."

Deena came over and took the flowers from him and busied herself putting them in a vase.

He reached out and held Caroline's small, birdlike hand. She gripped tightly. "How are you feeling?" he asked her.

"Better." She grinned at him. "Much better now you're here."

Steve felt an overwhelming sense of emotion. He loved her. But he'd have to tell her once more that they couldn't be together. He couldn't be her saviour. It just wasn't right.

But now wasn't the time.

Her mother tactfully left them together and they chatted easily, as if nothing had changed. Steve felt his heart tug when it was time to go. He didn't want to leave.

"I'll be back tomorrow," he said.

Outside, Deena grabbed him by the arm. "Thanks for coming," she said again.

"That's OK."

"I didn't want to call you really, but Caroline insisted; she said if she didn't see you she'd try again. She said it was all my fault for breaking you up."

Steve touched her arm. "It's not your fault. It's mine; I should have never started anything."

"No, you shouldn't have." Her previous anger had been muted, as if she didn't have the strength to argue anymore. "You know, you're her only visitor."

"Oh."

"I've phoned her dad again and again, but he hasn't even bothered to turn up."

She paused as Steve took in the information, and then continued.

"And she doesn't want her friends to know what's happened."

Steve couldn't think of any words to comfort her. All he wanted was to help Caroline get better. "I'll be back tomorrow," he said.

48

Katie carefully applied her mascara in the bathroom mirror. She stepped back and surveyed her appearance, considering her blue dress. It was a little creased on the sleeves, but she didn't have time to iron it. All the attention would be on Sam anyway, so she supposed no one would notice a few creases.

She smiled at herself in the mirror, checking that she didn't have any lipstick on her teeth, then went back into the bedroom.

Renée was standing with her back to the mirror, trying to do up the zip up on her dress. The fabric of the dress was already stretching over Renée's bump, and the zip was only a quarter of the way up.

"Do you need help?" Katie asked.

"Yes, please." Renée turned round and lifted her long dark hair up so that Katie could see what she was doing.

Katie pulled at the zip. It moved a couple of inches further up and then stuck. Katie stared at it. "I don't want to rip your dress," she said. "Do you have anything else you could wear?"

"I only have one dress with me. I bought it a month ago. I didn't realise I'd grow so fast." Renée put her hand over her stomach protectively.

"I'll try again," Katie said. "Breathe in."

"I shouldn't have had breakfast," Renée said.

Katie laughed. "I'm not sure that would have helped." She tugged at the zip, and this time it gave, and rushed up Renée's back. Renée grunted.

Katie looked at the time. "We'd better go," she said. She picked up her shawl from the bed and adjusted it in front of the full-length mirror by the door. She needed to get it in exactly the right place. Her dress revealed some cleavage, and with the shawl round her shoulders there was sometimes an unsightly gap of flesh between the pale blue shawl and her dress. She adjusted the shawl until her chest was completely covered. "OK, let's go," she said as she slipped her shoes on.

Downstairs in reception, Dave and Andy were already waiting. Dave sat on the sofa and Andy was standing in the farthest corner of the room, staring out of the window. Katie looked at Renée. She couldn't imagine how difficult this must be for her. Renée had woken her up frequently in the night with her tossing and turning. She must be worried about today.

James was nowhere to be seen. He hadn't turned up for breakfast, but Katie had thought nothing of it. She had only just made it down herself. Her head was pounding from her hangover, but she'd forced the food down. It was going to be a long time until the food at the wedding, and she didn't want her stomach to rumble during the ceremony.

Andy came over. "Have you seen James?" he asked her. He didn't seem to be able to bring himself to look at Renée.

"No," Katie replied.

"I'll go back and hurry him up then. I think he might have fallen back to sleep."

Andy left quickly, and returned with James ten minutes later. James reeked of booze and his white shirt was unbuttoned. Despite their heavy drinking session the night before, Katie hadn't expected this from James. It was out of character. At university he had been notorious for drinking everyone else under the table, but having no sign of a hangover the next day.

Something must be wrong. She would talk to him later and see if she could get to the bottom of it.

Renée had always been together too, and Katie started to wonder whether it was those who appeared to be most in control who were actually the least in control. It was like the world was a different place all of a sudden, and everything was the opposite of what you thought it was. She would talk to James at the reception. He was probably just relaxing because it was a wedding, but she felt the need to just check he was OK.

They finally left the hotel and made their way towards the church. The sky was cloudless and the sun shone through, unfettered. The men strode ahead, their shoes thudding against the pavement, not thinking to wait for Renée and Katie. Katie was wearing four-inch heels, which were completely impractical even for this short walk. She tottered along, holding her arms out comically and avoiding the cracks in the pavement. Renée walked beside her. Renée's dress was too tight round her legs, which also made walking difficult and slowed them down further. She lifted it up to her knees to make it easier as the men walked on oblivious.

Katie started to sweat in her sensible shawl, but she didn't want to go to the effort of unravelling it just so she could put it back on in the church. Churches were always drafty no matter what time of the year it was.

As she walked, the shawl kept riding up and she felt a breeze across her cleavage. She tugged it down, even though she could already feel it starting to unravel beyond her control. She knew it wouldn't look right by now anyway.

She hadn't talked to Renée about the pregnancy since the night before. But she now felt brave enough to ask the question that was bothering her.

"Renée?"

"Yeah."

"Why don't you take a paternity test?" It had occurred to her and Dave last night when they'd been drinking. Renée could just take a paternity test and find out whether Dave or Andy was the father. Then Dave might be off the hook. Andy and Renée would have slept together loads of times, whereas with Dave and Renée it had been just once. So it was unlikely that Dave would be the father anyway. If they could just confirm that, then Dave wouldn't need to worry anymore.

"Sorry?" Renée said, pretending her attention was fully occupied just by walking.

"The baby. You could take a test; find out who the father is."

"I'm too far gone," Renée said. "I can't do it until it's born."

"Oh. OK."

"Are you in a relationship?" Renée asked, changing the subject.

"Kind of," she said, thinking of Daniel. It was over between them, but she didn't want Renée to think she was alone, or that she was jealous because the baby might be Dave's.

"How's it going?"

"Fine," she said, and then added. "Actually it's great. Daniel's great."

"Good," Renée said, "I'm pleased for you. I was worried you might be annoyed about the baby. You know, because of Dave."

"Don't worry." Katie had to turn away to hide her glassy eyes. Renée began to walk just a little bit faster, and Katie knew that the conversation was over.

*

They arrived at the church before the bridal car, and she and Renée slid into a pew at the back, beside James, Andy and Dave. James stunk of stale alcohol and was lolling in the pew alarmingly. Renée looked at Katie, indicated towards James, and they both laughed. Maybe there was nothing wrong with him, Katie thought. She was probably being oversensitive.

The church looked stunning, and Katie saw that all Sam's

wedding preparations had paid off. Light shone through the stained glass window and illuminated the blue hydrangeas decorating the ends of each pew. The church was about half full, with family and close friends eagerly occupying the first few rows and the rest of the guests sitting at the back. Sam's side of the church was sparsely populated compared to Patrick's, and there were a few empty rows between the guests at the back and the family at the front. Katie wondered if they should move forward, but they had already caused a bit of disturbance by arriving late, and she decided it wasn't worth it.

She looked at Patrick. He was tall and moderately good-looking, probably in his late thirties. If Katie hadn't known certain things about him, she would have been quite attracted to him, but she was worried about the way he treated Sam. She observed him now, standing at the altar in his kilt, tapping his leg impatiently as he spoke to his best man.

She felt a rush of nausea. She had been intending to speak to Sam about Patrick before the wedding. Her memory was hazy, but she had a vague recollection of trying to call Sam from the bar the previous night. She paled. She hoped she hadn't called her up drunk the night before her wedding to ask her to call it off. She tried to interrogate her memory, but she couldn't remember clearly.

At the front of the church, she could see Sam's Aunt Liv repeatedly turning round and staring towards the church door and then checking her watch. There was no sign of Sam's mother, and Katie remembered Sam saying at the hen-night that her mother would arrive with her in the bridal car.

She looked at her own watch. The wedding should have started half an hour ago. She looked anxiously at the door. She really hoped she hadn't called Sam last night. What if she was the reason Sam wasn't here yet?

She nudged Dave, who was sitting beside her. "Last night . . . did I call Sam?"

Dave grinned at her. "No, you didn't. You wanted to, but we took the phone away from you."

She breathed a sigh of relief. If Sam didn't turn up now, at least she knew it wasn't her fault.

Sam was probably behind the door, preparing. Brides were always late, weren't they? She looked back to Patrick, who was stone-still beside the altar. No one was speaking to him anymore. They all stared at the door.

The door opened with a creak, and a woman in a red dress came in with her husband. There were tuts from the front of the church as the door swung shut behind them. From her vantage point at the back, Katie had been able to see outside when the door had opened and she had seen no flash of white dress, only the green and grey of the graveyard.

She turned to Renée and whispered, "I don't think she's coming."

"Really?" Renée's eyes widened. "I saw her yesterday."

"You did?"

"Yeah, here, at the church."

There was a snore from Renée's left and they realised that James must have fallen asleep. Renée nudged him awake.

"You know, I hope I didn't put her off."

Katie was intrigued. "Why? What did you say?"

"Just about me and Andy."

"The baby?"

"No, the separation, actually. It didn't seem that inappropriate at the time, the conversation just kind of flowed that way."

Katie smiled, relieved. Hopefully Sam had decided to call the wedding off on her own. She wondered where she was now. She hoped she was alright.

Dave leant over to talk to them. "Do you think she's a no-show?"

"I don't know."

Dave nudged James. "No show," he whispered theatrically. James started to stand up, but Renée pushed him down.

"Is it over?" James asked.

"No," said Katie and Renée, together.

The boys started a conversation about the football they were missing for the wedding. Katie noticed that Sam's aunt had left the pews at the front. Patrick was pacing up and down. The best man touched his shoulder, and Patrick spun round aggressively and then walked up the aisle and out of the church.

"Is it over now?" asked James, pulling himself out of his slump and sitting up straight.

"Yes," Andy said.

"Shall we go to the pub then?"

There was nothing better to do.

49

Sam stared at the pink floral wallpaper in the room at her mother's house. She had lain there all night staring at the ceiling, scared by the inevitable events of the next day. Finally, when the sun had started to shine through the thin curtains, she had realised that there was no going back. It was too late for anyone to come and pick her up and force her back up north to get married. She would not be marrying Patrick. At this point of certainty she'd finally been able to get to sleep, until her vivid dreams were interrupted by the sound of her phone ringing.

She looked at it suspiciously. Its insistent ringing symbolised all the pressure that had built up within her in the last year, and all the friends and family she knew she was letting down. The number was an unknown one, and when she looked at her watch she knew it would be the woman responsible for her hair and make-up wondering where she had got to. Luckily the hairdresser didn't have her mother's phone number and therefore couldn't make enquiries elsewhere. Instead she tried to ring every fifteen minutes.

Sam lay awake listening to the ringing, knowing that in one hour, when her mother came to pick her up from the hairdresser's, the ringing would intensify. She switched the phone off and eased herself out of bed. She opened the curtains and stared out onto the street. A boy cycled by and cars went about their daily business. The next door neighbour was watering his garden. It was the middle of a heat-wave, a sunny Saturday in June. The weather was even better than Sam had hoped for for her wedding day.

The night before, she had arrived at her mother's house just after midnight and let herself in. She had felt a wave of relief. The house she had been trying for years to escape finally felt like home. Despite the time, she had made herself a cup of tea and sat on the sofa and watched a repeat of *Coronation Street*. She decided the life of soap operas and tea that her mother led wasn't so bad after all. She thought of her mother and the bravery it must have taken to stand up to her father. For the first time she admired her.

She put on shorts and a T-shirt. She thought how hot she would have been in the huge layered wedding dress she had always wanted. Instead of sparkling high heels, she put on sensible sandals, and went outside into the sunshine. She felt free. She left her phone on the bed.

It was an ordinary Saturday, and out of habit she found herself making her way to the library. It was busy, with the Saturday children's session in one corner and a long queue at the desk. At first no one noticed her. But before she could go and hide in between the shelves amongst all the books, they spotted her.

"Sam!" The confusion was written on their faces.

"What are you doing here? I thought ... We thought ..." They looked at each other, unsure what to say next. They thought they had to cover for her today.

"I didn't go through with it," she said. She was surprised by how calm her voice sounded.

Their eyebrows raised simultaneously. Their eyes asked so many questions, and eventually an appropriate one slipped out.

Do you want a cup of tea?"

"Yes, please."

They all decamped to the staff room, leaving the Saturday girl to deal with the ever-lengthening queue.

*

After three cups of tea in the staffroom, Sam felt much better. She had thought the other librarians might disapprove of her last-minute change of heart, but they had all been supportive. The worst thing that could possible happen had happened, and it really wasn't so bad.

When the others had to go back to work, she volunteered to help out, stacking shelves and manning the check-outs. The library felt like home. And at five thirty, when she strolled home, it was still sunny. For the first time in ages she felt happy and free.

Then she saw her mother's car on the driveway, and she felt sick. She opened the front door slowly. Her mother must have rushed back from the wedding.

Her mother came to the door to greet her.

"Hi Sam."

"Hi."

Suddenly her mother's arms were around her. "Are you alright?" she asked.

"Yeah," Sam replied, surprised.

"We were all worried about you."

"I'm sorry."

Her mother hugged her harder. "What happened? Did he hit you?"

"Sometimes." She felt relieved to say it, to get it off her chest.

"You know, I noticed the bruise yesterday and I wondered. You couldn't quite conceal it with make-up. You tried the way I used to. I was going to ask you, but I didn't want to ruin your day."

"Thanks," Sam said.

Her mother hugged her tighter. "You were brave, Sam – a lot braver than I was. I should have chucked out your father years before I worked up the courage."

Sam nodded, understanding.

"People don't change," her mother said. "You're better off well away from him."

Sam thought of her father, and how much she had wanted him to come to the wedding. About how he'd never replied to her letters. Perhaps her mother was right.

50

Katie tried to roll over to snuggle back into the sheets, but they seemed to be weighed down and she couldn't get enough of them around her. She reached out to pull them harder and her arm felt the warmth the skin of another person.

Oh god. What had she done?

What day was it?

She started to remember. It was the day after the wedding . . . Had she slept with one of the wedding guests? Now the memories were slowly coming back. The wedding hadn't happened. They had all gone to the pub.

She opened her eyes slowly and observed the back of the head beside her. The way the dark hair curled round towards his neck . . .

It was Dave.

She wriggled a bit to try and get comfortable, but she realised that they were sharing a single bed. This was never going to work. She needed more sleep.

She found her watch on the floor by the bed and looked at the time. Five a.m. If she crept back to the room she was sharing with Renée now she would able to get a few more hours' sleep.

She knew from experience that it wasn't worth hanging around after she'd slept with Dave. In the morning there was half a sense of regret and half a sense that he just wanted to get on with whatever he had planned that day. She'd been here enough times before. He never wanted to linger in bed with her. She really should stop doing this to herself.

She stumbled across the bedroom to the bathroom. The other bed was in the centre of the room, and Katie vaguely remembered her and Dave trying to drag it across the room to make a double bed, before giving up and collapsing on Dave's bed. She observed herself in the mirror. Her make-up was streaked all over her face. She would have to take it off once she got back to her room.

She went back into the bedroom and found her dress from yesterday. It had a pale stain down the front that she suspected was white wine. She put her clothes back on. She found her shoes across the other side of the room and picked them up. It would be easier to carry them.

She surveyed the room once more. Dave was still sleeping soundly. She gave him one last kiss on the cheek, and left.

She wasn't going to do this to herself again. She had to move on.

*

Dave woke to the sound of his phone ringing. It was James.

"Mate, it's check-out time"

God. He glanced round the room. It was a tip. He'd have to pack all his stuff up quickly and then just get out of there. "I'll be down in a sec," he said.

Where was Katie? She'd come home with him last night, but she seemed to have already left. He frowned. She never left before the morning.

He liked it when she stayed and tried to make him stay in bed with her all morning. It made him feel wanted, needed. And anyway he had wanted to talk to her.

The others had gone to bed early last night, and he'd been left with Katie and James. He and Katie had talked and talked.

It had been good to just chat. He had almost forgotten about Renée and the baby and all the other things that were weighing him down.

When James had passed out, they'd put him to bed before heading up here. Luckily Dave was supposed to be sharing the room with Steve, so he had the room to himself.

Things had been the same as ever last night, but they had also been different. When he had been chatting to Katie, he hadn't only been thinking about that night. He'd been thinking past that night: how good it was to talk to her, how nice it would be to have dinner with her, how much fun it would be to spend more time with her. He had thought of Rachel and how manipulative she was, and how honest and genuine Katie was in comparison.

He'd needed to escape his life, and Katie was always a welcome escape. He loved being with her. She was always there. But now she wasn't. She had left him. He wanted her, but he couldn't have her. He felt a strange feeling of regret, and realised that he already missed her.

51

Katie turned her key in the lock and let herself into the house. She was relieved to be home after the weekend. She felt drained by all the emotion of it.

Without Steve's car, Andy, Dave and James had to take the train back with her and Renée. They couldn't find seats together on the train, and they had separated. She had slept all the way to London. When they got off the train they reunited to say goodbye and then went their separate ways. She hadn't spoken to Dave properly since the night before, but that was entirely normal for them. She had promised herself after university that she would stop sleeping with him if he didn't want a relationship. But seven years later, she was still in the same position. She wasn't going to do it again.

Despite sleeping through the journey back to London, her hangover meant that she still felt tired. Now she just wanted to lie down and go to sleep.

"Hello?" she called out, thinking it odd that her mother hadn't heard the door when she'd come in. She wandered into the kitchen and saw her mother sitting at the kitchen table, staring out over the garden. Something was wrong.

She coughed, and her mother looked up.

"Oh. Katie." Her mother wiped her eyes with the back of her hand.

"What's wrong?" she asked, fearful. She sat down in the chair next to her mother.

"It's you grandfather. He . . . he died." Her voice faltered.

Katie gasped and took her mother's hand. "When?"

"On Friday."

Katie thought back to Friday, when she'd spent a leisurely afternoon shopping and then taken the train up to the wedding. She hadn't wanted to be in the house with Daniel. But if she'd been there, could she have stopped it happening?

"What happened?" she asked.

"He just gave up, I suppose. Daniel put him in bed for his afternoon nap and he didn't wake up."

"Oh." She tried to digest the news. Her grandfather wasn't here anymore. He wasn't upstairs, asleep in her old room. He wasn't about to come down in his stair-lift. He wouldn't need bathing in the mornings, or need his meals cooked, or need help going to the toilet. He was just gone.

"Why didn't you tell me?" she said, thinking that she hadn't really needed to go shopping, that she could have gone home, said goodbye to him, helped out afterwards, looked after her mother.

"I didn't want to spoil the wedding for you."

She sat with her mother for a while longer before going upstairs. Once upstairs, she couldn't stop herself from peering into her old room. The bed was neatly made and her grandfather's clothes were folded on the chair. The large-print Agatha Christie book still lay on the bedside table, with a bookmark halfway through.

She shut the door and went back to her brother's room and lay down on the bed. So that was that. It was hard to absorb the news, hard to think that she wouldn't see her grandfather again.

She thought of Daniel. He had found him. What must that have been like? Was it strange for him, or was it so much a part of his job that he was used to it? She imagined him finding her grandfather, cold in the bed, and checking for a pulse. She knew he'd have been calm and known what to do. He had always seemed to accept the ebb and flow of life and death around him. She remembered him telling her about another one of his clients who had died. It must happen all the time.

Daniel wasn't coming back. When she had asked her mother what had happened, she had explained how helpful Daniel had been on the day, how he had helped with all the practical arrangements as well as comforting her. Katie had felt a tinge of jealousy at their closeness.

She wished she'd spoken to her grandfather more. She wished she'd learnt about his life before her and before her mother. Who was he before he was the frail old man? She hadn't seen him much when she was a child, so that was the only grandfather she knew.

Her mother had said she could have her old room back next week, but she didn't want it. Not yet. If she took it back it would be like he'd never been there, and he'd disappear into just a memory. If she stayed in her brother's room, she could pretend he was still there, snoring gently or reading his book.

As for Daniel . . . she wished she'd said goodbye. And she wished she'd had the chance to thank him.

52

Dave sat in his chair in the office pretending to be concentrating on the folders of paperwork that lay in front of him as he thought about everything that was going on in his life.

He had given up trying at work long ago. When he had starting stealing from the others it had seemed kind of pointless to keep up the pretence of being a good employee. It would have felt like he had double standards, like he was being dishonest.

He checked his emails. Rachel wanted to meet for lunch. He needed company. He needed distractions from his thoughts, and the chance to feel young again.

He replied. "Why not?"

When he was with Rachel he felt carefree. They stole pint glasses from pubs and rang people's doorbells late at night when they were drunk. The kinds of things that fathers never did.

Fifteen minutes later they were in the pub. Rachel let him buy her a drink and they ordered burgers, his with bacon and cheese and hers a veggie burger.

They sat and sipped their drinks.

"They know," she said.

"Know what?" he asked, studying the menu for real ales

and thinking he must come back to this pub and sample a few.

"About the money."

He was alert now. "Shhh . . ." he said, leaning forward and whispering.

She laughed. "You worry too much. They were always going to find out eventually. They always do."

Dave absorbed this, wondering how many times she had done this sort of thing before. He didn't want to ask.

She saw his worried expression.

"Don't worry, they don't suspect you. You're much too sweet and innocent. I read their emails. They suspect me." Her eyes flashed indignantly, as if she was deeply offended that they didn't trust her.

"What are you going to do?"

Their burgers came, and Rachel took the salt from the middle of the table and poured it liberally on her chips. She opened the burger and took the tomato out, placing it unceremoniously on the side of her plate.

"I'm going to leave. Tonight."

*

There was no movement except the gentle tap of Rachel's fingers on the keys. Everyone except she and Dave had left, and the open-plan office spread out before them, dark and hazy, except for the tiny flashing LEDs on computer monitors.

"What are you doing?" he asked, standing over her.

"Paying myself," she said, without taking her eyes off the screen.

He watched her go quickly through the system, pulling up her own file and increasing the figures under salary and bonus.

She was completely calm.

"Have you done this before?" he asked, unsure if he knew her at all. This was fraud, wasn't it? It was different from taking a tenner from someone's handbag when they weren't looking.

"I doubled my salary on my first day. No one except HR looks at the payslips and they don't know what they're supposed to say."

"Oh," he said, thinking of all the times she had sat doing nothing while he had got on with the filing and made the tea.

"Now I'm adding a bonus to this month's pay-packet. It's a bigger number. They might pick it up, but by the time they do, I'll be gone."

She turned to him. "Do you want to come with me?"

"Where are you going?"

"France."

Dave wanted more than anything to get away, to prove he was young and free. He pictured Renée and the curve of her stomach, the baby growing inside her. Could he leave it? Could he pretend nothing ever happened? Leave with a free conscience and run away to France?

"I'll come," he said.

53

Steve stepped off the crowded London bus with a sigh of relief. It had taken him over an hour, but finally he was at the hospital. He crossed the road quickly and strode towards the automatic doors.

Caroline was being discharged today, and Deena had suggested that he come to help. Unable to ignore such a clear signal that she was softening towards him, he had cancelled meeting some friends for lunch in favour of a trip to the large grey hospital.

When he arrived at the ward, he saw Caroline sitting on the plastic chair next to her bed reading a magazine while Deena busied herself, neatening the bedcovers and tucking in the sheets. He coughed, and mother and daughter turned simultaneously. Caroline jumped up, abandoning her magazine to wrap her arms around him and squeeze him tightly.

"I told you he would come," she said to her mother.

Deena forced a smile and came over to greet him.

"Hi, Steve." Her eyes were accusatory, as if by being late he had let Caroline down again. He unlocked himself from Caroline's arms and turned to face her.

"I took the bus," he said hurriedly. "It took ages."

She nodded curtly, dismissing him. "I think we're ready

now. Let's go." She turned to Caroline. "Are you OK to walk down?"

"Of course, I'm not an invalid."

They made an awkward trio, walking through the hospital corridors in silence, Caroline walking between Steve and her mother, setting the pace, clutching her magazine. Steve was carrying her small flowered hold-all; her mother was holding her discharge notes.

When they reached the car park, Caroline breathed in the fresh air gratefully and Steve reached for her hand. When he turned round to smile at her, he noticed she had tears running down her cheeks.

"What's wrong?" he asked, gripping her hand tighter.

She replied in a whisper. "Nothing. I'm just glad to have you back."

He didn't know how to respond. Her mother was beside him, looking for where she had parked the car. He wanted to kiss Caroline deeply, to tell her it was true, that he was back, but he didn't. He had gained her mother's trust and he couldn't lose it now.

Eventually Deena spotted her old Polo, obscured by the van parked beside it. Steve climbed into the backseat with Caroline. Her mother frowned at them in the rear-view mirror, but said nothing. The car lurched forward out of the parking space, and the brakes creaked as she took a turn a bit too fast.

"Where shall I drop you off?" she asked him.

"Anywhere near the tube is fine."

"Why don't you come back with us?" said Caroline.

Her mother frowned, and then glanced in the mirror and saw Caroline's tear-stained face.

"Yes, that's a good idea," she said. "I'll make you some coffee and you and Caroline can chat."

Twenty minutes later they pulled up outside a 1930s semi in Ealing, with a neat front garden and a dirty white facade.

Caroline had always been secretive about where she lived, and Steve entered tentatively, as if he were invading someone else's space. Inside, the house was warm and welcoming, family pictures of Caroline and her mother covering the every available surface. The whistle of the kettle drowned out the underlying hum of the motorway as Deena made him a cup of coffee.

*

Later that afternoon, they sat and watched TV together. Caroline's mother was wedged between him and Caroline on the sofa.

Steve looked at his watch. "It's late. I'd better be off. I've got work tomorrow."

He reached over and kissed Caroline's mother on the cheek, then paused and repeated the action with Caroline.

Caroline looked panicked. "Can't you stay here?"

"Well, no, I don't want to intrude."

Caroline looked at her mother.

"Steve needs to go, love. I'll just go and get the car out of the garage, so I can take him back. "

Her mother left the room and they heard the front door shut behind her. In an instant, Caroline was beside him, kissing him hard on the lips. He absorbed her hungrily, his feelings for her flooding his consciousness. It was a full minute before he came to his senses and pulled away.

"I've missed you." She grinned impishly.

He tried to remind himself that she was fifteen. It couldn't work.

"I've missed you too," he said. He heard the engine of the car outside the house.

He wanted to pause his life and hold this moment, before reality hit him. He leant forward and gave her a quick peck on the lips, determined to feel her lips against his for the final seconds before her mother came back into the house.

"You've got to go," she said, pulling away as they heard the front door open again, and her mother call out from the corridor.

"Yeah," he said.

He walked out of the living room and into the hallway, feeling an uncomfortable combination of elation and dread.

54

Renée sipped her coffee as she waited for Andy. The coffee shop was half full on this rainy Saturday morning. In one corner, students huddled around laptops and talked in loud voices about an assignment they were working on. At the opposite end of the shop, three older men sat on separate tables, papers spread out around them. A woman was feeding a baby at a table by the counter.

The last time she'd spoken to Andy had been in the pub after the wedding. He had calmed down a bit by then, and they had found a quiet spot and chatted. She'd explained carefully that the timing of her pregnancy meant that either he or Dave was the baby's father. He'd been angry, but more with Dave than with her. He'd avoided Dave for the rest of the day and had left the pub long before the rest of them. She had been tired of drinking lemonade and had thought about leaving too, but she had stayed to talk to Katie.

Andy had phoned the previous week, suggesting they meet up. She had been pleased to hear from him. A part of her was afraid that the wedding might have been their last meeting and that after that he would disappear from her life entirely. When they'd spoken at the pub, he hadn't mentioned all the plans he'd made to connect with the child. She supposed that if he wasn't the father, he wouldn't be interested, which was fair enough. She wondered what Dave would do if *he* was the father. She'd hardly spoken to him at the wedding and hadn't heard from him since.

Renée had returned to her previous conclusion, that the baby was hers and hers alone. A part of her felt relieved, and part of her was scared. She had already started looking in the outskirts of London for a place of her own for when the baby was born. Her parents had offered to let her move back in with them, but she knew that wasn't what she wanted. She'd be happier living independently. She'd bought all the baby books she could find, and was well-prepared for the sleepless nights and the crying.

She felt happier now, like she was working through things and sorting them out. She felt back to her old self. When Andy had rung her to suggest they meet, she had only felt familiarity when she heard his voice, rather than regret.

She still missed him, but in a distant way, and memories of him interrupted her at the most inappropriate moments: choosing tomato ketchup in the supermarket (Andy would only have Heinz); in the park when she saw children feeding the ducks; looking through other people's holiday photos. She was happy without him, or at least surprisingly content.

She still thought about him a lot, but she didn't think about getting back together. She thought of the baby instead. The baby was her future. Their future would be entwined no matter what happened. It made her feel at peace.

She saw Andy enter the shop, flustered. She didn't stand or wave, but watched as he scanned the tables until he spotted her. He waved and smiled and she smiled back. He came over to see if she wanted coffee and then went to the counter to get himself one. He seemed nervous and she felt herself tensing.

He brought back his coffee and sat down.

"How are you?" he asked.

"Good," she said, and nodded as if to confirm this to herself.

"And you?"

"Good, good." He fidgeted in his seat.

"So, how come you wanted to meet?" Renée asked, trying to sound businesslike.

"I've got the divorce papers."

"Here? Oh." Divorce seemed so final. There would be no going back. She felt her face flush.

Andy reached out and touched her hand. "It's only procedure."

"We never talked about divorce." She supposed it was the next logical step, but she hadn't thought about it.

"What else is there?" he asked.

"I don't know." Just a couple of months ago he had asked her to move in with him. She felt the tears sting her eyes and she could hear them exposing her in her voice.

"Renée, don't cry."

He put his arm round her, but it didn't feel natural. She leant away from him.

"I wanted to tell you in person," he said.

"Why?"

"Actually I wanted to apologise."

"Oh."

"I just wanted to say I'm sorry. I'm not sorry it ended, but I'm sorry I hurt you. That's all."

She said nothing, and silent tears rolled down her face.

"Is that it?" she asked, downing the rest of her coffee and picking up her bag. She felt tired and wanted to lie down.

"No. I also wanted to tell you something."

"What?"

He stumbled over the words. "If the baby's mine, I'd like joint custody."

Renée stared at him, shocked.

He continued quickly. "I've met someone. Her name's Sabrina. You'll like her, I'm sure. She's lovely. We're planning to move into the old flat in Wimbledon when the lease runs out. She'll help with the baby, so there's no need to worry."

"Oh." She couldn't think of anything else to say. One minute he was asking her to move back in with him, the next he was asking a new girlfriend. The last thing she wanted was Andy and his new girlfriend bringing up her baby in their old flat. They would soil the memories of the happy times she and Andy had had together there. She thought of all the hard work they had put in to buy it.

He couldn't just move his girlfriend in, she realised. Half the flat belonged to her.

"I think we should sell the flat," she said.

"Well, how about I buy your half out?"

"No," she said, although she couldn't think of a logical reason to object.

"Well, think about it. It will be good for you. It's gone up in value since we bought it, and you could use the money to put a deposit down for a place for you and the baby."

He'd thought everything through.

"I have to go," Renée said.

"OK . . . Just make sure you let me know the results of the paternity test when you take it."

"You know it won't be until after the baby's born?"

"Yes, you said." He sounded calm. "Once we know for sure, then we can talk about joint custody. But I have a good feeling about this." He grinned at her and patted her arm.

"It might not be yours," she said.

"I know," he said. "Just make sure you let me know."

She nodded, and then got up and left the cafe, fighting back tears. The baby wouldn't be hers alone, she'd have to share it with Andy and "Sabrina".

In another life, he would have seen she was upset and followed her out of the cafe, but that life was over now. When she glanced back, just once, he was still calmly sipping his coffee.

55

Dave sat alone on the old sofa in the living room of Rachel's house in France, drinking a beer. Outside, recycling trucks thundered by, sending tiny shivers through the house. It was warm, but Dave was reluctant to open the window during the day and let in the smog from the recycling plant at the end of the road.

He rested his feet on the small plastic table in the middle of the room, and it sagged slightly under his weight. Everything in the house was old, falling apart, or not there at all. The house had been completely empty when they moved in, and they were gradually acquiring furniture, piece by piece. Rachel slept in the main bedroom upstairs, on the only bed, whilst Dave was restricted to the sofa where he sat now.

He sighed. A life in France in the summer without any work should be idyllic, but it felt like circumstances were conspiring against him to make things difficult. He had thought he had escaped the daily drudgery of working for Craig and his life in London, but it seemed he had exchanged one set of irritations for another.

But he didn't want to go home. Home was a land where there were various axes hanging over him: the imminent birth of Renée's child, the possibility of his stealing being discovered, his confusion over his feelings for Katie. No, it was much easier here, in France, away from it all.

The front door banged shut, announcing Rachel's return. Dave heard the familiar sound of deep voices downstairs alongside Rachel's high-pitched laughter.

Rachel came into the living room, followed by the two dark-haired Frenchmen. Their green recycling plant uniforms were covered in dust. Dave suspected they had brought some old furniture with them, or else Rachel had conned them into fixing the leaky shower or the plumbing. Usually the presence of the local men meant something needed fixing in the house. Rachel could be charming when she wanted to be.

She opened three beers and handed one each to the men, keeping the remaining bottle for herself.

"Merci," she said, clinking her bottle with each of theirs in turn and ignoring Dave, who stayed rooted to his spot on the tatty sofa. The sofa creaked as Rachel sat down beside him. The men leaned nonchalantly against the walls and began a rapid conversation in French, punctuated by Rachel's laughter and the occasional glance at Dave. He knew they were talking about him, but he had no idea what they were saying. His skin tightened over his knuckles as he gripped his beer bottle harder.

Eventually it was the end of the lunch hour and the men finished their beers and went back to work. Rachel and Dave sat beside in other in silence, drinking their beers.

"What are you planning to do today?" she asked.

"Not much," he replied, his voice almost drowned out by the sound of a lorry rattling down the road. "How about you?"

"Not much either, I guess. I might go to the pub later."

It was a statement, not an invitation. "OK," he said.

He took another sip of beer and thought back to when Rachel had first invited him to France. He wondered why she had done it. He suspected that, like most things with Rachel, it had just been a whim, a spur-of-the-moment kind of thing. He had agreed because it had sounded like an escape, a bit of fun. He had taken pleasure in telling his parents he was moving to France, in some way asserting his independence.

And somewhere, not too far from the surface of his mind, he had harboured fleeting fantasies of sleeping with her. She was attractive, daring, and fun to be around. And she was inviting him to live with her. It had seemed like a given.

He glanced sideways at her. Now he was living with her, any attraction he'd felt had vanished.

"So . . ." Rachel said. "Good morning?"

"Yeah," he replied. "Bit noisy though."

Rachel rose to it instantly, like he'd known she would.

"I don't see you complaining about having free accommodation." She had been as surprised as he had been to find that the village had been purpose-built for the workers at the plant. She had bought the property through an estate agent when she was still in the UK. She had paid for it outright.

"Maybe you should have done a bit more research before you put all your money into the house," he said.

She frowned. "It seemed like good value for three bedrooms."

"There was a reason for that."

"I'm the one who's earned enough to have my own house."

Dave swallowed, an unfamiliar feeling of anger rising within him. He was repulsed by her sense of entitlement. All her money was stolen, but she spoke in the tone of someone who'd been working for forty years.

She caught his expression and continued their familiar argument.

"It's not that easy. I've had to work in crappy jobs for crappy bosses for years, so I could build up a fund. And it's hard work not getting caught. You've got to always get temp jobs with the same HR system installed so you can hack in easily. It takes a lot of research."

He looked at her. She seemed to want congratulating for her cunning. Instead, he felt irritated that she had built up so much so quickly, when he'd been working for nearly seven years and didn't have a penny to his name.

"But you've only been working in your university holidays. I've been working for years."

Rachel laughed. "You still think I'm a student?"

"Aren't you?"

"Of course not! I'm in my thirties." She laughed again. "Even now, you just don't get it, do you?"

Dave swallowed. He glanced at her one more time, got up, and walked out of the living room and then the front door, into the glaring sun.

He walked briskly down the road, not caring where he was going. She was in her thirties? It didn't make any sense.

But then things started to fit together. She had always looked older than her years, always talked down to him as if he was a child, always regarded the others in the office with a casual disdain.

He was angry. Angry that she had fooled him like she had fooled all the others. Angry that she held him in the same contempt as she had held Craig and everyone else at the office, angry that she didn't think he was clever enough to see through her. But mostly he was angry with himself that he hadn't even suspected. She'd never sounded or acted like a student. He had only believed her because she had told him, and even when he had got on the plane to France with her, he hadn't thought otherwise.

He paused outside an internet café and considered booking a flight straight home. He went inside and sat down at one of the state-of-the-art computers. He wanted to talk to someone.

He opened up his email account and scanned through his emails. Aside from a whole bunch of marketing emails, the only other one was from his mother, enquiring about his new life in France. He sighed. There was nothing from Katie.

He wondered how much flights were, but he decided not to look them up. He had no intention of going home, back to the questions from Craig and the imminent birth of Renée's baby. He'd be able to make a life for himself in France, to do whatever he wanted, whenever he wanted. Perhaps he could fix up the house for Rachel, or perhaps he could run some kind of tourism website for Brits. He had options in France. His life was in his control.

He thought of Katie, and wondered what she was doing. The last time he had seen her they'd been in bed together. He missed her. She was the opposite of Rachel.

Since the wedding, she hadn't contacted him. Was it about the baby? Perhaps she didn't want to get involved with someone who might soon be a parent. Had the baby changed everything?

Maybe he should email her. Perhaps she could come out and visit him. She loved travelling. If anyone would visit, it was Katie. He imagined having her around the house, messing about and laughing. He turned to the computer and started composing an email.

56

James tossed and turned in bed. Clive had called a meeting with him first thing tomorrow, to discuss the results of the investigation. The inevitable scenario of his being fired was playing through his mind on a continuous loop.

He looked across at Meera's sleeping form and had a sudden desire to wake her up. Even Phoebe was sleeping soundly. A part of James hoped that Phoebe would wake, start crying and disturb Meera's sleep. Then he would have the chance to talk to her and explain what was happening.

But his wife and daughter looked so peaceful. He couldn't wake them. This was their last chance to be contented, safe from the worry he would inflict on them from tomorrow, when Clive tore up everything he had worked for.

Instead of waking them, he tossed and turned, trying to get comfortable. The sheets felt sweaty and too hot around his body. Five minutes later, he pulled back Meera's hair from her face, kissed her cheek, and slid out of bed, creeping silently over to Phoebe's cot and lifting her out. She murmured, and for a second he thought she would wake and scream, but he held her to his shoulder and she settled against him. He twisted his neck round to kiss her soft skin, then put her back in the cot.

He tiptoed downstairs to the kitchen and took the battered

plastic bottle from behind the bleach under the kitchen sink. He opened the bottle and smelt it, breathing in deeply.

He went into the living room, sank into the comfortable leather sofa, and drank it, gulp by gulp. He didn't try and hide it any more. He didn't mind if Meera found him. It would only bring the consequences of his actions forward by a few hours.

He felt better.

He surveyed the living room: the stylish wallpaper, the modern art, the antiques. It was his empire. It had taken him years to build, but tomorrow it would be gone. By tomorrow afternoon he wouldn't have a job; he would be gone by ten a.m., but he wouldn't be able to go home then, so he would probably go to the pub. In the evening, when he finally went home, he would have to tell Meera what had happened. He would lose her. He would lose Phoebe.

James took a final gulp of the vodka. His future was inevitable. He laid his head on the sofa and fell unconscious.

When he woke up, the light was streaming through the window. It was six a.m. He went upstairs and checked on Meera and Phoebe. They were still sleeping soundly. He gave them each a kiss on the cheek. Meera stirred but didn't wake.

He showered quickly, picked up his keys from the side and left the house. It was still early, but it was better to get out of the house before Meera saw him. He was sure she would notice that something wasn't right, and he couldn't bear her questions. It was best to get to work and get the inevitable over with. He would face Meera later.

*

At nine thirty a.m. Steve had already been in the office for two hours and was thinking about getting a coffee from the shop on the ground floor. He would just finish the paragraph he was writing and then take a break. He hummed to himself as he typed. Things were starting to improve. His house had finally been sold and he was packing up his things to move to a new flat. Deena was softening towards him, and he visited Caroline regularly after work. In a few weeks she would be sixteen. He felt a shiver of hope and excitement when he thought about it.

He jumped when Clive appeared suddenly above his desk. He stopped humming. Clive was the director of HR, and had never had cause to speak to Steve. He hoped he wasn't about to lose his job. Not now. Not after everything that had happened.

"Hi Steve. How are you?" Clive had a reputation for being jovial, but today he looked flustered.

"Good, thanks."

Clive got to the point. "You know James well, don't you?"

Steve breathed a sigh of relief. Clive didn't want to talk to him about his job. "Yeah, I do."

"Right. Do you know where he is today? We had a meeting at nine, and he hasn't turned up."

Steve looked at his watch. Nine twenty-one. The meeting must have been important for Clive to be chasing it up in person so soon after it was supposed to happen. "I don't know; perhaps he's stuck in traffic."

"Maybe, maybe," said Clive. He started to walk away, and then turned round. "Would you mind doing me a favour?"

"Sure."

"Can you give him a ring at home and tell him I'm looking for him?"

"OK."

Steve watched Clive walk away. He tried James's mobile first. No answer. Then he tried the house phone.

"Hello." The voice was muffled. He thought it was Meera's, but he couldn't be sure.

"Hi, is that Meera? It's Steve."

"Hi."

She was in tears. Steve had a sinking feeling. "What's wrong?"

"It's James."

"What's wrong, Meera?"

"Steve – it's James – a lorry hit his car."

"Is he in hospital?" As he spoke the words, Steve already knew the answer. If he had been in hospital, Meera would be there with him.

"No. He's not in hospital." She choked on the words, her sobs echoing down the phone. "He . . . he died at the scene."

"Stay there," he said. "I'm coming right over."

He grabbed his keys from his desk.

57

Dave pushed open the church door. Most people were already seated, arranged in some intuitive hierarchy: Meera and Phoebe at the front with James's family, and Meera's family in the row behind. On the other side of the aisle were the empty seats, reserved for the pall bearers.

Dave scanned the church until he spotted the back of Katie's head. She was seated about halfway down, and Dave walked slowly down the aisle towards her, taking care to tread softly, so his footsteps didn't echo round the church. He slid into the pew beside Katie and Renée, and they both looked up and nodded, the light reflecting off Katie's watery eyes. They murmured hello and then returned to staring forward, lost in thought.

He looked round the church. The gentle murmur of voices contrasted with the tense silence when they had waited for Sam at her wedding. The church was adorned with white lilies, hauntingly beautiful. A baby screamed at the back and his mother took him outside, his screams echoing around the waiting mourners. Dave's eyes followed the mother out and then he glanced at Renée. She was a lot bigger now. Soon that would be her.

He looked around for the father of the screaming baby.

He sat with the empty pushchair at the edge of the back pew, holding a bottle of milk. In a few months that could be him.

In front of the father sat a row of older men, who looked like they might be James's colleagues. They talked in whispers; then one laughed, and then clamped his hand over his mouth as he remembered where he was.

The first bars of the funeral march echoed, the church doors opened, and in came the coffin. The people rose in unison with a synchronised creak. James's brothers led in the coffin, staring straight ahead, eyes glazed, as if in another world. Behind them, James's father and uncle, and behind them, Steve and Andy. They walked rhythmically, Andy shell-shocked, Steve with tears running down his face. Dave watched, mesmerised.

Later, Steve delivered a speech. He begun by saying that he had been best man at James's wedding three years before, in a church just like this. His hands shook, and he dropped his piece of paper. He scrabbled around for it on the floor, but by the time he picked it up his face was red and his voice choked. He continued regardless, stumbling over each word of his speech, determined to pay James the tribute he deserved. When he finished, he returned to his pew at the front, put his head in his hands and sobbed. At this point, Phoebe started to scream. The vicar waited patiently while Meera calmed her down.

*

It was over in an hour. They all stood in the rain and watched as the coffin was lowered into the ground, while the priest delivered the final prayer under a red and white golfing umbrella. Meera threw the first earth, and the sound of it hitting the wood of the coffin was drowned out by the rain, which beat against the coffin and the more appropriate black and navy umbrellas of the mourners. Dave watched the earth turn to sludge and slide down the edges of the coffin.

That was James, he thought. *That is James.* But his mind couldn't quite comprehend it. He didn't expect people his age to die. He couldn't quite believe that he wouldn't see James again.

They returned to James and Meera's house; he took a taxi with Katie and Renée while Andy and Steve stayed behind and talked to the vicar.

The house seemed cavernous and empty, despite being full. Most of the people from the church had come back, and they stood around awkwardly in small clusters, nibbling at sandwiches. Meera was constantly accompanied by her mother, who seemed to be monitoring all conversations. Phoebe had been put to bed, and Dave wondered if Meera was glad not to have to deal with Phoebe's needs on top of everything else, or was already missing her daughter, her only connection to James and her excuse to leave awkward conversations on the pretence of a soiled nappy.

Dave had always been jealous of James. He seemed to do things so easily. He was motivated enough to work the long hours to get to the top, he had a beautiful wife and daughter, and he was always friendly, calm and easy-going. But now he knew that underneath his success he'd been hiding an alcohol problem. Steve had told him that James had been six times over the limit when the lorry hit his car. And he had been on his way to work.

He thought back to their university days. James had always been able to hold his drink better than anyone else, and seemed sober even after ten pints. Had he had a problem even back then? He had always assumed it was just another aspect of James's superhuman constitution. It fitted in with everything else in his life: he had landed the best job, he had a happy marriage – and he was the best at taking his drink.

Dave thought about how pissed James had been at the wedding. He had hardly been able to stand up. How much had he had to drink that night? And why hadn't anyone said anything? He couldn't remember them even talking about James, except to laugh at his hangover. They had all been distracted by the other dramas: Renée's baby; Sam leaving Patrick at the altar. Should they have done something?

He didn't really feel like talking to anyone, and yet he stood within the huddle of his friends, nodding in the right places. They all agreed that Steve's speech had been just right. They all thought the food was good. None of them could believe what had happened.

There didn't seem to be much to say.

He took a sip of water. Although alcohol was provided, most of it remained untouched, out of respect.

Renée was talking to Andy in the corner of the room, away from everyone else. Andy reached out and touched her stomach, and Dave felt a twinge of jealousy. The baby seemed so much more real now that Renée was bigger. It must be due soon. Would it look like him? Would he recognise it as a part of him as soon as he saw it? Or would it look alien to him, regardless of who the father was?

Realisation dawned. He wouldn't even see it for the first few months, at least. He had a plane booked back to France the next day.

He watched as Renée and Andy talked. This would be his last chance to speak to her before he went back. Katie was behind him.

"Go," she said.

"What?"

"I know what you're thinking. You need to talk to her. Go." She gave him a nudge in their direction.

When Dave reached Renée and Andy, Andy was describing all the things he was planning to do when the baby was older. "I can't wait to teach him to play football," Andy said, pointedly ignoring Dave.

"Him?"

"Well, if it's a boy. And I think it will be," Andy said confidently.

Renée shifted her weight awkwardly. Dave thought about walking away. Perhaps he'd got things wrong. Perhaps they had already taken the paternity test and the baby was confirmed as Andy's. Perhaps he was embarrassing himself.

"Shall we sit down?" Renée said suddenly, gripping her back.

"Yeah," he and Andy said in unison, and they went to the corner of the room where some wooden chairs had been laid out. They sat down, Andy on one side of Renée and him on the other. He needed to talk to Renée before the child was born.

"Renée," he said.

"Yeah?"

"If it's mine, I want to be involved."

Andy was respectfully silent.

"But you're living in France," Renée said, reasonably.

Dave thought of France, and Rachel, and the huge, empty house. "I'm not going back," he said.

"OK," she said, nodding.

"OK?"

"Yeah. You can see the baby, but on my terms, when it's convenient for me. Is that OK?"

"Yes," he said, surprised at his elation at her response.

There was an awkward silence, and then Renée stood up again. "We should speak to Meera," she said.

The three of them stood up and crossed the room to where Meera stood, elegant in a black dress.

"I'm sorry," Renée said.

"Thanks," Meera said.

"It must have been awful," Andy said, and Dave nodded.

"Yeah."

There was an awkward silence.

"If there's anything at all we can do, let us know," Andy said.

"Yeah," said Dave, impotently.

"I will do," Meera replied.

Steve and Katie appeared, and added their voices to the

condolences. Then Meera was whisked away by her mother to talk to a member of her family.

"It's awful," Katie said.

They all nodded, and Dave thought how incomplete the English language was. There were not enough words to describe pain, and each word spoken sounded empty and unsatisfactory.

"I can't believe he's gone," said Steve.

"Do you think we should have realised?" Katie asked in a whisper.

"He was really hung-over at the wedding," Renée said.

"Was he?" asked Steve, and Dave remembered he hadn't been there.

"I meant to speak to him after, but I didn't. I just forgot." Katie said, visibly shaken.

"What could we have done?" Andy replied.

58

Katie said her goodbyes and made her way out of the house onto the driveway. She heard hurried footsteps behind her, and turned.

"Hi Katie."

"Hi Dave." She looked at him quizzically.

"That was pretty intense."

"Yeah."

"I'd normally see if you wanted to go for a drink, but it doesn't seem appropriate."

"No, not today."

They ambled down the street together, in a comfortable silence.

"I'd offer you a lift, but you know I don't have a car." He grinned boyishly.

"I guess you don't need one in France."

"No, I suppose I don't."

"Well, I'm taking the bus and then the train," she said, matter-of-factly.

"Oh. I'm staying at a hotel." He pointed out a hotel across the road.

She knew what he was hinting at, but she wasn't cooperating anymore. She smiled to herself. "No, Dave, not this time."

"Oh." Dave stared at his shoes.

She felt liberated. It was the first time she'd ever done this successfully. She was proud of herself. Maybe she'd finally learnt her lesson with Dave. She didn't need him.

They walked towards the bus stop together. "I thought you were staying at the hotel."

"Yeah, I am."

"It's over there," she pointed.

"So it is." He didn't change direction. When they got to the bus stop he checked the times.

"Your bus isn't due for ten minutes. Come back to the hotel and talk to me, just for ten minutes."

"I'm visiting you in France soon, remember?" She had agreed to that, but she had told herself that she wouldn't sleep with him under any circumstances. There was no chance of it, anyway. He was shacked up with some girl over there.

"You can't come to France."

"So I'm uninvited because I won't go back to your hotel today? What do you want me for Dave, just sex?" It was the first time she had said it, but as the words tumbled out of her mouth she realised how true it was. It summed up their whole relationship.

"No," Dave said. "You can't come to France because I'm not going back to France."

Her curiosity was aroused. "Why not?"

"Well, partly because of the baby and partly because of you."

"Me?" She didn't want to go down this road again.

"Yeah you. I think we should try to make a go of things, you know, not just sex. A real relationship."

"You mean like going out to dinner, watching TV together? That kind of thing?" She frowned.

"Yeah, I guess I do. I realised I don't only like sleeping with you. I like being around you too."

"Well that's a compliment."

Katie could feel herself being won over, and tried to resist. Dave had never said anything like this to her before. In all the years they'd been sleeping together he'd never hinted that he wanted anything more than sex, although she had always been looking for indications that he felt otherwise.

"Why don't I take you out tomorrow?"

"Don't you have plans?"

"Not anymore. I was supposed to be on a plane."

She saw her bus coming, but chose not to notice it. Dave must have seen it too, because at that moment he leant in to kiss her. Not a drunken kiss in a dark corner of a nightclub. A full-blown sober kiss, in front of a queue of people at the bus stop. She looked up at him and smiled. Maybe he'd grown up.

People in the queue were piling onto her bus, and she pulled away from him and hurried to rejoin the end of the queue.

"I'll see you tomorrow then," she called out as she stepped onto the bus.

59

Steve and Andy piled the final bag of James's clothes into the back of Steve's car.

"That's everything," Steve said to Meera.

"Thanks," she said. "I couldn't have done it on my own."

"That's OK," Andy said. "You know we want to help."

"Do you want to come in for a bit, have some tea? Phoebe's asleep."

"OK," Steve replied, and they followed her back into the house to the living room and sat down on the sofas. Memories flashed through Steve's mind: introducing Caroline at the Christmas meal here, James offering him a job, the room crowded with guests after the funeral.

Meera brought out the tea on a tray and sat opposite them. "I wanted to ask you something," she said.

"OK."

She paused, and studied their faces. "Did you know how much James was drinking?"

Steve swallowed, a rush of guilt submerging him. He should have known. He should have noticed something was wrong. "I knew James liked a drink, like we all do," he replied. "But I didn't know how much he was drinking. I didn't know he had a problem."

He thought back to the boozy lunch he'd had with James. He had been more concerned about being caught out by the management than about James himself.

"I lived here and I didn't notice a thing," Andy said, his face drained of colour. "I'm so sorry, Meera."

She nodded, and stared into her tea. She was demure, sitting up straight on the sofa, and Steve knew how hard it must be for her to hold it all together.

"It was always hard for him," Meera said. "I'm not sure if you knew, but his brother was an addict. It was drugs for him, not alcohol. Coke. It tore his mother apart. And I think James . . ." She paused, holding back tears. "And I think James . . . he must have been scared of hurting her again. Scared of hurting me. He couldn't tell anyone."

Steve nodded, and Meera continued.

"His brother recovered, of course. Went to rehab. But James always felt that he had to be the steady one. For his mother."

Steve wondered why he had never known this, why James had never mentioned his brother. He thought back to the funeral. Two of James's brothers had been pall bearers. Steve could only picture their dark black suits and the backs of their heads. Their faces were a blur.

He went over to the sofa and put his arm round Meera. "It's OK," he said.

"How come I didn't notice?" she asked him. "How come I didn't see the signs?"

"None of us saw the signs," Andy said. "He hid it well. You can't blame yourself."

"Thank you." She was making a huge effort to remain composed.

"That's OK," Steve said awkwardly.

"I mean it," she said. "Thank you. I needed to ask you."

They drank the rest of their tea in silence. When they had finished, Meera seemed a little better and they asked if she wanted them to stay. She insisted that she needed time alone, and they got up to leave.

On their way home, they stopped at the bottle bank at the supermarket and emptied the half-full bottles of whisky and vodka they had found stashed around the house into the big green bin.

*

Steve got back to his empty house and paced up and down. The house had been sold, and hallway was full of boxes. Most of his things were packed, and he was now living in an upstairs bedroom. He was due to move out to his rented flat in four days' time, and the house no longer felt like home.

He wanted to just sit down, pour a glass of wine and relax. But he couldn't stop thinking about James. The number of spirits bottles hidden around the house had been startling. He didn't know how Andy had lived in the house and failed to notice James's problem. It seemed impossible. But then James had been good at hiding things.

Steve thought back to his first day at work, when he'd gone out for lunch with James. The clinks he'd heard from the boot of James's car must have been spirits bottles. James had become drunk and shaky, and yet he still hadn't put two and two together. When they'd gone for a drink after work, he had just gone on about his problems with Caroline and hadn't considered that James might have his own problems.

His phone beeped, interrupting his thoughts. The text was from Caroline:

Do you want to come over?

He needed to get away. He tapped out *yes* without thinking, and got straight in his car. When he arrived at Caroline's, she opened the door excitedly.

"Hello." She reached up and gave him a kiss on the lips and then disappeared into the house. He followed her.

"Mum's out," she said, turning to him and grinning broadly.

Steve felt his heart quicken. Since she'd been discharged from hospital, her mother had never left her side, a shadow behind them, always watching.

He looked at her, and she raised her eyebrow suggestively. There was nothing more he wanted when she leant in to kiss him. He felt the stress of the morning leaving him as he relaxed and forgot about James for the first time since the funeral. Before he knew it, she was unbuttoning his shirt.

He had promised himself he would wait until her sixteenth birthday. "No," he said. "Caroline, we can't."

She giggled. "But I want to."

"Caroline." His voice seemed weak compared to hers. She ignored his protests and grabbed his hand. Wordlessly she led him upstairs.

She had bunk beds, and she lay down on the bottom one and pulled him on top of her. He swung his legs round awkwardly to avoid hitting the wooden ladder that led to the top bunk. She pulled his face towards her and kissed him deeply, already unbuckling his belt.

Her eyes met his, and he grinned. There was no going back.

*

Afterwards, they lay squashed together in the single bed and Steve contemplated the wooden slats above him. He couldn't sit up properly because of the bed above, and he shifted his weight around awkwardly to get more comfortable.

Caroline turned to him, her face a couple of inches from his. "My friends said you were just using me. You weren't, were you?"

"No."

"You slept with me and then you left."

Was that how she saw it? "I left because you were under-age."

"I'm under-age now."

"I know."

Steve felt a familiar tension in his chest.

"Do you love me?"

"Yes," he answered honestly, thinking how soon she would be sixteen. He was suddenly hopeful and lightheaded.

"Do you think we'll get married?"

"Maybe later. You're too young." He brushed a stray strand of hair away from her face.

"You're too old." she said, irritated.

She looked at him. "Can I move in with you?"

Steve's thought about the new flat he had found. It could easily fit Caroline too. He thought how good it would be to see her every day.

"I'd like that," he said, stroking her hair.

60

Renée woke up woozy and tired. Her eyes felt glued together. She opened them slowly. Around her, grey-black objects started to identify themselves in the dark. She was in hospital.

She looked to her left and saw Elizabeth lying in her cot. She eased herself out of bed and went over to her. She marvelled at the baby's tiny hands and feet and screwed-up pinkish face. She could hardly believe that just the previous day Elizabeth had been wrapped up inside her, not yet real. Now that she was out in the world, she looked so innocent and fragile, fast asleep. Renée hoped that her life would be happy and contented. There was so much ahead of her.

She touched Elizabeth's cheek softly, as a wave of love washed over her. She was beautiful. Renée could pick out her own features in her: her rounded nose, her dark hair, the dimple on her chin. She looked for signs of Dave or Andy too, but could see none.

The nurse had explained to her how to order a paternity test. Soon she would have to share Elizabeth with one of them. She felt an irrational jealously. She didn't want Andy's girlfriend, Sabrina, anywhere near Elizabeth. She didn't want to share her.

She had sold her half of the flat to Andy, and he and Sabrina were now living in her old home in Wimbledon. She tried not to think about them sharing the bed she and Andy had bought together. She didn't want anything to do with him anymore. But if he was the father, he was destined to be part of her life forever. Andy wanted the three of them to meet to discuss custody. He'd told her that she'd like Sabrina, that they'd get on. But Renée had seen a picture of Sabrina, with her large, pert breasts and her bleached blonde hair. She didn't want to share custody of her child with her.

The only people Renée had told that the baby had been born were in her immediate family. Andy had been texting her daily for updates, but she had stopped replying. She would tell him tell him tomorrow. She needed time to herself first.

She leaned over the cot and kissed Elizabeth on the forehead. The baby woke, and started to cry. Renée lifted her out of the cot and held her in her arms, appreciating their time together before they found out who her father was; before everything changed and things got complicated once again.

61

Katie rolled over in bed and opened her eyes. The world was hazy in the sunlight that came through the faded green and yellow curtains of Dave's childhood bedroom. She looked round the room at the remnants of Dave's youth: the school football trophies on his desk, the shelf of CDs from the 90s. She felt closer to him than ever.

She looked at him and admired the way his wayward dark hair curled over the pillow. She moved closer, until she could feel his light breath on her face. She wrapped her body around his and watched his eyes shoot back and forth beneath the lids. She wondered if he was dreaming about her.

She indulged her desire to touch the side of his face and run her hands over the coarse stubble that was starting to appear. He smiled in his sleep, and she smiled back at him.

It was ten years since they'd first met, on a rainy day in Bristol. She was planning to take him on a day trip to revisit their old haunts for his twenty-eighth birthday the following week. She was going to give him his own personalised nostalgia tour, starting with the road where they had briefly shared a house in the second year, then on to their favourite student café for dinner, before finishing up at the club where they had had their first drunken kiss.

She looked over at him, sleeping. She knew he would love the trip. She reached over and gently stroked his hair away from his eyes. She wanted to kiss him gently awake, to see his eyes flick open and feel the warmth of his casual smile.

The beep of her phone startled her and she scrambled over to the other side of the bed to pick it up. The text was from Renée.

Elizabeth May, 7lb 10 oz. Back at home now and feeling fine x

Katie's breath left her body.

She felt restless, and decided to get up. Dave's parents were away for the weekend, and they had the house to themselves. Perhaps she would cook breakfast. Then she could tell Dave the news. There was no need to wake him up for it. She padded downstairs to the kitchen. She smiled at the empty bottle of wine left halfway up the stairs, the only evidence that remained of the good time they had had last night, after they had returned from the cinema. The evening had finished with Katie splayed across the kitchen table. She coloured slightly as she looked at the table now. She flicked the kettle on, and then picked up a cloth from the sink and gave the table another wipe down.

She opened the fridge to find it devoid of anything that could be made into a breakfast. She wondered if she should pop to the shop. She fancied scrambled eggs, and she could use the fresh air. She pulled on her boots and was about to leave the house when she realised she didn't have a door key. She took her boots back off and turned to see Dave behind her, his hair messy, his eyes blinking. His bare chest was neither thin nor fat, neither toned or flabby. She appraised it objectively as he walked towards her. She looked up and met his eyes and felt a smile stretch across her face as he grabbed her in his arms.

"Back to bed?" he asked.

"Yes." She laughed, forgetting the tea, forgetting the scrambled eggs, forgetting Renée's text message.

62

Renée picked up her plastic bags of shopping from the hallway and hurried to the bathroom to put away the multipacks of disposable nappies. She shoved them in a cupboard, and then returned to the living room to gather up the leaflets which were spread round the flat. When she left the hospital, she had taken every available leaflet on caring for a newborn baby. But she hadn't had the time to read a word. Elizabeth woke every three to four hours through the night demanding a feed, and Renée was in a state of permanent exhaustion. She put the leaflets into a neat pile on the kitchen table, and hoped she would get round to them eventually.

She looked round the flat. It could do with a vacuum, but there wasn't time for that. Katie would arrive any minute. She'd better tidy away the gifts she had received for Elizabeth. They were spread across the sofa, many still unwrapped. She gathered them in her arms and piled them up neatly under the coffee table.

She noticed that the morning's post was still on the mat. She hadn't even heard the postman come down the drive. She picked it up and sorted through it. All bills. Except for one letter, with the logo of the online paternity test company emblazoned across it in huge green and yellow letters.

The envelope contained the blueprint for the rest of her life.

Once she knew who Elizabeth's father was, both their lives would change beyond measure. It would no longer be just the two of them.

She wouldn't open it now. She wasn't ready. She put the envelope on the kitchen table. She would open it when Katie had been and gone, when she could digest the news in private.

She looked at her watch. Katie must be running late. Renée's new flat was in a converted house in Ruislip, some distance from the station, so it might take Katie a little while to find it. She planned to live here until she found somewhere to buy with the money from the sale of her half of the Wimbledon flat.

Elizabeth started crying, and Renée went to her cot in the bedroom and picked her up. She had soiled her nappy. Renée took off the old nappy and wiped Elizabeth down. She had the new one in her hand when the doorbell rang. She tried to hurry, but she didn't put the nappy on tight enough and it slipped when she picked Elizabeth up. She put her down and took it off again as the doorbell rang a second time.

Katie would have to wait. She placed the spoilt nappy in a plastic bag and got out another one. She put this one on more carefully and then lifted Elizabeth up, kissed her gently on the cheek, and placed her back in her cot. She took the plastic bags of dirty nappies and put them in the kitchen bin, then returned to the bedroom to check she hadn't left any mess there.

The doorbell rang again.

*

Katie gave Renée a quick kiss on the cheek, and handed her a bouquet of flowers and a box of chocolates.

"Thanks," Renée said. "I'll put the flowers in water."

"They're from both of us," Katie said, keen to give her an indication that Dave cared about her and Elizabeth.

"How is Dave?" Renée asked as she rummaged around in the kitchen cupboards for a vase.

"He's good. We're going to Bristol tomorrow, for his birthday."

"That will be fun," Renée said, her voice neutral.

"He's got a job interview today, for a consultancy role. Otherwise he would have come too and seen Elizabeth." Katie smiled as the white lie slipped out. The week before, she had taken a swab from the inside of Dave's cheek and watched as he had reluctantly signed the consent forms for the paternity test. She wasn't sure he was quite ready to be a father yet. He still wanted to be involved in Elizabeth's life if she was his, but now that she had been born and he was faced with the paternity test kit, he seemed shell-shocked. Katie was sure he would come round.

"Hmm," Renée said, putting the vase of flowers in the middle of the kitchen table. "Do you want to see Elizabeth?"

"I'd love too."

They went into the bedroom. As Katie stood over Elizabeth's cot, she found herself searching for signs of Dave. The baby had dark hair, but other than that it was hard to see any resemblance.

"She's gorgeous."

"I know," Renée grinned.

Katie was glad to see her looking so happy.

"Do you want to pick her up?"

"OK."

Renée picked the baby up and handed her gently across. Elizabeth immediately started to cry, and Katie tried to comfort her, rocking her gently in her arms. It didn't work, and after a few minutes she handed her back to Renée, who calmed her and put her back in her cot. They went back through into the living room.

"You look well," Katie said.

"Thanks."

"It's a nice place you have here."

"I sold Andy my half of the flat. I'm renting this until I find somewhere to buy."

"Oh?" Katie remembered Renée being adamant that she wanted to keep her half of the Wimbledon flat.

"He's moved his new girlfriend in."

"Shit, Renée, I'm sorry." She smiled sympathetically.

"You know, I really think I'm over him now. It's just that, well, Elizabeth kind of complicates things."

"Have you got the results yet?" Katie asked gently.

Renée's eyes strayed to rest on the kitchen table. An unopened letter sat on top of a newspaper.

"Are they in there?"

"Yeah."

"What does it say?"

"I don't want to open it."

"Why not?"

"Because whatever it says it ties me to Andy or Dave for the rest of my life."

"Dave isn't so bad."

"But Andy . . . And *Sabrina* . . . she's awful, Katie."

Katie went over to the kitchen table and reached for the envelope. Renée got up to take it off her, but she was too slow. Katie felt her heart beating faster as she opened it.

She scanned the page to find the words she was looking for. She felt her face flush.

Renée's voice interrupted her spiralling thoughts. "What does it say?"

"There's a match. Dave's the father."

Renée went pale. She stood up and started to pace the room. Finally she turned to Katie. "At least it's not Andy's," she said.

Katie stood up and put her arms round Renée. "Dave will be a great father." Her voice wavered.

She thought of the birthday trip to Bristol the next day, and knew that it wouldn't be the light-hearted event she had imagined. The news would cast a shadow over their day. But she smiled at Renée. "Elizabeth will be an early birthday present for him," she said.

Acknowledgements

Although writing is often a solitary pursuit, 27 would not be what it is today without the support of many people along the way. Thanks to my partner, Lewis Nicod, who has been a steady presence throughout and possesses a rare combination of open-mindedness and pragmatism. Without him to take me out when I was taking it all a bit too seriously, I wouldn't have been able to prise myself away from my computer.

A particular mention should go to my beta readers. Without them, the editing process would have been considerably shorter than 18 months and a vastly inferior book would be on the market today. Thanks to Michael Oren (author of *The Dallas Mercenary* and *Dudlham Sings*), Leela Dutt (author of *Only a Signal Shown*) and Chris Savory, who had the patience to see through the errors in an early draft and offer encouragement and constructive criticism. Thanks to Emily Allen, Denise Leonard, Victoria Arr, Samantha Naik, Pam Nixon, David Hadrian, and Puiyin Labial for reviewing the novel and providing invaluable feedback.

As an independent author, I couldn't have produced this book without the help of professionals from the industry. Thanks to Kirsten Armstrong for her invaluable advice, my editor Martin Ouvry and my cover designer, Becky Chilcott. Martin had an uncanny knack for understanding the intention in my writing and communicating it clearly and concisely. Becky not only applied her expertise and vision to cover design and typesetting, but also went far beyond her brief to offer me support and advice on the whole publication process.

Thank you finally to my family and friends, for always being there for me, whatever I decide to do.

Lightning Source UK Ltd.
Milton Keynes UK
UKOW031905300812

198299UK00010B/10/P